FALL OF A GAY KING

Visit us at www.boldstrokesbooks.com

FALL OF A GAY KING

by

Simon Hawk

A Division of Bold Strokes Books

2014

FALL OF A GAY KING

ISBN 13: 978-1-62639-076-8

This Trade Paperback Original Is Published By
Bold Strokes Books, Inc.
P.O. Box 249
Valley Falls, NY 12185

First Edition: July 2014

Credits
Editors: Greg Herren and Stacia Seaman
Production Design: Stacia Seaman
Cover Design by Sheri (graphicartist2020@hotmail.com)

This book is dedicated to Patrick.
Also a special thanks to Greg and Stacia.

CHAPTER ONE

Alex's Journal, Entry 1

They had me the moment we entered the shower house. Bobby latched onto the waistband of my jeans and pulled me toward the showers. Max followed behind us, grappling with my T-shirt, rolling it up my back and slipping it over my head. As he pulled it off and flung it through the air, Bobby unbuttoned my fly and yanked down my zipper.

I moaned as Bobby slipped his fingers down into my boxers, fondling me gently. "Relax," he said, nailing me with his catlike green eyes. "We want to play with you, Alex."

Max slipped around behind me and ran his hands over my chest. He tweaked my nipples, then slid his fingers down into the waistband of both my jeans and my boxers and peeled them down, exposing my hard, throbbing cock. I knew exactly what he meant when he said, "Just like old times."

Lakewood was deserted now, closed down for the season, but we had climbed over the fence to sneak into the place where we'd spent so many summers of our boyhood. I could clearly remember the night we had gone skinny-dipping at Lakewood summer camp. It had been Bobby's idea that night. Max and I had accepted his dare, both of us knowing that a summer camp filled with kids and counselors was a dangerous place for three horny fifteen-

year-old boys to play naked in a moonlit lake. But we'd managed to pull it off.

And now three years later, we were three eighteen-year-old young men, playing naked in Camp Lakewood shower house, horny as hell and all fired up for some action.

Bobby kneeled down in front of me. He laughed as he pulled my boxers and my jeans down to my ankles, then slid both over my sandals, removing all three. Stripped so quickly, I relaxed then, leaning back against Max.

Max's fingers fluttered up over my chest, tickling both of my erect nipples. He then brought his index fingers up and slipped them into my mouth, wetting them before removing them. I closed my eyes, feeling his moist fingertips swirling over and around my nipples. He quick-flicked in a maddening frenzy until I was breathing rapidly, sucking in and blowing out as he used butterfly skims, driving me up and down on the balls of my bare feet...

Logan Walker closed the book. The late-afternoon sun shone through the window of his den, shafts of hazy, lemony light drifting through ghostly ribbons of steam rising from the mug of Kenya AA beside him.

Seated at his desk, he studied the front cover of the book. The leather-bound tome had a strange, gold-embossed seal with intricate loops of Celtic knotwork on it, and yet the dragon, and the lion it embraced, looked slightly Egyptian.

Moments ago, he had opened the large manila envelope he'd discovered on the porch of his cabin. Logan suspected it had been left by someone connected to the story he was researching. He'd opened the mystery envelope after brewing a pot of coffee and read the first portion of the journal.

Placing the journal down on the desk, Logan picked up his coffee mug and stood up. He peered out through his front picture window, staring for a moment at the reflection staring back at him. Tall, lean, shaggy-haired, and ruggedly handsome, he had just turned thirty-five, coming to the sad conclusion that he would spend the rest of his days hidden away as a recluse, writing novels that would never be recognized by the masses.

He smirked at his reflection, then looked beyond the glass to his front lawn and the river beyond.

November winds plucked the last of the yellow leaves from the oaks standing along the Platte River. His cabin, nestled in the bluffs of eastern Nebraska, was about fifty yards from the river's edge. Two mallards paddled by, drifting downstream. A lone hawk perched in the tree above them.

Logan waited until the hawk launched from the branch to soar out over the wide river before taking another slow sip of his coffee and returning to his desk.

He opened the brown leather book and began to read again.

...so there we stood now, back in Camp Lakewood's shower house.

Max, with his broad shoulders, narrow hips, and the lean waist of a gymnast, reminded me of one of those wild surfer boys from California. He was cute, with his hair flowing in tiny wavelets on the sides and a shock of thick blond hair that spilled down and over his forehead in unruly tangles.

Besides having the slender, hardened body of a surfer boy, Max also had the blue eyes of ocean water. Blue eyes that I looked into many times while he blew me. And "blow" would be quite an injustice when describing Max performing oral sex. Max was a slurper. He deep-throated and tongue-waggled with long, slow motions. I especially enjoyed his facial expressions while he was between my legs making slow, gentle love to my cock.

Dark-haired Bobby, with the lean, sleek body of a panther, had the finely chiseled features of a young model. He reminded me of an Egyptian prince or a wild, rascally Gypsy boy. He was raven-haired with slight wisps that cascaded down to his thick eyebrows, then rippled back along both sides of his head, hanging just below his ears. Whenever he started something between us, he peered so seriously at me with his piercing blue Paul Newman eyes, I always wilted beneath the heat of his intensity. He was demanding, knowing exactly how he wanted each move of our session to start, and then was rather firm with his hands and a few verbal directions to get me into the positions for his rather strenuous sex play. And yet, once I complied with all of his instructions, Bobby's broad grin was infectious, carrying me along into some of the best domination sex I had ever had. Yes, I often imagined Bobby an Egyptian prince having his way with me as his captive.

This dominating personality of Bobby turned me on so much that I was compliant and willing to do whatever he demanded of me. Bobby would say things like, "Stand. Lie face down. Kneel. Place your legs over my shoulders. Push your cock forward. Hold still. Pump in my hand. Faster! Faster! Slow now. Real slow. Stop!"

I did anything Bobby said. Any position he wanted me in, I quickly assumed it. Not because I was afraid he'd punish me if I didn't comply, but because Bobby knew exactly what he was doing. He was a true master at giving pleasure. And then after a long session of Bobby boldly playing sex with a Simon Says attitude, he would melt my heart with a sudden burst of laughter and always kissed me on the brow afterward. It was his way of saying, "Sorry I started out so rough, but now you know it was for your own good, and in the end we both ended up loving it."

Bobby and Max had come prepared. They stripped out of their clothes and removed the plastic bottles from Bobby's backpack. They grinned at me like impish pranksters, knowing full well that I was now theirs to do with as they pleased.

I stood there naked before them, my erection aching to be toyed with. Max's nipple flicking had left me with a warm feeling in my balls. I was surely going to shoot a power load tonight. But that would be a long while later.

The last rays of the sun trickled in through the windows of the shower house, and Max made sure the water streaming down from the showerhead above him was warm. He then reached out and slid his soapy hand around my fully extended cock. Tugging, he moved me over next to him, beneath the warm water.

While Max doused me with thick globs of green herbal shampoo, Bobby moved in behind me. He squirted lavender-scented body wash all over me, covering me in the thick goop. My head and ringlets of black hair. My broad shoulders. My firm chest. My lean waist. My pubic region. He then poured a gob in his hand and packed it up under my balls, working sudsy fingers all the way up into my ass crack. There, he lingered for long moments, poking in and up, in and up, just fingertipping me until I reacted by sighing.

Bobby then gave a silent signal to Max, and they wildly ran their hands all over me, slipping and sliding and going into such a crazed frenzy that I didn't know what part of me felt the best. I began to moan. And swayed back into Max behind me, then leaned forward into Bobby in front of me.

They hugged me between them then, moved the three of us under the water. As suds, body wash, and shampoo ran off our sleek bodies, Max leaned forward and sucked gently on my neck, then nibbled my ear. Bobby held me tightly and slid down the entire length of my body, bringing his lips within inches of my waiting cock. He licked my hard, round knob, then placed both of his warm, wet lips over my pleasure spot. He froze there, not tonguing, not sucking. Just held me with his lips while his piercing blue eyes bored up into mine. Then he struck.

His moist tongue whipped between his pursed lips. Just the very tip lazily rolled over my sperm duct. I let out a whimper. They both laughed wickedly. Bobby made his move again. Pulling his lips free of my pleasure spot, he moved his head up and down, darting, dashing, lashing all six inches of my hardened manhood with his slippery, snakelike tongue.

I rose up on the balls of my feet. Bobby teased and

never took me fully in his mouth, licking, flicking, and butterfly kissing my fully enlarged cock. While I made little mewling sounds and turned my head from left to right, Max cupped my butt cheeks in his hands and spread my legs wide. Having full access to my ass crack, Max slid his middle finger into my soapy butt ring. He probed gently. Pulled out smoothly. Probed gently again, going knuckle-deep in my hole. Plucked his finger from my sphincter's embrace with a fluid move. He then drove in with a plunge that made me gasp.

Bobby rose up then, embraced me and planted his mouth on mine, frenching me deeply and passionately. He came up for air to say, "Keep fingering him, Max."

Max jammed his middle finger all the way up into my ass.

As if on cue, Bobby bowed his head to furiously work over both of my nipples. Keeping his finger in my ass, Max kneeled down behind me. Turning himself around so that he was looking up at me, he stuck his head up between my legs and began tongue-flicking my left ball.

I arched my back and made my front side more available to both of them. Bobby tickled one of my tits, barely skimming it with his tongue. Snick. Snip. Flick. He pulled off and switched tits, doing the same slow skim. I let out a low moan. But he stayed the course, not letting up or hurrying his pace. I whispered things into the air. Muttering. Mumbling. Gasping.

Then I grunted in surprise as Max sucked the entire six inches of my cock into the warm, wet confines of his sweet mouth. Even as he skillfully gorged himself on my rock-hard rod, he finger-fucked my ass, driving in again with his middle finger. Probing. Withdrawing. Probing. Then swirling. Twirling. Jamming me deep with long, swift jabs.

"Don't cum yet," was all Bobby said, then with a smirk he went back to his slow tit flicks. After a few seconds he sped up finally and went crazy with some wild tongue

action that drove me up and down, back and forth, almost dropping to my knees.

Totally aware of my state of pleasure, Max reached up and wrapped his hand firmly around my dick. Holding it tightly, feeling my pulse, he lifted his face and began kissing my inner thighs. While bending my cock down and tapping it against his face, Max lightly sucked first one ball and then the other. He then tongue-lashed me between my ball sack and my ass crack.

Bobby pulled off my tits and placed a strong arm behind my back, forcing me to lean back into his partial embrace. Max released my boner, tweaking it playfully before sliding one finger down the front. Bobby grabbed my bobbing shaft and tugged, leading me over to a mattress on the nearby floor.

"Get on all fours," Bobby commanded. "On your hands and knees, with your ass up in the air."

Max helped me, leaning in to lower me to the mattress.

I assumed the position, making like a dog, my ass in the air, exposed and vulnerable to Bobby behind me. I heard a gurgle of body lotion squirting out of the bottle, then felt the warm, wet liquid splattering all over my butt cheeks. Then Bobby used his fingers to lube up my ass crack.

Fingering me several times before pulling away, he told Max, "Go under him. Take him from below. Nice and slow."

Max immediately slid down beneath me, worming his way between my knees so that his face and mouth were directly beneath my cock. I raised my head, looking up at the last of the day's sunlight spilling through the window. Max blew his hot breath across my pelvic region, then on my dangling balls. He sent little puffs up and down the underside of my cock. It felt good. I shivered with pleasure. I also shivered with anticipated pleasure. I knew he would eventually take to sucking me.

Bobby lowered himself onto my arched back, sliding his cock down into my greased butt crack. He prodded with his hardness, his meaty knob smacked my butt ring. Sliding down and off me to kneel behind me, Bobby spread my cheeks with his strong fingers. His stiff cock slid up into my puckered hole, just the mushroom head. But it made me grunt.

Max, knowing what Bobby intended for me, began sucking wildly, working his tongue all around my head and shaft. He knew his frantic efforts would relieve my pain. He knew if he gave me pleasure, I could take all eight inches of Bobby up inside me. Maybe with one quick thrust.

Bobby leaned over me and slowly began pushing his rod up into my anal cavity. I sucked in, and Bobby drove deep.

"Uhhh!" I grunted, nearly collapsing on Max's upraised face.

"Shhh!" Bobby whispered, starting to hump. He pushed in me and pulled back. Pushed in and slid an inch back. Pushed in and slid three inches back. Nearly out of me. He gripped my ass cheeks with both hands and shoved himself deeper inside, then humped madly, pumping his rod all the way up into me.

Max worked his magic beneath me. He not only maintained his tight, wet lip lock on my cock, but he lightly ran his lotion-covered fingers all over my ball sack and beneath it.

"I'm cumming!" I gasped, and Bobby shouted, "So am I!"

And he did. Spurting warm sperm up in me, even while Max powerfully sucked sperm up out of my balls and through my throbbing shaft. I gasped. Bobby gasped. Max slurped and sucked.

"Okay," I whispered. "I'm done, Max. It's over."

Max let my cock go. I still remained on all fours, shuddering and tingling as Bobby slowly pulled his spent cock out of me.

"Now," Bobby said, "wasn't that fun? Rest about five minutes, Alex, then we'll do it again."

Logan placed the book on his desk. It was no coincidence this detailed account of a three-way sexual encounter between the three young men came his way when it did. Someone was leading him closer to the truth he had been searching for the past four months. Some anonymous donor had been depositing two thousand dollars in his PayPal account each month, so far leaving him an eight-grand incentive to keep working on the story.

Stay focused, he reminded himself. *This is just one facet of this story. This is just one piece of the overall puzzle. I have to keep reading this journal to find out where it takes me.*

He stood up and stretched. The sun had set in the west, thick shadows now gathered beneath the ancient oaks near the river. He took a drink of his coffee, finding it had gone cold while he'd read from the book.

He started to sit back down when his eyes were drawn to the river.

There, amidst the black trees, the cherry of a cigarette glowed.

Someone was standing there watching him. Logan closed the blinds.

He turned and crept down the hallway to his bedroom, feeling much safer once he had retrieved his 9-millimeter pistol from his nightstand.

He chambered a round and sat there in the dark, waiting.

CHAPTER TWO

W hen Logan Walker first received the proposal to ghost write this particular story, he scribbled down two questions on his notepad. He was amused at the time, thinking he had finally stumbled upon a conspiracy more complex than anything he could concoct. In fact, the old saying *You just can't make this shit up* ran through his head.

Question one: If I write this story, could I be sued for slander?
Question two: If I write this story, could I end up dead?

He then wrote down an answer to both of the above: *yes* and *yes*.

Logan was thinking about the latter possibility as he watched his mysterious stalker fading away into the woods. He was still thinking along these lines the next morning when he sat down with the two private investigators who had flown in from Chicago to have a sit-down with him, expecting him to turn over a disk to them.

A disk that Logan didn't have.

He had chosen a local coffeehouse in the Old Market area of Omaha for their meeting. Both men had entered the shop dressed in long, black trench coats with briefcases tucked beneath their arms. Logan had arranged for backup shortly after receiving their first call to set up this meeting. Sure, over the phone these guys claimed to be private investigators simply wanting to talk to him about the disk, but the words *hit men* came to mind as they joined him at his table in a remote corner of the coffeehouse.

Logan's backup sat across the room at his own small table, casually reading a newspaper and sipping quietly from a steaming cup. Noah Standing Bear took up most of the corner where he was seated. Big and brawny, Noah looked rather unconcerned about the meeting taking place forty feet from him. The big Lakota sized up the two investigators with a brief glance, swept his long braided ponytail over one broad shoulder, and continued reading.

Truthfully, Logan thought, *I'm almost hoping these two morons will get angry at me when I don't give them what they want. Noah's ready to spring like a cobra.* Mike Carrol, who politely introduced himself as the lead investigator, was a lean guy with dark hair. He was pretty-boy handsome and had an easy-going smile. Logan figured he was the good cop.

Which made his steely-eyed partner the bad cop. Brad Helman glared at him from behind his wire-rimmed glasses as he said, "Tell us about the disk, Mr. Walker."

Logan said, "The disk is the diary of Sean Murphy, the twenty-seven-year-old young man who first proposed I write this story. Sean claims he's written a lurid account of his sexual relationship with an older man, one that began when he was thirteen. It continued until he was nineteen. The sexual activities between the two stopped, but they continued to have an amicable friendship. The diary, according to Sean, has details involving the man's high-level associates in the Omaha area and their pornography connection in Thailand. The most blatant accusation Sean is leveling against his former partner is that the man has HIV and allegedly infected several unsuspecting youth. Sean is now threatening to expose the man and asked me to ghost-write a book about his abuse of young boys, using his diary."

Mike said, "Of course, there's nothing unusual about a spurned younger man coming out of the woodwork all these years later to accuse an older man of sexual abuse and severe emotional damage. In most cases, blackmail is the motive for threatening to go public with such damaging allegations. Hush money keeps such cases from ever going to court. How much money is it going to take to make Sean go away?"

"Well," Logan said, "the older man Sean wrote about is Franklin Anthony Judson, the CEO of Odin's Ring, a multimillion-dollar corporation. The Ring, as it is commonly called, was founded by Franklin after he sold Judson Machinery, the family business his grandfather started in the early sixties in the small town of Beatrice,

Nebraska. It was big news when Judson Machinery was sold to the Strong Motor Company for a grand total of four hundred and fifty million.

"Franklin sank his newly made profits into his new corporation, Odin's Ring, and in just a short year, made another three-hundred-and-fifty-million-dollar profit on a deal he cut with a Japanese corporation. Frankie, who'd grown up as a little gay boy in the small town of Beatrice, had risen up through the ranks and become a maverick in the world of business. It seemed everything he touched turned to gold.

"To most in the business world, Frankie remained closeted, but if there had been a fellowship of gay businessmen, Frankie would have been the CEO. He was notorious for including his gay associates, attorneys, architects, doctors, judges, and even a few politicians as guests at his mansion here in Omaha. Frankie is a beloved figure, too. He's a good guy. He treats people right. He is fair in his business dealings. Everyone loves Frankie."

Logan paused. "Including Sean Murphy. When he met him at the age of thirteen, Frankie invited him to his bed late one evening. Sean went willingly, and though Frankie was thirty years his senior, he fell in love with him. Their relationship lasted for the next six years. And though they eventually grew apart when Sean turned nineteen, Frankie continued to support his ventures financially, paying for his college expenses and other needs.

"During this transition period, Sean attended Frankie's parties at the mansion here in Omaha. Parties which involved sex between young gay boys and high-level older gay men. Sean was privy to information that could have landed Frankie in prison, but due to the attention Frankie was still giving him, Sean was quite pleased to stay quiet.

"Sean finally came out with a damning accusation that threatened to send the gay maverick down in flames. By then, Frankie was worth six hundred million dollars and his empire was going strong. And when Sean asked for his support to start up his own nonprofit corporation, Frankie told him to first research and explore all his options in marketing and selling the anti-drug, youth-oriented books that he wanted to promote. Sean believed Frankie would eventually grant his wish.

"Sean set to work putting a board of directors together for his nonprofit corporation, which he named the Haven. It was a major book publishing venture, using books to reach kids in detention and drug centers, institutions, and alternative schools."

Logan took a long, slow sip of his coffee.

"However," he said, "soon after Sean and Frankie spoke about such an investment in the book venture, Frankie contracted HIV, and his lawyers circled the wagons around their king, not allowing Sean anywhere near Franklin Judson. They were afraid he was joining the ranks of the many young men demanding hush money for sexual favors they had provided for Frankie when they were younger. Every boy who had ever shared Frankie's bed came out of the woodwork, demanding a handout for services rendered.

"One of these boys dropped a real bombshell for Frankie's lawyers to deal with, too. He claimed he was infected with HIV and contracted the virus from sleeping with Frankie. He wanted help in a most desperate way. This boy was threatening to go to the authorities. Against his lawyers' advice, Frankie caved in to this boy's demands. He set him up to be treated by his own doctor, bought him a place to live, and provided for all his needs. Frankie used money from his own nonprofit corporation to provide for this boy.

"In the past, Lighthouse had provided grants for hundreds of young men and boys. Legitimate grants providing education, living, and sometimes automobile expenses for young men who applied for assistance. But Frankie made one big mistake when he urged the board of directors to provide grants for this one particular boy."

Mike looked out the window to watch cars passing by on the street. "Sounds like a complicated mess. You sure it was worth getting involved in?"

Logan shrugged. "I was just asked to write the story, and I bowed out when Sean told me he intended to blackmail Judson."

Brad snorted. "Let's cut to the chase here, Walker. Just hand over that disk."

Logan said, "Sorry, but I don't have it. Sean never mailed it to me. If that's all you guys came here for, then I'm sorry I wasted your time. I've been waiting three weeks for Sean to send the disk my way. He never did."

Mike asked, "What will it take to make Sean go away?"

Logan knew he wanted him to place a price on how much it would cost the Odin's Ring Corporation to pay Sean off.

Brad said, "Just give us the goddamned disk before we include you as a key player in this conspiracy to blackmail Franklin Judson. Cooperate with us, hand over the disk containing Sean's diary, and we won't turn you over to the feds."

Logan knew he was in no real trouble. He'd contacted his attorney before attending this meeting.

"Have a sit-down with Sean and Frankie," Logan said. "Sean looked up to him like a father. I think this whole matter can be dealt with if Frankie would just listen to what Sean has to say."

Mike replied, "That won't be happening."

"Fine," Logan said. "But I think you're making a big mistake. Let Sean and Frankie meet."

"Not a chance," Brad said.

Mike became very serious as he looked at Logan. "Don't play us, Logan," he said. "In the end, this is not going anywhere near good."

The two private investigators walked out of the coffeehouse. Noah Standing Bear joined Logan at his table. "I'm wondering just what is on this disk to arouse such interest. And how much is this Judson fellow worth? Four hundred million, maybe six? When someone is threatening a rich king like that, hard telling how far he might go to hang on to his riches. Sounds like a complicated mess. You sure it is worth doing a story on, Logan?"

Logan answered, "No, not really, but so many bits and pieces keep getting thrown my way, I can't help but be a little intrigued about where this whole thing might be going."

Standing up, Noah said, "It was fun playing your bodyguard, but I have lessons to teach in the next fifteen minutes down at the dojo. Be careful, Logan. Be very careful. There's something I can't quite put my finger on regarding these two PIs. They're not quite right."

Logan watched the big Lakota walk out of the coffeehouse, and muttered, "This whole situation is not quite right."

A moment later, his cell phone rang. He answered it on the third ring. "Hello?"

"Logan," Sean Murphy excitedly said, "good job with that

interview! Mike Carrol called and assured me I'd be given a trust by Frankie! Tonight, Frankie and I are actually having a sit-down to work out our differences. But I have to hand over my diary."

Sean assured Logan that he would. And knowing Sean, Logan figured he would place another copy in a safe place somewhere, for leverage in the future.

"So," Sean said, "once we reach an agreement, I'll be silent, and the gay King of Kings can make more gold with his magic ring. If Baxster Crown doesn't topple him from his throne first."

"Who?" Logan asked.

"Baxster Crown," Sean said. "The other thorn in Frankie's side."

CHAPTER THREE

He started to undress. Logan stopped him, saying, "Let's just talk."

"Talk?" he said, his slender fingers frozen over the button of his faded jeans. "You don't want to have sex with me?"

It was not the typical thing one hears from an eighteen-year-old boy. He stood there, his small and slender frame nearly swallowed whole by his large black hoodie and his baggy, faded jeans. He had a smooth, hairless face, and his blue eyes and silky raven hair reminded Logan of angels, though he knew this kid had been working the streets for two years.

What disturbed Logan most was the hunger in his eyes. The kid wanted sex. He'd followed Logan up to his hotel room fully expecting to be naked moments after he entered the room. He had thought at first this wasn't the kid he'd been searching for. He'd assumed the Alex who wrote the journal was a little more rough, with more muscle to his frame. But this kid was short and almost frail-looking.

Logan told him, "I don't want to have sex with you. But I'm willing to pay you for your time." He already knew the answer to his next question. "By the way, what shall I call you?"

"Alex," he said. "Pay for my time? Oh, you just wanna watch me get off? Okay."

His hands once again dropped to his waist and he began unzipping his jeans.

"No," Logan said. "I just want to talk."

"You a cop?"

Logan smiled. "I'm not a cop. Would you please sit down? I'm actually a writer. I'm doing a story on young boys who sell themselves to men."

"Writer?" Alex asked. "You're like an reporter, right? So if I talk with you, is what I say gonna end up in a book or magazine? You ain't using my name, right?"

"A book," Logan said. "And no. I wouldn't use your real name."

Alex sat down on the edge of the bed.

Logan pulled the journal from his backpack and Alex's eyes widened in surprise.

Alex frowned. "They sent it to you, right? They said they were sending it to someone to sort it all out. You are that writer, correct? How far have you read?"

"Just entry one," Logan replied. "I'll read it all, but care to share with me how you got started?"

"How I got addicted to sex? Sure, I'll start from the beginning. I'll tell you everything if it will help get me out of this mess."

Logan began to read the journal aloud:

Alex's Journal, Entry 2

I stood in the crowded hallway at Grover Parker High School as my friend Max latched onto me, pulling me out of the mass of students rushing down the halls to get to their next class. Leading me to one side of the hallway, Max said, "Alex, he needs your services again."

He leaned in close and whispered, "How about we make that happen?"

Max led me into the nearby boys' bathroom.

Tall, blond-haired Baxster Crown stood there waiting for us. "You've got two seconds to decide," he said. "If you stay, for the next forty-five minutes, you are ours to do with as we please. Okay?"

I stood there, my dick already hard. I nodded. "I'm okay with this."

Max circled behind me, placed both hands on my shoulders, and gently lowered me to my knees.

Baxster unzipped his jeans and slowly lowered them

and his boxers all the way down to his ankles. "You have such soft-looking lips, Alex. Get some saliva going in that sweet little mouth of yours."

Baxster shoved his seven inches of hardened flesh directly into my face. I noted his blond pubic hair and the way his pre-cum glistened on his perfectly round head. I could not help myself then. I was rock hard as Max kept me down on my knees and Baxster shoved his protruding erection against my lips. "Suck me," Baxster commanded. "Slob my knob, little bitch."

Max slipped his hands down inside my T-shirt, his fingers brushing the tips of both of my nipples. He flicked them back and forth, working both tits into hard nubs. "Relax, Alex," he whispered, lowering himself to his knees behind me. "Open your mouth and pretend your tongue is a slithering, slippery snake. Slither it all around Baxster's head and pleasure spot beneath it."

Baxster prodded my face with his slick head. He pulled back slowly, leaving us connected by a string of white pre-cum. "Do it, little bitch boy!" he said firmly. "Suck me off now!"

I leaned forward, opened my mouth wide, and Baxster plunged inside me, burying his head all the way to the back of my throat. I gagged. Baxster relented ever so slightly, withdrawing a few inches, but then driving back in. I gagged again. "Deep-throat it," he coached me.

I did so and swallowed all seven inches of Baxster, until my nose was resting in his pubes.

We remained locked that way for several long moments. I froze, my mouth full of cock. Baxster stood poised above me, a smile on his face. "Excellent, bitch boy," he said. "You look like you are enjoying this. You are, aren't you, little bitch boy?"

I breathed through my distorted nostrils, giving a slight nod of my head. I then went to work, slathering Baxster's entire length with my tongue. I worked my lips, suctioning up and down, back and forth, running my slithering tongue around his head and over and over his sperm duct. I bobbed my head. I opened my mouth wide, taking him in, spitting him out, and taking him deep inside again and again.

With Max still working my tits in a mad frenzy, I arched my back and began to writhe while keeping a firm lip lock on Baxster's hard cock. "He's loving this!" Max laughed, speeding up his flickering, driving me mad with pleasure.

Baxster grasped me firmly with both hands, working his fingers into the long strands of my hair. He fiercely began bucking his hips, catching the momentum of my sucking just right. "Aw, yeah, bitch!" he crooned. "Suck that cock! Churn that sperm! Suck me dry!"

My slurping sounds filled my ears. Above me, humping my face with mad little thrusts, Baxster was moaning with pleasure. Behind me, Max began whispering nasty comments, and with every sentence he completed, he swirled his tongue into my ear.

Baxster groaned loudly. His knees buckled and he had to reach down and steady himself by grabbing my shoulders. I knew he was peaking, that all my effort was now resulting in Baxster's orgasm. I gave myself over to the feeling of being connected to the older boy whose cock was stuffing my mouth. I sucked furiously and Baxster exploded inside my warm, wet mouth, spurting blast after blast of his sweet-tasting sperm.

"Oh, God! Oh, bitch boy, suck that cock!" he whimpered with pleasure. "Oh, you beautiful boy!"

Baxster held my head in place while he humped in tiny movements, shooting the rest of his load down my throat. Our eyes met and I actually grinned, my lips still wrapped around Baxster's meaty cock. One last spurt of sperm forced me to close my eyes and quickly swallow.

Then Baxster left me kneeling there. He sauntered out of the bathroom without a backward glance.

Before following him, Max said, "Nice work, Alex. We shall contact you again. Okay?"

I nodded submissively. "Okay," I softly said.

Two days after giving Baxster a blow job in the bathroom, I was walking home from school when a car pulled up beside me on Center Street. I looked over at Baxster in the driver's seat of a maroon Mustang. Baxster did not say a word. He simply crooked his finger, indicating that I should join him in his ride.

I got hard before I even closed the door behind me.

Harder still when Baxster nodded at me in approval, then drove off down the street, still not saying a word. I was startled by the shrill ring of Baxster's cell phone. "Yo," he said. "Yep, found him. The bitch boy is willing to offer services again. We'll be there in five. Get the tub ready for the kid. We'll have some fun tonight."

I actually jumped as Baxster reached over and lightly ran two fingers over my lips, twiddling them to elicit saliva from them. Slowly, he pulled them away, a line of spit connecting my bottom lip with Baxster's two fingers. "Slick," he said, grinning. "Moist and gooey."

Baxster said nothing more as he drove us to a large, two-story house in the Loxley Woods housing district. He pulled into the driveway. Turned off his car. Climbed out. Crooked his finger. I climbed out of the car and followed him up five wide stone porch steps to the house's front door.

The door opened and Max appeared, naked and sporting an erection.

He latched onto my right wrist, drawing me inside the foyer of the large house.

An older guy named Ridge Majors came out of the den, also wearing nothing. Tall and muscular, he reminded me of a gladiator, with a thin, wispy beard and a Marine-style haircut. He walked directly up to me, brushing his rising boner against my crotch. "Ready for some fun with us?" he asked, peering expectantly into my eyes.

I lowered my eyes and nodded.

"Strip him, boys," Ridge ordered. "Get the little bitch boy naked. Once he is unclothed, take him to the hot tub. Let the jets drive him over the edge."

Once they had me naked, Max and Baxster took hold of my bare legs, and together, they hoisted me up off the ground so that my stiffening rod was hanging down pointing at the floor as they carried me between them.

In the den where they hauled me, Ridge Majors was seated behind a camera, adjusting the focus on a rather large hot tub situated in the sunken garden at the back end of the den. His eyes traveled the length of my naked body. "Turn him around, boys," he ordered calmly. "Let me see his package."

Max and Baxster complied at once, turning me and twisting me so that I faced forward, trapping my arms behind me, both of them using their legs to nudge me forward so that my entire front was exposed for Ridge's appraisal. He smiled in approval. "Nice. Six inches. Nicely haired, too, with small balls. His butt?"

Max and Baxster turned me around between them, using their legs to spread mine wide, still grasping my arms, which they spread to my sides. Ridge said, "Ah, nicely sculpted. A bubble butt, for sure. He shall do just fine. Play time. Let's see how much stamina he has. See how long he lasts."

I still had said not one word. I allowed the two boys to raise me up and over the sides of the green-tiled hot tub. Baxster eased into the silky green water and helped guide me in beside him. Max followed us into the warm water, purposely sliding against my backside as Baxster pulled me over to one of the finely molded seats between two jets.

"Climb into my lap, bitch boy," Baxter gently coaxed as Max helped me to straddle him.

I felt Baxster's stiffy prodding me and figured I was about to get fucked by the three of them. The prospect scared me because I wondered if they would go easy on me or simply savagely rape me. I had been fucked repeatedly by Max before, but I did not want them to force their thick, long cocks inside me, especially if my ass could not stretch to let them in. I knew, though, that once they got started on

me, they would all three pound me furiously until they had
spurted their seed into me. And then more than likely take
me again before they released me to go home.

"Relax, tiger," Max said, moving up behind me, his
long, slender fingers spider-walking down and over my
shoulders as I sat perched there in Baxster's lap. "We
brought you here tonight for your pleasure fest."

With that said, Max planted two moist fingers on my
nipples. He then made tiny flickering motions, working
them into tight little nubs. Even as he worked over my
tits, Baxster snaked one middle finger into my butt crack.
He swirled it round and round my ass ring, slipping in,
pulling out, slipping in, pulling out. I spread my legs wider,
straddling Baxster's lap, offering my butt for the taking.

When he finally thrust in with long jab, my mouth
opened in a silent gasp. With Max flickering my tits and
Baxster fingering my hole, I practically performed a lap
dance, bucking up with each plunge of Baxster's middle
finger. Over and over. Until I was whimpering with
pleasure, not even realizing I was making any noise.

Max said, "And now, it begins."

As if on cue, Max took hold of my left arm while
Baxster clamped his free hand onto my shoulder. In this
way, the two boys hoisted me up and halfway out of the
water.

Turning me around for Ridge to get a full shot of
my boner and balls, they held me there while the camera
continued to roll. At a nod from Ridge, they spun me
around, and while Baxster placed me in a full nelson,
Max took hold of my boner and directed it into one of the
jets spewing water into the hot tub. Baxster applied more
pressure, forcing me forward, and as my cock entered the
hole of the jet, Max drove a finger into my ass.

I froze for a moment, feeling my dick being furiously
fondled by the agitated water. I moaned five times in a
row as Max began finger-fucking me with mad passion. I
squirmed and writhed, so overcome with wild pleasure I
also began to whimper and whine. It went on and on for a

very long time. I bucked back and forth, grasped so firmly by Baxster that I had no choice but to fuck the hell out of the water jet. I spread my legs wide to allow Max open access to my ass, feeling his three fingers swirling around inside me. I threw my head back, closed my eyes tightly, and began a steady moan that caused the other two boys to laugh out loud.

Just when I was about to go over the edge, I tensed up.

It was the sign they had been waiting for, and Max and Baxster worked in unison to dampen my fire. Max swiftly withdrew his fingers and Baxster pulled my very hard dick out of the confines of the jet. Baxster slid his arms from a full nelson to wrap around me in a tight hug. "Hold it in, bitch boy. Don't cum yet or you'll ruin the final moment. Hold. Hold. Hold."

Max helped Baxster to hold me by my shoulders, both of them staring down at my reddened cock to make certain I complied and did not spurt sperm yet.

I needed badly to cum. But I held it in as commanded and allowed the orgasm that threatened to rack me to subside and slip away, taming it by willpower alone.

"The trick is," Max said, "to bring you to the edge over a dozen times, and then when you can't stand it any longer, when you cry and whimper to allow us to let you cum, we do so, and it will be the most powerful orgasm you've ever had. Believe us, Alex, you will thank us afterward."

I was planted back inside the jet. I bucked once most wildly, then began to do spastic little dances within their grasp. They worked me in that manner for over an hour, firing me up, tamping me down, bringing me to the brink, letting me down slowly.

By the time they were almost finished with their play, I was calling out their names, begging them to finish me off.

Max and Baxster got the final nod from Ridge Majors, and they spun me away from the water jet and moved me over to the side of the hot tub, where they lifted me and offered me to Ridge.

    Naked, Ridge lowered himself into the water, taking my well-worked-over dick into his mouth. While the other two sucked on my tits, Ridge swallowed my cock all the way to its base. He furiously sucked, even while ramming his index finger up into my ass.

    I went wild, writhing, squirming, letting out cries of pleasure.

    When I exploded inside Ridge's mouth, I wailed in delight, throwing my head back and arching my entire body. Spreading my legs wide, I felt Ridge's jamming finger working its magic. Thrusting my cock deeper inside, I felt Ridge furiously working the warm, wet confines of his mouth.

    With one final cry, I spurted seven long and full eruptions of sperm down his throat. The feelings racked me over and over, lasting longer and being more powerful than anything I had ever felt before. I felt like tiny furry fingers were working their way through my hair, down over my scalp, sending quivering motions over my jaw, down across my throat, spidering down and over my chest, and centering there in my crotch.

    I nearly passed out from the powerful orgasm. In fact, I thought maybe I had blacked out for a moment, for when they finished with me, I did not remember being guided over to the side of the tub and the three of them lifting me out of the warm, sudsy water. But there I stood, naked before them, my cock slowly dwindling in size and shriveling up considerably.

    "That," Ridge said, placing an arm around my shoulders, "was the beginning of your training, Alex. A couple more sessions like that and you will be turned into a very willing boy prostitute."

    And still overcome with the long moments of pleasure, I simply asked, "When will you guys do this to me again?"

Chapter Four

L ogan finished reading with a heavy sigh.
   "And that's how it started," Alex said, running a hand through his silky black hair, brushing his long bangs out of his eyes. "Any questions so far? By the way, I didn't even get your name."

"Logan Walker," Logan told him. "I am the author of several books. Mostly in regard to at-risk behavior. Drug abuse. Alcoholism. HIV. Not your typical bedtime reading material." He pulled a hundred-dollar bill from his wallet. "Now," he said, "it's a matter of trust between us. You can either help me out with some answers to my questions, or you can go out that door."

Logan was relieved when Alex stayed put. Alex looked so much like a typical high school kid that Logan almost forgot the kid was there because he sold himself on the streets.

"First question," Logan said. "How much do you charge for your time on the street?"

"I've got certain rates," Alex said. "Blow jobs usually earn me forty or fifty. Add a fingering while I'm doing the deed, another twenty gets tacked on. If I get ass-fucked, I get sixty to eighty. If we do a sixty-nine and my client and I both get off, I can usually jack him up to ninety or a hundred. Depends how horny I get him when I start negotiating."

Logan scribbled on his legal pad. "Are you still in school?"

"Grover Parker," Alex responded. "Full of gang-bangers and the most ignorant, intolerant gay-bashing skinheads on the planet. Last place on earth you wanna be out at. You know, with the Mexican bangers it's like a macho thing. Can't be a real man if you're a faggot. Those bangers would beat up any gay kid just because it's, like, offensive to their manhood. But the skinhead bastards? To them, gay kids are the scum of the earth that need to be wiped out. Nazi-type, Hitler-like shit, I kid you not! Those skinheads are twisted freaks!"

Logan scribbled down a few more words. "So, who first got you started hustling?"

Alex said, "It got to be almost an everyday thing with me and Baxster. I'd fooled around with Max before I even hit puberty. I liked gay sex and was probably gay before I was ten. It's just one of those things you know inside your head. Baxster, though, he really put me through the moves. And every time we'd do stuff, he'd get to talking about how we could make money doing it with other guys. We cruised the Old Market. First guy we ever did couldn't believe his luck. Two on one wasn't what he expected. But he left a satisfied customer. Even tipped us an extra fifty bucks."

Alex coughed self-consciously. "Yeah, I know, most kids are being grounded for not doing their homework. Or looking forward to weekends when they go on sleepovers with friends. Maybe hanging out at home, blasting away zombies on a video game. Not having sex with older men. Some guys are only five years older than me. They're actually good-looking, decent men who treat me pretty cool. You people who look down on this sort of thing seem to get all bent out of shape on the age difference crap. You think it's just dirty old men who come down to the Market looking for sex?

"Well, I don't see what the big deal is in how old anyone is if they willingly want to have sex with each other. Baxter calls some of the most older guys chicken hawks, because like a hawk they prey on young twinks like me. But really? Some of those guys are the nicer ones. Most younger men just tell you what they want you to do. Not that way with some of the older dudes. Sometimes they even ask you what you like and ask if it felt good afterward."

❖

They continued talking for another hour. Alex opened up and started sharing details about his street hustling, in no big hurry to leave. The payment might have been his incentive, but Logan thought he really enjoyed just sitting there being able to let down his guard.

Logan believed Alex told him his most sordid acts he'd been paid to perform, to see if there was a limit to what he could hear. But Logan was not there on a crusade to save street kids. Nor was he there to persuade him to get himself off the streets and change his unsafe sexual practices. He was just there to get his story.

When they finished speaking, Alex snatched up the money from the desk. Once Alex had his money in his pocket, he seemed reluctant to leave. "Mind if I ask you something, Logan?" he asked, sitting on the edge of the bed.

"Sure," Logan replied. "What would you like to know?"

"Are you gay?" Alex asked, looking him directly in the eye.

Logan kept his eyes locked on Alex's. He wanted to shrug it off and ask him what difference did it make? His second thought was that he shouldn't divulge any information to this kid. If he told him he was gay, Alex would think he had other motives for inviting him to his room. When he smiled, Logan knew he'd waited too long to answer.

"I knew it!" Alex said, smirking. "I could tell. I picked up your gay vibe."

Logan laughed.

"So," Alex said, "any of your books got any porn scenes in them?"

"My last book," Logan said, "had to do with AIDS and suicide among gay and lesbian teens."

Alex said, "No wonder you haven't hit it big yet. Maybe with the info I give you, you can write a hot and steamy porn novel. That would probably sell really good, don't you think?"

Logan handed him his business card, which had his web address listed on it. "Keep this," he said. "If you want to check the status of this current book I'm writing, I'll post the publication date on my site. Email me, and I'll send you a copy."

"For real?" Alex said, taking his card and sliding it into his pocket. "Cool! Will you sign it, too?"

"Of course," Logan replied.

Alex, was slow to get up from the bed. Even more slowly, he shuffled toward the door. Just before reaching for the doorknob, he grinned and asked, "Hey, before I go, do you think I might ransack your room's liquor cabinet?"

"No, Alex," Logan said. "Sorry."

He opened the door, and the question that Logan had been wanting to ask since he'd entered the room came to the surface "Alex?" Logan kept his voice calm and even. "I forgot one last thing."

Alex turned to face him. "Yeah, and what's that?"

Logan held up a finger. He rummaged through his hastily scribbled notes, putting on quite a performance, acting a little fuddled. He let out a quiet "aha" as he flipped open his notepad to the page he'd been pretending to search for. "Baxster Crown," Logan said, purposely keeping his eyes fixed on his notes instead of checking Alex's reaction.

"Yeah," Alex said, boring a big hole in Logan with his piercing stare. "What about him?"

Logan finally raised his eyes to meet Alex's now suspicious gaze. "You said he got you started with Baxster, right?"

"Yeah," Alex said, still holding the door open.

Logan looked down at his notes, saying, "So did Baxster actually retire from street prostitution?"

Alex bluntly stated, "Baxster quit because he got the virus."

Logan acted surprised. "So do you still stay in touch with him?"

Alex responded, "Leave it alone. Don't go there, Logan Walker. Just leave it alone."

He left, the door closing behind him.

CHAPTER FIVE

After meeting with six other young boys who sold themselves in the Old Market, Logan checked out of the hotel to head back to his cabin, thirty miles from Omaha. Two of the street prostitutes had belonged to a rival pimp. When he'd mentioned Baxster Crown to them, they cursed his name, claiming he was a big star in the porn industry. This made Logan more curious as to how far-reaching the boy trade was in the Omaha area.

As he approached his Pathfinder in the hotel's parking garage he was cut off by two men. The one appeared to be a grungy biker, big and red-haired. The other man was clean-cut, with a neatly trimmed beard and a Marine-style haircut.

The biker had rage simmering in his dark eyes. But it was the cold, calculating stare of the other man that sent chills up Logan's spine. "My name is Ridge Majors," he said. "I hear you've been asking my boys questions?"

"I'm writing a book," he told Ridge. "Asking your boys questions is part of my research. I'm just trying to get a clear picture of the sex trade and boy prostitution in general. Anything you might like to add?"

"Yes," the biker snorted as he lashed out to strike Logan, his fist aimed for the center of his chest.

Having spent considerable time training with Noah, Logan was prepared. He simply reacted, performing a backhand sweep with his right hand, efficiently deflecting the big man's punch.

"Dirk!" came a voice from behind the two men. "Stop that!"

The biker froze, glancing back at the dark-haired man

approaching them. Ridge Majors simply rolled his eyes and muttered, "Murph, you're interfering in my business!"

Murph was a Catholic priest. Dressed in the usual black suit with the white collar, he appeared to be in his late forties. Tall and slender, he wielded the black cane he held with a certain grace, swinging it up and planting it rather firmly against Dirk's thick chest.

"Ridge? Dirk?" Murph said, "We need to talk."

Ridge Majors gave Logan a long, hard silent look. "Be careful, writer. You get to snooping too deep and you might not like what you find."

As Logan climbed into his Pathfinder, the priest launched into a heated lecture. Ridge and Dirk stood there looking like two altar boys who had been caught sampling the communion wine.

He drove out of Omaha with that image in his head.

❖

When he arrived back home, he killed the engine and sat there for several minutes peering out toward the dark waters of the river. Too many thoughts were whirling around inside his head. Too many questions he needed answers to. He wanted to go inside, crank up the computer, and write, but he needed time to allow the dust to settle on everything he'd learned from the boys. He wasn't certain he could keep digging into the dirt. He justified his research with the notion that he was on a crusade to expose Franklin Judson, doing society a favor by revealing to the world that such activities did exist and were more common than most realized.

Although he wasn't attracted to young boys, some boys were attracted to men and sought out their company and instigated these sexual liaisons. In some cases, the boys were more aggressive in their pursuits than the men.

Once he was back inside the cabin, he picked up the leather-bound book and began reading.

Alex's Journal, Entry 3
*   After a little more fun in the shower house of Camp Lakewood, Max suggested we go skinny-dipping in camp*

lake. I readily agreed that a swim in the cool waters of the lake would be nice. The night was hot. Summer night hot. July in Nebraska hot.

The three of us were actually sweating by the time we gathered up our clothes and followed the path down from the shower house. Dropping our clothes in a pile on the sandy shores of the pristine lake, we stood gazing at the place we'd first explored our young bodies together. Where we first discovered and accepted our unique sexuality.

A million stars speckled the smooth black surface. A full silver moon hung in one corner, between the nearby docks and the distant pines running along the banks on the far shore. Tall and dark pines. Spiraling up into sharp peaks like the turrets of a castle. Standing like ancient guardians, who had many times witnessed our late-night sessions in the lake. They kept our secret well, those trees. Never whispered a word about us playing naked beneath the moon and stars. They watched us now, like old friends, remembering when we were young and daring.

Bobby stood staring up at the camp lodge fifty yards beyond the lake. "You guys go for a swim. I'm going up there to play around with the audiovisual equipment that Lakewood raised all the money to buy last year. It's supposed to be used for camp security, but I think Jungle Jim just wants to record all the boys for his viewing pleasure later."

And as Bobby headed up the path to the lodge, Max was the first to dive into the lake. Knifing through the air, soaring out over the glassy surface, his perfect form sliced down through the kaleidoscope of brilliant stars. He shattered them for brief moments, his body sinking beneath the water and sending waves up to disturb the photo-like quality of the summer night sky reflected in the lake's face.

I stood, my toes scrunching up sand between them. Waiting. Watching. Holding my breath. Until at last, Max surfaced and came up for air, his long, blond strands plastered to his forehead. He shook his head like a dog, casting little pearls of glistening moonlit droplets in all directions.

Max's white-blond hair shone like the silken strands of an elven lord. He rose out of the water, his green eyes bright with mischief. Like a wickedly grinning, smirking Puck, he lunged up at me, his hardness sliding down between my legs, gliding over my inner thighs. His round, shiny hard knob prodded gently at my hole.

He leaned forward into my embrace. Kissed me gently. I instantly became hard. He pushed his upper body away, still holding on to my shoulders with both hands. Still attached to me by his fleshy rod crammed between my legs.

I clamped my thighs tighter. Captured him. Pinned the entire length of his hard cock between my legs. Felt him throbbing. Felt his shaft all along the underside of my ball sack. Felt his knob poking at my ass crack.

Max pumped in and out. In between my legs, all the way. Out, up to his head, almost pulling free. In again, sliding his cock like a slippery eel between my inner and upper thighs.

He tricked me then. Ducked his head down and slurped rapidly all over my left nipple. I lost my leg grip on him. He pulled free. Yet I could still feel his throbbing hardness on the tender part of my thighs. It felt like he was still stabbing, jabbing, and pumping there.

I gasped when Max wrapped a fist around my cock. He bent me downward at an awkward angle, just rough enough to tease me. Spinning around to face the lake, still holding me firmly in his tight fist, he scooted himself back against me.

With just a slight guiding nudge, Max slid my shaft between his legs. Clamped down hard on me. Held me firm. Captured my dick as I had his, only with me taking him from behind this time. He eased his thigh muscles slightly, enough to give me playing room. I prodded slowly. He reached down between his own legs from the front and lightly shoved my cock up, wedging it beneath his balls.

I drove forward. Max leaned back into me, taking my hands from his shoulders and pulling my arms around himself.

I ran my hands all over his front side. Flicking his tits. Caressing his flat stomach. Tickling his firm chest. Ever so gently I cupped his balls, lightly skimming beneath the skin of his sack, using both index fingers to make him sigh. He did. Softly. Loudly. Softly again.

I wrapped one arm around his upper body. My free hand I wrapped tightly around his curved shaft, spiking up like a scimitar pointed at the moon above. I pumped slowly at first, keeping a tight lock on the entire seven-inch shaft. I went up. I pulled down. Taking a firmer grip on his chest, shoving my own cock deeper between his legs, I worked him over in a frenzy of speedy pumps.

I got caught up in the moment. Max cried out. Arched his back. Puffed and huffed. And jizzed a gusher, shooting white ropy strands out into the black water, where they drifted lazily like milk in black coffee. Max cried out as I wrung out every last droplet from his spurting dick head.

Gasping, he said, "Enough, Alex. Really. I've had enough."

He leaned back and kissed me on one cheek. "Let me go," he whispered. "And I'll do you now."

I released him. He removed my cock from between his legs and turned to face me. Latched onto me at once with a cum-covered hand. Smeared it all over my head and down the length of my shaft. Bent down, swirled a skimming, darting, jabbing tongue all over my right nipple. Began at once to run his gooey fingers all over my head, across my pleasure spot, down my shaft and over my balls.

I shoved my erection at him. Jabbed at him with it. Into his grasp. Into his firm hand. Pulled back and jabbed at him again. Max planted his entire mouth over my right nipple, sucked and slurped and made sluicing, smacking loud noises with his tongue and thin, wet lips. I went a little crazy. Thrusting. Humping his hand. Arching my back. Tried to stay upright on my widely spread legs. Went up and down on my bare feet, digging my toes into the sand to find purchase.

Max switched to my left tit. Sucking hard, he went for the kill. Sliding his tight-fisted grip all the way down my shaft, slick and shiny from his cum, Max worked me in a frenzy. Worked me like I did him. Sucking my nipple and pumping my cock, he aimed my head at his belly. I spurted all over him. Shot one strand after another all up and down his lean, hard stomach. I let out a grunt like a bull.

I gasped, "Okay. Done now."

My words ignited a spark of mischief in Max. He returned my earlier favor, toying playfully with my sensitive spent cock. Using my cum, he plastered my head with goo. Just the head. He went crazy then, swiveling his fingers around and beneath and over and under, and then taking my cock head between two fingers, he ran his thumb all over my very tip.

It was far too much. Way too unfair. Max was making me dance in place. Making me gasp, pant, and cry out, "Enough! Please, I've had enough!"

Max laughed, but stopped. Placing an arm around my shoulders, he led me down into the cool waters of the lake. We dropped in the water, rinsing off. Looking into each other's eyes. Pleased with each other for pleasing each other.

Logan found himself drawn into Alex's journal and wanted to find out where this intriguing narrative was going. After brewing a pot of strong Colombian, he poured himself a cup and took a few minutes to prepare it his favorite way.

Taking a jar of orange marmalade from the fridge, he scooped out a teaspoon and dropped the sweet-smelling glob into a small strainer, then heated two teaspoons of coffee creamer in a small espresso cup and added this to the strong black coffee. After spooning in just a tad of brown sugar, he poured the combination of Colombian coffee, heated milk, and sugar over the marmalade in the strainer, allowing it to slowly drain down into his small metal coffeepot.

He repeated this process three times, taking on a Zen-like calm as he did so, pouring the mixture over the marmalade, back and forth from metal cup to his coffee mug.

When he finished this familiar process, Logan stood at the kitchen counter, sipping and savoring the strong coffee with just a hint of orange flavor in it.

The phone rang. Logan picked it up on the third ring. "Hello?"

"Are you safe down there, Logan?" Noah asked seriously.

Noah Standing Bear's cabin was situated at the foot of the bluffs half a mile from Logan's riverside home. "Three separate vehicles parked in three separate locations out along Bluff Road. If they were friendly folks, they wouldn't be so sneaky. I've got a suspicion they're here to do some mischief." Noah lowered the phone on his end. "Say, Mountain? Want to go out and check the woods for bad guys? Our friend Logan has himself in a situation needs sorting out."

Logan grinned when he heard Noah's massive wolfhound bark in the background.

"You stay in where it is safe," Noah said. "I will check in with you later."

Logan took his coffee and sat back down at his desk to read more from the brown leather book.

He nearly choked when he looked out the window and saw a dark, hooded figure standing on his porch, staring directly at him.

CHAPTER SIX

Logan cautiously opened the front door. He sighed in relief when he saw Noah towering over his late-night intruder.

"Howdy, neighbor," Noah said. "Look what Mountain brought to my doorstep."

The small, dark figure in the baggy sweatshirt had his ample hood drawn up so it shadowed his face. Noah's wolfhound appeared beside him, a low rumble coming from his deep chest.

"Says he's come here looking to find the writer," Noah said. "Says he was sent by someone. Claims you need to hear what he has to say. If you want, I can escort him back to the car he left parked outside the fence on the road. Or you can listen to what he has to say. Either way, me and Mountain are on patrol duty tonight."

Noah walked off the porch, his large wolfhound trailing behind him.

Alex removed his hood and offered Logan a sheepish grin. "I followed you out here after you left Omaha."

Once inside the cabin, Logan offered Alex a seat on his lumpy couch next to the wood stove. Logan said nothing as he loaded up the stove and rekindled the fire inside it. Alex asked, "You are still reading the journal, right?"

Logan closed the twin doors on the stove. He stood up and nodded slowly. "Yes," he said, "though I haven't made it past entry three."

He walked over to his desk and picked up the leather-bound book.

Alex said, "They thought if you heard it straight from the source it would be more appropriate. They also said if I approached you and explained my journal to you, you could keep me out of the story."

Logan said, "You've mentioned 'they' twice. Who are *they?* And how do they factor into this?"

Alex anxiously asked, "Shall I read to you from my journal?"

Logan held the book up and seated himself on the opposite end of the couch.

Alex slowly removed the book from his hands and began to read.

Alex's Journal, Entry 4

When we joined Bobby up in camp lodge, he was already busy playing with the switchboard of Lakewood's security cameras. Bobby zoomed in on the camp lake. "I watched you in the lake," he said. "If I could figure out how to record with this thing, I'd say we had a real fine porno in the works!"

I looked from the image of the lake to Bobby. "Hey, are you sure this system didn't record our little fling in the lake?"

"No," Bobby assured both me and Max. "These are only turned on during summer hours. Can you imagine the tapes they would need to keep this system up and running in the off-season? Naw, this ain't set to record, but it sure is fun doing a visual sweep of the entire camp."

He showed us the new cabins of East Camp. Then switched to Ranch Camp. The archery range. The pop stand. Campfire area. And just as he was zooming in on Lakewood's challenge course, there came a flash of light on the center monitor.

"Whoa!" Max gasped. "What in hell was that?"

Bobby moved the angle of the camera back.

There in the trees was a movie set. Lights. Cameras. And action, lots of action, that appeared to have a method to the madness. A tall, lean director seated in a chair to one side of the set shouted, "Action!" And immediately a cameraman zoomed in on four dark-clad figures struggling to restrain what appeared to be a young man dressed in the garb of a thirteenth-century outlaw from the wilds of Great Britain. In fact, the young man looked like a wild, blond-haired Robin Hood as he struggled to break free from his captors. The abductors soon subdued the wily outlaw and held him firmly between them.

"Someone's filming a movie there on the edge of Lakewood!" Max said.

"Yes," Bobby said knowingly. "Baxster told me they were shooting the flick tonight. It's the main reason I brought you guys here. It's a movie set, and they've got tight security up there in that part of camp. I'm going to record it from here."

"Yeah," Max said, "but they don't know all the back trails that we do. We could ditch security guards if we had to. Let's get a closer look at this movie shoot."

Bobby remained glued to the console while Max and I slipped out of camp lodge.

By the time we stopped on a high knoll overlooking the movie set, the Robin Hood fellow slumped submissively in the grasp of his dark-cloaked, hooded captors.

Hidden behind thick bushes, Max turned to me and mouthed the word "Baxster."

I nodded. "Yes," I whispered, "Baxster."

One of his captors shouted, "We have him at last! We have captured Prince Corin, son of the French king! We have a hostage that may very well end this bloody war!"

Prince Corin/Baxster struggled once more to break free, but the four men closed in around him. "You squirm like a little lass!" one of the men said. "Your lordship is as pretty as one, too! Golden locks! Smooth-skinned cheeks! Ah, and the firm ass of a dainty maid!"

"Enough!" came a voice from the shadows beneath the trees beyond the clearing. A moment later, a tall and slender raven-haired young man made his entrance onto the set, stepping out from beneath the pines. He was dressed in tight-fitted leathers and moved with the grace of a swordsman as he approached center stage. He was extremely handsome, but for the moment, his features *were fixed with a look of outrage as he stopped in front of the prince.*

"It's Prince Corin, my lord," one of the men said. "We captured him after the battle on the ridge. We were just having some fun with him, King Richard. We're sorry if we offended you."

King Richard commanded, "Strip him!"

"No!" Baxster wailed as his four laughing captors removed his clothes. He stood there between them naked, his pale and lean body bathed in a spill of silver moonlight from above, his manhood slowly beginning to stiffen.

Richard dismissed the four men. "Leave us, now," he said. "As the King of England, I will be the one to warmly welcome him to his captivity."

The four men bowed submissively, stepping off the set.

Richard deliberately stepped up so that he was facing Baxster, the only thing between them his straight and lengthy erection. A smirk on his face, Richard lowered his eyes. "Nice," he softly said. "Very nice. Smooth. Long. Round head, with just that little tip of a curve to your shaft. That little curve is a nice attribute when you're entering and thrusting." Richard smiled. "You are now my hostage, Prince Corin."

He wrapped his right hand around Baxster's meaty erection. Baxster's breath escaped in a pleasurable sigh. Richard slowly pumped his shaft with long, gentle pulls. Baxster's eyes rolled upward; he lifted up on his toes, settled back down, lifted back up, sighed, began to softly whimper.

At once, Richard stopped, releasing his hold on Baxster's cock. "Nice balls, too," he said, sliding his hand down beneath his legs, tightly cupping both of his rather large, dangling balls.

He used the splayed fingers of his left hand to smooth Baxster's pubic hair, purposely brushing his shaft with feather-light touches as he pushed the hair down flat against his pelvic region. Baxster sighed again. Richard

*playfully wobbled his balls around in his cupped hand,
then curled up his fingers to gently tickle beneath the
tender orbs with light, swift strokes.*

Baxster leaned his head forward, resting it
submissively on Richard's chest.

"Remove my clothes, Corin," Richard whispered into
his ear. "Make me as naked as you."

Baxster did as he was told. In seconds, they were
standing naked before each other, their well-toned, slender
bodies glistening with sweat, their rock-hard cocks grazing
each other. Richard moved forward, thrusting his stiffness
into Baxster's, but he placed both hands on his broad
shoulders, forcing him to remain at arm's length. "Slowly,"
Richard whispered. "Let's just take this slowly."

Once again, he thrust his straight shaft at Baxster,
and this time, Richard shifted his cock so that their heads
grazed each other. Back and forth, he bobbed his cock
across Baxster's head, his shaft, down beneath his balls,
and back up so that his head, slick now with pre-cum, slid
smoothly over his pleasure spot. His eyes widened at the
sensation.

Hands planted still on his shoulders, Richard looked
down and Baxster followed his gaze to see a slender,
gooey tendril of sperm connecting his shaft with Richard's
round, smooth, moist head. Richard's hands dropped from
Baxster's shoulders and encircled both of their erections
in a strong, two-handed grasp. Locking the sperm-slick
shafts together, he worked furiously, pumping, pulling,
jerking, until both men were gasping breathlessly. He then
stopped, smiling at Baxster as he kept a firm grip on their
smooth-skinned throbbing sticks of manhood.

Baxster was not having it, though. He wrapped
himself back around Richard in a fierce embrace,
continuing to drive his hardness into anything that felt like
flesh. Panting. Gasping. Moaning.

"Easy there, tiger," Richard said, with a breathy
laugh. "I think you're ready now, don't you?"

"Ready?" Baxster curiously asked.

"*Oh, yes,*" *Richard purred, teasingly sliding one finger down the entire length of Baxster's stiffness. "Ready to have me inside you.*"

"*Well, I—*" *Baxster started to say, when Richard pulled him close and went wild on his left nipple with a tongue-lashing that left Baxster whimpering and letting out low moans of pleasure. "Yes!*" *he gasped, throwing his blond head from side to side. "Yes! I want you to drive deep inside me!*"

Richard made sure his spell of tit-sucking had its intended effect. He continued for several minutes on Baxster's left nipple before switching quite suddenly over to his right, this time slurping in a mad, sloppy frenzy. "Ahhhh! Ohhh! Yessss!" *Baxster's gasps came out in reedy whispers.*

Suddenly, Richard pulled off Baxster's tits, gently took hold of him, and lowered him to the ground. "The first time," *he said, "will probably be best received if you're on your back, Corin.*"

As Richard hovered over him, Baxster hesitantly leaned back and spread his legs wide. "What is that?" *he asked, watching Richard reach over and take a small metal tube out of the pocket of his leather breeches.*

"*This,*" *Richard said, opening the tube and squirting a creamy white liquid into the palm of one hand, "is to provide moistness. Here. Smell it. It's made of oranges and herbs and some greasy concoction. But it works well to slide myself in and out of you.*"

Baxster sprawled out on his back, slowly lifted his legs in the air, and fell silent as Richard worked the cream around the rim of his hole and up and down his crack. For good measure, he then leaned forward and tongue-flicked Baxster's stiff cock.

"*Will it hurt—*" *was all Baxster managed to say as Richard took his cock in his mouth, engulfing it with one swift gulp. And then Baxster let out a mixture of rapid breathing and deep groaning as Richard began to methodically work his fingers up and into his anal cavity.*

First one finger, then two. Back to one. In and out. In and out. Then two fingers. He increased his intensity with his cocksucking and gently slid three fingers in and deep.

Baxster responded by raising his legs higher, as if to open himself up even more. Soon, his bent legs were rising and falling in motion with Richard's slowly bobbing head and his gently probing fingers. "Ah, yes! Yes!" Baxster sighed as he bucked and swayed, completely overtaken by the deep, steady finger-fucking.

He was still mouthing the word "Yes!" when Richard released his cock from the warm confines of his mouth and withdrew all three fingers from the warm confines of his ass.

Baxster lay there, looking down the length of his body as Richard kneeled between his upraised legs and slathered the cream on his jutting erection. "It's so big," Baxster whispered. "Will it fit?"

"Shhh!" Richard urged him. "Lie back now. Just relax. Just relax and let me in, Corin."

Baxster did as he was told, his raised legs the only thing moving now that Richard was kneeling over him, prodding his lathered rim with his own lathered shaft. He poked. He prodded. He poked again, found purchase with his slippery dick head, then slid free. Baxster reached down and planted Richard's head up against his ass rim. "It's there," Baxster said.

Richard pushed forward, slowly, carefully, but also skillfully, knowing that soon Baxster would likely writhe in protest. But still, he thrust inward, first his purple head, then two inches of shaft, and then Baxster spasmed and let out a little yelp.

"Easy, tiger," Richard crooned. "Open! Open!"

Four inches of his shaft buried inside, and Richard froze, working on Baxster's tit with a wild frenzy. Baxster began to writhe, pulling on his shoulders, shoving his ass up against him, opening himself all the wider. Richard switched tits, moving to the left nipple with quick, repeated flicks that drove Baxster into another little fit of pelvic thrusts.

Richard shoved all eight inches of throbbing meat into Baxster's anal cavity. They froze like that for several seconds, Richard stabbed deeply into Baxster, penetrating him with his hardness. Richard let up on his tit sucking, raising his head to peer into Baxster's eyes. He pulled out, shoved in, pulled out, shoved in, checked Baxster's eyes, grunted loudly, and began to madly hump.

Baxster flopped about for long moments, his legs thrashing, his hands slapping down onto Richard's bare back with meaty little thwacks. "Uhhh! Uhhh!" he muttered, his head turning from side to side. Baxster almost wept. "Hump me! Hump me!"

And Richard did as he was told, and soon Baxster was going spastic beneath him as they shot their loads simultaneously.

And after a long pause, the director on the set managed to quietly say, "Cut!"

He then added, "And that, my friends, is a wrap!"

CHAPTER SEVEN

L ogan wanted to hear more, but first he needed a drink. He thought about another cup of coffee, but opted for something a bit stronger. He walked into the kitchen, asking, "Would you like something to drink?"

"A soda," Alex said. "If you have one."

Logan poured himself a shot of Crown in a frozen glass he took from the freezer. He added half a glass of 7 Up to the cold concoction and took a long, slow sip. He snagged another can of soda from the fridge and returned to the den.

Alex was thumbing through his journal.

"Before you continue," Logan said, handing him the soda, "mind if I record the rest of this?"

Opening his soda with a quiet *zzziiippp,* Alex said, "Uh, I'm not sure. Sorry, but you'll understand why when you hear the rest."

Seeing the genuine fear in his eyes, Logan said, "Fine. I'll listen without taping you."

"Thanks," Alex said, sighing in relief. He took up his story from where he'd left off.

Alex's Journal, Entry 5

Max and I found our path cut off by the security guards Bobby had warned us about. There were three of them. Big, burly guys, too. If we could have just slipped past them, I'm sure we could have moved like deer, so swiftly down trails we were both familiar with that we could have lost them in a heartbeat.

But as it was, they lit up cigarettes right there between us and the one trail that would take us back to main camp and the lodge, where Bobby was probably anxiously waiting for us.

We crouched down there off to one side of the trail, blending with shadows, playing like ninjas just like we did in our boyhood days. An hour later, the movie set was packed away and crew, actors, and stage hands were filing out down the road leading to the Deep Woods parking area. We waited, listening to cars and trucks starting up and driving away.

Max whispered, "Let's go."

I nodded silently and stood up to leave.

We both froze, however, when in the clearing below two figures stepped out of the shadows. One of them was the actor who had played Richard, the dark-haired king. The other one was Baxster.

Now that they thought they were alone, the two embraced and shared a long, slow kiss.

It was Richard who first pulled away from Baxster, slapping him on his ass.

"Hey!" Baxster yelped. "Easy, tiger. You'll have me doing something nasty to you if you're not careful, my lord."

The two laughed. Richard said, "You did really good tonight. I mean, if this was really your first time acting, you were dead-on."

The lean, blond-haired Baxster smiled, his white teeth flashing in the darkness. "When," he asked, "do you think we'll get paid for this, Todd?"

Todd, the raven-haired young man, gave a short laugh. "Paid? Hell, wasn't it enough to get the best fuck of your life? Now listen to you! You think we did this for money?"

Baxster looked a little surprised. "What? These guys who shot this flick are going to make plenty off it! You're kidding, right?"

Todd stripped off his black T-shirt and tossed it to one side of the clearing. "Come on, I'll pay you right now."

Baxster stopped Todd's roaming fingers as he undid his zipper. "No, Todd. I'm serious. These pornos make good money. Sex with you was great. But there's got to be some pay involved, right?"

"Yes," Todd said. "I was just shitting you. Payday is two weeks after this first shoot. It'll be hefty, too. So don't you worry your pretty blond head about it, Baxster. You'll get paid good for services rendered. Way better than you would if you were working the streets on the lower east side of Omaha."

Todd and Baxster were about to go for seconds down there in the moonlit clearing, and Max and I were just about to sneak off down the trail, when a deep, booming voice came from the trees to one side of the clearing below. "Baxster Crown?"

Baxster looked like a startled deer. He ran like one, too. He just up and left Todd down there in that clearing, his jeans down around his ankles.

Baxster Crown came swiftly up the trail. Running directly toward us. Max and I had no chance to slip aside and hide. He was on us that fast. There was terror in his eyes.

Max was plowed over by Baxster. I sidestepped both of them as they went down in a tangle of arms and legs there in front of me. "What the hell!" Max snarled, and Baxster gasped, "Alexander? Maxwell?"

He overcame his surprise. "Shh!" he desperately urged. "If you want to live, be quiet!"

The three of us stood there, staring back down into the clearing. Todd was struggling to get his boxers and jeans back up when a massive figure stepped out of the trees beside him. "Baxster Crown?" the giant said, making it sound like a question.

"Jeessuss!" yelped Todd, so scared he stopped fiddling with his boxers and jeans, and just stood there staring in fear at the big man before him.

"Baxster?" the man said, posing it as a question.
A gun appeared in his large hand.
*   Todd saw it and gasped a second later as the*
man shoved its cold metal barrel up against his slowly
dwindling erection.
*   "Baxster Crown?" the large man asked.*
*   "No!" squealed Todd. "No!" he yelled now. "I'm*
not!"
*   "Oh yes," the big man calmly said, "you are."*
*   He stepped back a few feet and fired his pistol point-*
blank into Todd's surprised face. He fired again, and Todd
crumpled and fell lifeless to the ground.
*   "And now," the shooter said, "you're dead, Baxster*
Crown. You can't scam the old man for one more damned
dime, you stupid little prick!"
*   The three of us stood frozen, forgetting to breathe,*
horrified by what we'd just witnessed.
*   When I did draw a short, shallow breath, I realized*
how close I'd come to fainting. Sparkling motes swam
in my vision. The sounds of the forest came alive around
me. Things came back at me with startling clarity. Max
grabbed me by one wrist and Baxster placed his hand over
my mouth. "Shh!" he hissed. "He's gone! But he hears us,
he'll come back!"
*   I nodded. His hand came away from my mouth. I*
looked directly into his catlike green eyes. He met my gaze,
and I saw terror in his look. I realized he'd just barely
escaped being assassinated back there in the clearing.
The big guy had been after him. He'd mistaken Todd for
Baxster.
*   "Let's get the hell outta here!" Max hissed, and*
Baxster and I followed him down the trail leading past
Todd's prone body and on to the pathway that would lead
us back to main camp.
*   Bobby met the three of us on the trail. He was excited,*
nearly bowling us over as he came sprinting down the
trail.
*   "Holy shit, you guys!" he gasped as Max and I caught*

him, both of us taking notice of the small black object he held. *Righting himself by propping himself up between us, Bobby looked over at Baxster and said, "That was not part of the movie, was it, Baxster? I mean, the guy getting shot, that was for real, right? That guy really shot your... friend...or whoever he was to you?"*

Baxster said, "Acting associate. He was the one who got me the gig to shoot the flick. I don't honestly know who the big guy was with the gun. But evidently—"

"Evidently," I said, "the guy was gunning for you and yet he took out your associate instead. Why did he come after you in the first place?"

Baxster peered around at the darkened cabins and nervously said, "I will explain that, but can we just get the hell outta here first? This place gives me the creeps."

Max followed his gaze, searching the shadows for any sign that the gunman might be lurking nearby. "But we need to call the police—"

"No!" Baxster nearly shouted. "Leave the cops outta this! Do you wanna get ticketed for trespassing and maybe get an accessory to murder charge?"

Bobby looked at Baxster warily. "No, even if we get trespassing citations, we need to turn this over to the cops. It's proof of what really happened out there."

As he said "this," he held up the black item, a disk case. "I started taping your steamy sex scene and the camera kept rolling all the way through to the actual murder. It's definite proof that this man actually shot your friend."

Max and I looked over at Bobby. "Do you realize," I asked, "that if we turn this in, we will become witnesses in court? Are you prepared to go through with this, Bobby? I mean, we could turn this disk in anonymously, and no one would be the wiser. Because what if this has some kind of mafia connection?"

At this statement, Baxster Crown actually laughed out loud. "Unless of course, there is some kind of gay mafia running around out there. No, but if you do turn this

*disk in, it could get some psycho killer hunting you down,
too. Come. Like I said, I'll explain this if we can just get
the hell outta here."*

*We nodded in agreement and soon we led Baxster off
through the trees and exited camp the same way we had
entered, by slipping through an opening in the fence.*

*We approached Bobby's car cautiously, thinking that
any moment the gunman was going to spring out from
between the trees and blast us away as he had the poor
guy back inside Camp Lakewood.*

*But Bobby managed to drive us safely down the back
road and then back onto the highway that would take us
back into Omaha.*

*Before turning onto Highway 50, Baxster said, "Tell
you all what the murder was about if you don't head into
the O just yet. There's a cabin tucked away down the road
from here, and I've got the key to the door. Drive me there,
and I'll tell you everything you want to know about this
shooting you all witnessed."*

*Max wanted to take the disk directly to the cops.
Bobby was leaning toward turning it in anonymously. And
I was about to side with Max when Baxster said, "Any
of you like to drink expensive beer? There's a whole lot
of rare beers stored in the icebox at the cabin. And while
we're tipping back some cold ones, I can fill you in on the
details of this murder. Then maybe you'll all see why you
can't just turn it in."*

*The cabin turned out to be more or less an expensive
mansion snuggled deep in the hills near Louisville. It
was one of those two-story log-built homes that I always
dreamed about having somewhere in Colorado, not in the
foothills of Nebraska.*

*But Baxster produced a key to the cabin, and after
showing us around the huge place, he offered us beer from
the icebox and led us to directly to the hot tub.*

*There, he shucked off all his clothes, offered us all
a corny smirk, waggled his slowly growing erection, and
slipped into the bubbling water.*

"Come on, guys," he urged us. "Make yourselves comfortable and get in here with me."

Bobby and Max removed their clothes, but I wanted to know who the place belonged to and if we could expect to have any company out there in the near future.

"Owned by one of my older clients," Baxster said. "And unless he comes back from his summer home in France before winter, no, he won't be showing up here anytime soon. The place is mine for the next three months. Strip yourself and join us, Alex. You won't be sorry."

I did as he said and followed Max and Bobby into the large hot tub. Baxster guzzled a beer that I couldn't pronounce, let alone ever tasted before. Bobby, Max, and I sipped our foreign beers and Bobby finally asked, "Okay, we just saw a murder, and while you don't seem to be too concerned that your friend was mistaken for you and then shot by some psycho gunman, we are slightly shaken up by what we witnessed. Please tell us, what the hell is going on?"

CHAPTER EIGHT

Logan crunched the last of the ice cubes in his glass, the aftertaste of whisky lingering. "That's the ultimate question," he said, interrupting Alex's story. "Just what the hell was going on?"

Alex offered him a sheepish frown. "I'm getting to that, Logan. May I call you that? Sorry, Mr. Walker just doesn't seem to fit you."

Logan studied Alex, wondering if he was playing him, thinking how easily he had wormed his way inside his cabin, wilted before him when he'd showed him the journal, and proceeded to tell him in colorful detail about the night he'd witnessed the murder there at the summer camp.

"Alex," Logan said, firmly, "continue reading."

Alex settled back on the couch.

Alex's Journal, Entry 6

Baxster finished off three more beers while he told us all about his scam to get rich at Franklin Judson's expense. He told us in lurid details of all the sex he'd had with the guy, calling him the King of Gay Kings.

Bobby had to fill me and Max in on exactly who Franklin Judson happened to be. Bobby's dad, being a corporate lawyer, had once represented the man during one of his Nebraska business deals. So Bobby knew all about his Midas touch and all his business deals turning to solid gold.

"He's worth millions!" Baxster crowed with a stupid giggle. "But he wouldn't lift one finger to help me out. I

was the Boy Wonder back when I was sharing his bed. I simply asked Frankie for a loan after one heated fuck, and his mansion doors were closed to me ever since. So I threatened to go public with a sex abuse allegation, and evidently, Frankie sent someone to snuff me out."

"So," I asked, not sure I wanted to know more about this crazy situation, "your friend, Todd—"

"Acting associate," Baxster repeated. "I had no attachments, despite the steamy sex scene we performed. I am sorry he's dead. But hey, better him than me, right?"

Bobby and Max exchanged uneasy glances. Both looked to me to gauge my reaction to his flippant attitude. I nailed him with a rather cold stare and asked, "You mean you were blackmailing Franklin Judson, threatening him with exposing him as a pedophile, and Todd got killed because of it? This Judson would actually hire a hit man to have you eliminated as a threat? And you don't care that your scam got an innocent person killed?"

Baxster drunkenly laughed. "Who said Todd was innocent? He's been a porn star since he was sixteen! And I spent many nights in Frankie's bed, so he owes me for getting his rocks off on my hot, young body! One million dollars would have kept me quiet. He should have just paid me, and then Todd wouldn't be dead and I wouldn't have involved all of you in my troubles."

Bobby nearly gagged on his beer. "Us?" he asked. "Hey, we're not involved in this, Baxster."

"You're not?" Baxster asked. "Two of you watched the bad guy gun Todd down. And you, Bobby boy? What are you gonna do with the disk you recorded in that camp lodge? Throw it away?"

Baxster allowed his words to sink in before adding, "Before, all I had was my word against Franklin's that he'd had sex with me when I was an underage boy. Now with this disk, I have some leverage to really play with. How much do you think Frankie might pay to get a copy of this disk?

"Also, who might pay for that video of Todd getting

snuffed out? The murder of Todd at Lakewood is sure to be front-page news. Todd, murdered shortly after starring as the lead actor in a porn flick filmed out there at Camp Lakewood. We could sell this tape to a very high roller, one who will pay a considerable amount of cash to take possession of this tape before it reaches the proper authorities. What father in his right mind would want the public to know his own son was the star of a gay porn flick?"

He paused for effect. "Especially Todd Guildman, son of Nebraska Senator Douglas Guildman, who serves on the Nebraska Legislature."

Bobby's eyes widened. "Are you crazy? You want to try and sell the evidence of the murder of a state senator's son?"

"Oh, come on," Baxster said, scooting over toward him and reaching beneath the water to fondle him.

"Hey," Bobby said. "Stop that. Don't try to manipulate me by—"

Baxster lowered his head to suck ferociously on his left nipple. Bobby tried to push him away, but Baxster had a firm hold on his erection, and his tongue action had him glued to the side of the hot tub. Bobby tried to extract himself but Baxster snaked himself around Bobby in a playful manner, whipping his tongue back and forth over both of his nipples.

He then dove below the water and his head shot between Bobby's legs. Bobby gave in to what must have been some great cocksucking. He dropped his hands flat on Baxster's arched back and made a face that spoke volumes about what he was feeling.

Baxster finally surfaced, but even as he drew in a breath, he climbed up into Bobby's lap, hugging him fiercely as he began to hump him. Bobby began to resist, but Baxster remained so intent on subduing him that even as he squirmed his way out of the hot tub, Baxster stayed glued to him.

Bobby tried repeatedly to push Baxster away, but

by then he must have been drunk enough to give in to Baxster's insistent pelvic thrusts. Max and I sat there, a little turned on by the wrestling match the other two were having.

Bobby and Baxster ended up sprawled on the cushions scattered across the tiled floor. Bobby tried to pry Baxster's mouth off his hard cock. He gasped, "Whoa, slow it down some, Bax! I like it slow and easy, not fast and furious!"

Baxster pulled off Bobby's cock. He started to lean back, but Bobby locked him in place, shoving his rock-hard cock back toward Baxster's pursed lips.

Baxster turned his head from side to side as he took quick snips with his wet tongue, performing feathery kisses all over the head and the shaft of Bobby's long cock.

"Ahh," Bobby began to croon. "Oh, yes! Nibble on my balls!" Baxster did so, first nibbling tenderly on Bobby's left nut and then gobbling up his right nut in a slow, steady suck that had Bobby writhing on the floor.

Baxster then latched onto Bobby's bobbing hard-on, and with a little force, he spun him over onto his face and chest.

Baxster planted his face in Bobby's butt crack and began rimming him like there was no tomorrow. Bobby was facing us so Max and I could see his face, all scrunched up, his eyes tightly closed. "Ahhh," he panted. "Ohh. Unnhhh! Oh, my. Oh, yes!"

With a quick flick of his erection, Bobby was flipped back over onto his back. Baxster worked his cock like a magic wand, turning it this way and that. He then slid down to eat his meat with noisy gulps and slurping sounds.

By then, Bobby was so far gone, he would do anything Baxster wanted. And like a gymnast, moving smoothly, Baxster crawled up over him, placing his dick head into the pucker of his butt.

Humping him slowly, so that dick head and butthole were sporadically touching with ever-increased friction,

Baxster whispered, "Hey, one of you? Help us out here. Fetch that lube over there on that futon, will you?"

Max climbed out of the hot tub, snatched up the tube, and quickly joined the two over on the cushions. "Yes," Baxster gasped as Max smeared lube all up and down his butt crack.

"Unnhh," Bobby crooned as Max then lathered up his raging hard on with more of the slick stuff.

Baxster and Bobby let out simultaneous groans as Bobby slid into Baxster. Pumping up and slowly back down, Baxster elicited more pleasure-filled moans from Bobby.

He played then, Baxster did. He rode up and down on Bobby's thick shaft, scooting high and shoving down low. Burying all of Bobby's cock inside him and then slowly inching his hardness out of him. Back and forth he wiggled his butt, working a slow motion that had Bobby panting.

Baxster then rose high, nearly pulling the rod out of the close confines of his ass. Bobby tried to rear up to keep them connected, but Baxster shoved him back down and then performed a slow, slippery slide down on the full length of Bobby's boner.

Baxster then went crazy. He humped madly, thrusting and pounding, his arms wrapped around Bobby's upper body, his face buried in his chest, mouth working one nipple. He humped frantically, his ass rising up and down in furious thrusts. At that point, it was hard to tell who was getting fucked. Bobby was sprawled flat on his back, his hands digging into Baxster's butt cheeks as he bucked beneath him. Baxter was working Bobby into a frenzy, his fully penetrated ass making little sucking sounds as he rose up and down.

Just when it seemed Bobby was about to shoot his load, Baxster pulled himself off Bobby's impaling shaft. Before Bobby even realized it, Baxster pulled on his super-sensitive knob and spun him over onto his stomach. Wiping the lube from his ass all over his cock, Baxster romped down hard on Bobby, pinning him to the ground and penetrating him at the same time.

Bobby let out a loud groan, and Baxster reached around and pulled and plucked at Bobby's slick and shiny cock.

Baxster rapidly pumped and pushed inside him while Bobby spewed a load as Baxster beat him off.

Baxster remained inside Bobby and lowered him back to the cushions beneath them. "Prop your head up on a pillow," he commanded. "Yes, like that, then raise your ass up against me. Okay, yes, like that. Now hold very still."

Pressing himself forward into Bobby's raised ass, Baxster worked his lube-coated fingers all over his back, fingering with feather-light skims all the way around to his nipples.

Bobby raised his hips, matching the fingering Baxster was performing on his tits.

And then Baxster lurched forward, sending Bobby's face into the pillow, and Baxster worked himself into a frenzy, laughing as he finally came.

CHAPTER NINE

L ogan sat there on the couch. Alex might be there, as he'd said, to add credence to what he'd recorded in his journal, but he detected lust in his blue eyes every time he glanced at Logan.

This young man was hot, no doubt, but Logan was not inclined to cross a line like that. It had been seven years since his former lover, Jimmy West, had left him for a younger man, and Logan missed him at times. He had been living alone for seven years before Jimmy, and seven more after he'd left. Even so, he wasn't so desperate as to consider messing around with the young man on the other end of the couch.

"Todd?" he said. "The other actor was actually the son of Senator Guildman?"

Alex nodded and held up his empty soda can. "Could I maybe get another?" he asked.

Logan nodded. "Sure." He pointed at the leather-bound book. "There's more written down in here?"

"Yes," Alex said. "I've got one of those photogenic minds, I remember everything in great detail. I want to become a writer some day. I just hope I live long enough."

Logan walked into the kitchen and retrieved two cans of soda from the fridge. When he handed one to Alex, his fingers brushed up against the back of Logan's hand, purposely. Logan settled in on the opposite end of the couch, opening his own soda. "Now, as you were saying…"

After taking a sip from his can, Alex read more of his story.

Alex's Journal, Entry 7

Baxster sat there, watching the sun climb over the hills to the east. He said, "So do you all wanna hear about my first time?"

We sat there in the hot tub, looking out the window beyond Baxster, seated like good schoolboys across from him. All three of us nodded sleepily, for we'd stayed up the rest of that night talking about what we going to do with the disk of Todd's murder.

Baxster watched our faces as he told us, "When I was just thirteen, I was at a Boy Scout camp not far from here. My tent mate that night was a hunky older kid named Chase. He was one year older than me, and Chase and his fellow Scout Jason had a definite plan that night. I joined them there in the shower house, thinking that was all we were doing. Taking a shower.

"Chase started out by grabbing my crotch, while Jason prodded and pinched my ass. I got a boner right away, and as the two of them cornered me there in the shower stall, I knew something was going to happen. They left me alone, though, there in the showers. But on the way back down to our tent on the walk back through the woods, Chase kept whispering, 'Gonna give us some of that tonight, right? You're gonna spread them ass cheeks wide and let us pump up inside you, right? I've got a jar of Vaseline, and we'll go nice and easy on your tight little butt.'

"And they did, nice and easy three times before the sun came up. After that, I was hooked and could not seem to get enough."

Baxster looked at the three of us and smirked. "I shared that story with my two tent mates at the reparative therapy camp my father forced me to attend just this past year. And those two were so turned on by my story, they reenacted it right there in the middle of Camp Reborn late one summer night last July. There we were, three eighteen-year-old boys left alone in the shower house, our counselors fast asleep. Carl and David, two Catholic boys, were there at that camp, just as confused as I was as to why our families would send us to a camp full of young men to try to repair us, to force us to be born-again and change our orientation. When I shared with Carl and Davey my first-time experience, they listened to every detail there in the shower house.

"On the way back to our tent, I stopped right in the middle of the trail, leaned against Davey, and shocked him by frenching him long and deep. He didn't have the sense to put his arms around me. Just stood there, letting me tongue-fuck his mouth. When I finished kissing him, Davey ripped my shirt off me, then clawed at my gym shorts, shucking them and my underwear off and stripping me completely naked there in the middle of the trail.

" 'Pick up his clothes,' Carl ordered, and then he darted after me as I sprinted down the trail. There I was running stark naked through the camp with two horny boys trailing behind me. When I got back to our tent, I dove into our pile of sleeping bags, placing my ass up in the air, offering them a great view of my butt. They stripped out of their clothes quickly. Davey was first to mount me, slavering globs of Vaseline all over my ass crack while fingering me with his pinkie. He was then inside me, pumping and grunting and shoving my face down into the pillows beneath me. Carl lubed up his fingers and began running them up and under my ball sack. He pulled down hard on my boner, bending it back and working it like he was milking a cow.

"As Davey came inside me, I pumped furiously into Carl's tight-fisted grasp. When Davey pulled out of me, Carl grabbed me by both hips and plunged inside me. He ran his hands all over my upper body until his hands locked into my hair. He pulled my head back and then planted his lips on my neck, licking all the way up to my ears. He was a little rougher than Davey, but I was turned on by his dominance over me.

"Davey snuggled down between my spread legs, planting his lips under my ball sack, and began sucking fiercely, and then Carl went into a mad, crazy frenzy, ramming deeper and deeper. Davey stopped sucking on my balls and then snaked himself up and under me until just the tip of his tongue was slithering over my left nipple, then my right, then back to my left.

"I don't honestly know when I came, but with Carl going for broke on my back and Davey licking the hell outta of my tits, I finally collapsed on top of Davey, my sperm plastered all over him.

"Together, the two of them turned me over, checking my face to see that I was still conscious. I remember Davey saying, 'Is he okay? Is he still awake? Or did he pass out?'

"Carl laughed. 'Oh, he's okay. Lather him up some, and we'll take him again.'

"And they did. Spreading me out on my back between them, Davey planted a glob of sticky Vaseline down into my ass crack. He pulled on one leg while Carl pulled on my other leg, spreading me wide. Very slowly, even gently, Davey slid his index finger into my butt ring. I looped my arms around both of their necks, forcing their faces down onto my chest. I reared up, leaning onto my upper back while making my ass more available to Davey's steady fingering. And he was building momentum, chuckling softly as he heard me blow and mutter and gasp as the sensations rocked my entire body.

"Carl bit me softly on my right nipple. Davey breathed hot air on my left, flicking ever so lightly across my erect tit with the very tip of his tongue. They both seemed to know they were onto something, for they worked my nipples for a full twenty minutes, both giggling when I panted and begged them to keep going, not to stop, not ever to stop.

"I started rearing up, trying to stay connected to Davey's two fingers jabbing repeatedly into my ass. My *legs thrashing in the air, barely restrained by their hands as they tried to keep me under control. Davey laughed. 'He's going crazy over this!'*

"Carl merely grunted and said, 'Enough playing with him! I want some payback!'

"They must have followed some silent signal between them because the moment they quit nipple sucking me, they hauled me up onto my hands and knees. Carl slapped my butt with his raging hard-on and commanded, 'Open up again, kid!'

"He snatched me by my hair and I opened my ass to have a hard cock shoved into it. I tried to stay on my hands and knees, but Carl forced me forward onto my face and chest. It lasted longer this time, but I was feeling no pain. Carl kept licking my ears as he came inside me, and when he withdrew, Davey flipped me over onto my back.

"Crawling up over me, Davey reached down and fingered my boner up into his crack. I remember watching his face above me, and even in the shadows I could see he was grinning as he forced my prick up inside him. He kneaded my chest with his fingers, skimming lightly but never touching down solidly on my nipples. He began to move up and down, going so slowly I felt like my dick was a banana being peeled inch by inch. Davey leaned forward and hugged me, gasping once before his mouth glided over mine and his tongue snaked down until I nearly gagged.

"Penetrating him and his tongue penetrating me, I lost it. I began to writhe and squirm, and this turned Davey on. He began short, quick thrusts, forcing my dick straight up his ass. I nearly screamed with pleasure when Carl shoved one of his middle fingers directly up my ass without warning.

"He worked me furiously, and Davey broke off our lip lock as he grunted and shot hot splots of sperm all over my chest and my face. I came then, too, crying out until Davey cupped a hand over my wide-open mouth. 'Shh!' he warned. 'Keep it down! We got a whole night before us,

if we don't get caught. Quiet down. Relax, and we'll play some more, if you like.'

"*I did like it. In fact, Carl and Davey played with me for two more hours before all three of us must have passed out from the pleasure we'd shared.*"

CHAPTER TEN

Two things saved Ben Donovan's life that chilly autumn night: a falling star and the big Indian. The star, a bright green streak in the late-night sky, caused Ben to glance up toward the wooded hillside above him and he caught just a glimpse of the two shadowy figures within the black trees.

A second later, a brilliant flash momentarily blinded him. Ben was dropping down to his knees when the first silenced round zipped above his head. He closed his eyes, willing the bright spots to stop swimming through his vision as he hugged the tree at the bottom of the hill.

Ben knew a second shot would soon be coming. He waited. Listening. Forcing himself to remain calm and still. He heard a *poof!* and the second round passed above him, striking the cottonwood behind him.

Slowly opening his eyes, Ben glanced to his left and right, then down at his black leather jacket hugging his huge frame. He had three choices. Rolling to his left would place him behind a clump of vegetation to one side of the deer trail.

Crab-crawling to his right would send him sliding down into a deep ravine on the other side of the trail. And unzipping his jacket to remove his own weapon would expose him to the men above him. Ben flinched when he heard the shrill squeal of pain coming from the wooded slopes above. Another sound drifted down from the hillside above him. It was a growl, an animalistic one, causing goose flesh to rise on Ben's neck and shoulders.

"Oh, Holy Jesus. Call your dog off, man!"

Then a scream. And silence.

Ben reached up to unzip his black leather jacket. His hand was shaking. *Get a grip, man!* he told himself. He did feel much safer once he had his 9-millimeter Glock in hand.

Silently, Ben released the safety on his pistol. He slowly raised the Glock in front of him with a two-handed grip and stepped out from behind the tree, peering into the inky blackness of the forested ridge above him. He waited. He listened. Narrowed his eyes. Thought he saw a shadowy figure slither out from beneath the trees. Released his breath and slowly took a step forward.

Crack! The dried branch popped beneath his boot. *Oh, now,* he chided himself, *that tears it! Whoever's out there knows exactly where I am!* The sudden growl from his left made him swivel in that direction. Ben couldn't see anything but a wall of blackness. Ben Donovan felt quite helpless, thinking about cutting and running. Something he hadn't done in close to twenty years.

No, when Ben Donovan was hired to do a job, the mark was a good as dead. He hadn't failed to come through for a clients in the last forty-two hits. He was cold, ruthless, and extremely professional. Benjamin Donovan was a natural-born killer.

A sudden noise came from the dark trees directly behind him, and Ben wheeled around fast. Too fast. He slipped and fell backward to the ground.

Something dark and large appeared directly above him. He had only one option.

The dog snarled. A low growl rumbled deep in its chest. Its huge lips peeled back to reveal sharp, pearl-white canines.

He leveled his gun at the beast and gently fingered the trigger.

"Don't shoot my dog," a deep voice rumbled.

Ben's finger froze.

"Back off, Mountain," the voice commanded.

At once, the large, grizzled wolfhound stood down, big black eyes fixed on Ben.

"Drop your gun," said the enormous man stepping out from between two nearby trees. "If we had wanted you dead, you'd been standing before the throne by now, Ben."

Lowering his gun, Ben looked up at one of the largest Native Americans he'd ever seen. The long-haired, dark-skinned Indian stood well over six feet tall with a lean, muscular build, not an ounce of fat on him.

Dropping his Glock beside him, Ben asked, "How did you know my name?"

The big man looked over at the wolfhound. "Mountain? Should we let him stand up? He doesn't look all that dangerous sitting there on his ass, does he?"

The wolfhound offered Ben one last warning snarl.

The giant offered Ben one massive hand and pulled him to his feet. "I thought you'd be bigger," he said. "The way those two men on the ridge above talked about you, I was expecting someone a little more threatening. You do know your plans to assassinate my writer friend were to include a cleaner crew? Only question is, who sent Mike Carrol and Brad Helman to silence you after the deed was done?"

Ben stood there. Only one person knew he was coming here tonight. "Come with me, Mr. Donovan. My friend, your target, needs to meet you."

"You want me to meet this writer?" Ben asked.

The giant nodded, picked up Ben's Glock, and headed off through the woods.

"What about Carrol and Helman?" Ben asked.

"Both are a little tied up at the moment. It's best we leave them that way."

CHAPTER ELEVEN

When Noah Standing Bear knocked on Logan's front door, Alex shot off the couch like a gun-startled deer. Logan went to his desk and slipped his pistol out of the middle drawer.

"Is that loaded?" Alex asked.

Logan walked to the front door. "It wouldn't be much use otherwise."

"I need a bathroom," Alex said.

"First door on the right," Logan said, wondering if the panicked kid was going to escape out the bathroom window.

He swung the door open, and the massive form of Mountain came inside. The big wolfhound snuffed in friendly fashion at Logan's lowered hand, allowing him to run his fingers through his rough fur. The dog bounded up onto the couch, his huge brown eyes locked on the two rather large men coming through the doorway.

Noah used the barrel of his Winchester rifle to gently prod Ben Donovan into the den and ushered him over to Logan's easy chair. "I was right about those men," he said, forcing Ben to seat himself. "Told you something was very wrong about those investigators. They are not legit. Carrol and Helman were out there in the woods, waiting to gun down this guy here. A cleaner crew, wiping out the hit man sent to wipe you out, Logan. His name is Ben Donovan."

"You didn't use excessive force, did you?"

Noah said, "Mountain did. I left those other two cuffed to a tree out there near the old rock quarry."

Ben said, "You should have killed those sons of bitches!"

"I," Noah said, "should have killed all three of you. But my writer friend has a conscience, so I thought you two should have a sit-down to sort this thing out. So, Ben, how do you feel knowing the man who hired you also sent two men to eliminate you?"

"Hurt," Ben responded.

"According to those two investigators up on the ridge," Noah said, "you are a professional hit man. But how come I get the sense that despite your God-awful reputation, you are really a teddy bear at heart?"

"More like a grizzly," Ben corrected him. "Your regards for me are touching, Chief. If my soft spot for dogs hadn't kicked in out there, this would have turned out quite differently."

Mountain's lips curled back in a fierce snarl. "My dog tells me you still have killing on your mind, Mr. Donovan. I think you need to turn over your other piece. Take it out nice and easy, or you will be eating a slug."

Logan trusted Noah knew what he was doing.

"The best way to deal with three hired gunmen is to eliminate them. I do not appreciate the ruthlessness of a man who hired the three of you just because my writer friend has uncovered some nasty truths. Killing my friend is unacceptable. Killing the three of you just might be a justifiable option." Noah stared intently at Ben Donovan.

Ben casually raised his left pant leg to reveal the small-caliber pistol in a small leather holster strapped to his ankle. He slowly reached down and removed the pistol with a two-finger pinch, placed the pistol on the floor, then kicked it across the hardwood floor.

Logan stooped and picked it up, then placed both guns on his desk. "Would you care for a drink, Ben?"

Ben eased himself back in the chair. "You're not mad that I came here to snuff you out?"

Logan walked over to the liquor cart situated near the kitchen entry. "On the contrary. You coming here confirms I'm onto something fairly big. Franklin Judson has only dug himself a deeper hole by sending you and those other two men. Doesn't it make you curious about the man who hired you? What more does he have to hide?"

As Logan reached for a bottle of Jack Daniel's on the cart, Ben said, "Any kind of soda would suit me. I've been clean and sober going on twelve years now."

Logan handed one can of soda to Ben and the other to the likewise clean and sober Noah Standing Bear, saying, "Mountain seems content now, so I think you can take things down a notch, don't you, Noah?"

Noah lowered his rifle.

Ben spotted the leather-bound book on the couch where Alex had left it. "Ah, a little late night reading?" he said, an amused grin on his clean-shaven face.

"Yes, some unknown source sent me this journal. And placed me in a great deal of danger."

Ben's dark eyes remained fixed on the images on the front of the leather book. "You're in more danger than you know. Judson may have been behind this hit I was hired to carry out tonight. But the folks connected with that symbol are far more lethal and far more thorough than Franklin Judson. I'd say you are in quite a mess, Mr. Writer. That symbol there is the sign of the Pagan Princes."

"And who are they? A Middle Eastern biker club?"

"No," Ben said seriously. "The princes are homosexuals into some secret order shit. You've heard of the Masons? The Illuminati? Well, these guys are an order that's been around—some say longer than the freemasons. You've heard of temple prostitutes, right? Female and male? Well, that's where they started, back in the biblical days. You've certainly heard of phallus worship, right? Remember all those pillars of Egypt? Shaped like cocks? There's some tie-in there, and some royal prince loved his boys. He started this order that's flourished throughout the centuries."

"You're kidding, right?" Logan asked.

Ben gestured at the book. "That's porn, right? They put their stamp on porn. Books, films, even documentaries, anything that will help establish their order. They even believe in it like a religion. Do you know the story of Ganymede?"

Noah grunted and said, "The little Greek boy abducted by Zeus to serve as his cupbearer?"

"Or as some perverts would say," Ben said, "the boy who served as Zeus's cup. Because of that story, the Greeks made a popular sport of abducting young boys to use as their playthings. Man-boy love was alive and well in ancient Greece."

"Man-boy love," Logan said, "is still alive today. It's just swept under the rug. I studied it briefly. There's a big difference in between what a pedophile and an ebophile happen to be. Pedophiles prefer prepubescent boys, while ebophiles prefer boys who hit puberty. I once did a report on sexual abuse concerning the Catholic Church. It's not just the Catholics, but Lutherans, Methodists, Pentecostals, and every denomination where boys are placed under the authority of men. Including the Boy Scouts of America."

"Exactly," Ben said. "So you knew nothing about that symbol until just now?"

Logan nodded. "How did you know what this image represented, Ben? A dragon embracing a lion?"

Ben shrugged. "Well, let's just say it was a priest of the princes who sent me out here tonight." He gave an angry snort. "And now it appears the scrawny little fucker has set me up. You and I have a common enemy."

CHAPTER TWELVE

L ogan closed the door to his cabin.

Placing his pistol back inside his desk drawer, Logan wondered if Noah had done the right thing. The big Lakota had brokered a deal with the hit man, telling him he could have his guns back if he gave his word to simply walk back to his car and just drive away. Ben had argued at first, saying he wanted to follow Noah back to the old quarry to eliminate the two investigators cuffed to the tree.

"Let them go," Logan had told Noah. "Just send them on their way. There's no way in hell you can just shoot them and drop their bodies in the shafts of the quarry."

The moment they were gone, Alex emerged from the bathroom. "That was the guy who killed Todd! That was the same bastard who came to Lakewood hunting for Baxster!"

Logan nodded. "I figured as much, but what would you have me do? Call Crime Stoppers and turn him in based on what? Do you still have the DVD of him doing the actual shooting?"

"Bobby does," Alex told him. "But if he turns it over to the cops, Baxster is threatening to turn in all the DVDs of us!"

"DVDs of you?" Logan asked, puzzled.

"Yes," Alex said. "Sit down and I'll tell you about it."

Alex sat on the couch. Logan checked the clock on the wall. It was nearly two a.m. Alex began reading.

Alex's Journal, Entry 8
    By the time Baxster had shared his camp experience

with us, the three of us had boners. It was quite a story he'd told us, and we all could relate to the three-way play.

And although he offered to suck us all off, Max and I just stood there and watched as Baxter went down on Bobby.

Max slipped around behind me, pressing his dick up against my butt, and then he did me like we used to do when we were kids. Smearing pre-cum all over his index finger, he lightly skimmed over my sperm duct. Over and over.

Pushing my hard-on down at just the right angle, he worked one finger right across my trigger. I had no choice but to lean back into him and allow him to play.

"Remember the first time we did this?" Max whispered in my ear, swirling his tongue around for good measure. "Remember how I made you cum?"

"Uh-huh," I moaned, remembering he had been spending the night, and we ended up in a wrestling match dressed only in our boxers. My boner got so hard, I thought it would rip right through the silky fabric. Max had pinned me to the floor of my bedroom, holding my arms above my head and leaning forward so that his own hard cock was peeking through the slit of his boxers. We wrestled some more, throwing each other off nearly a dozen times, before our pretend fighting turned into something more. I just stopped and stared up at Max as he yanked down my boxers, slipping them down past my knees, over my feet, and tossed them in a corner. I latched onto the band of his shorts and peeled them down and off him. Max came back down on top of me, our dicks connecting and sending electric thrills through both of us. We humped each other for quite some time before Max whispered, "Let me see you cum, Alex. Okay? Just let me watch."

He had such an eager look in his eyes that all I could do was nod and regret the fact that he was climbing off me to watch me perform for him.

Although I had beat off every night since I had turned twelve, I had never quite cum like I did that night. I turned into a super horny boy there in the darkness of my room. I pulled on my cock and just went for broke. Not knowing why it felt so good. Not knowing if it was right or wrong. Just gripping and pulling and tugging wildly until sweat dripped off my brow, dribbled down between my balls. My feet twisted at awkward angles. My skinny naked legs moving up and down. My chest and stomach clenched almost as tightly as my fist on my throbbing, slick shaft. Until at last, I felt my load shoot up through my shaft. Spurt into the air. Over my belly. All over my pumping arm.

And so there in the cabin along the river, with Max reminding me of our first time together, Max crawled up over me and smeared pre-cum all over us. Pretending to grimace and telling him to stop, I felt him rocking and grinding. I finally just relaxed and Max wrapped both arms around my upper body, tongued repeatedly at my left ear and my neck, and humped me until he was panting and gasping. Just when I thought he was going to shoot, he slid off me, grabbing me by my dick.

I had no choice but to rise onto my hands and knees. Still clutching my cock in a tight-fisted grip, Max moved up behind me, forcing me to lean back into him. He bent my dick at a downward angle and ran just the tip of his cum-smeared index finger over my sperm duct, fingering evenly at my trigger.

I arched my back, allowing him to run his finger over my spot just below my dick head. "Feels so good, doesn't it?" Max asked me as he played. "That's your sperm duct. It's what makes you shoot your load, Alex. Am I hitting it just right?"

"Oh, yes," I gasped, turning my head so that I could look back into his eyes. He ignored me, though, as if he could only focus on the cock fingering he was so intent on performing. I think I lasted for a good five minutes before I was sucking in and blowing out, writhing and begging him to finger faster.

When I came, I let out a bellow and Max became so

turned on that after I'd shot, he forced me back down on my face and stomach and humped my butt until he, too, had cum all over me.

Max and I both laughed as we heard Bobby moaning again somewhere else in the room as Baxter gave him head.

When we were all done cumming, pretty well spent from all of our playing around, Baxster sat us all down and outlined a business proposition for us.

"How would you guys like to make tons of money," he said, grinning wickedly, "just for having fun like we just did?"

Bobby, Max, and I momentarily forgot about the disk of Todd's murder that we still were not sure what to do with, and we listened intently as Baxster said, "How would you guys like to star in a porno flick?"

Bobby and Max were a little turned on by the idea.

I, however, was not so sure. I mean, who would see it? And would our faces be blacked out? How legal was it? I had a million questions going through my mind.

Baxster said, "Relax, guys. I'll introduce you to my producer tomorrow evening. He can tell you how things work in the industry. Then you can make up your minds if you want to act in his porn flicks or simply back out. His name is Brian Peters, no pun intended. He's the Gay King's Jack of Spades or Queen of Hearts, depending on how one looks at it."

Alex stopped and adjusted himself slowly, almost dramatically.

"The first flick," he said, "was produced under the direction of Brian Peters. It was filmed by Ridge Majors and financed by Franklin Judson."

Logan nodded. "And these productions were shown where? In Frankie's mansion? On the Internet?"

"Not sure," Alex told him. "I just know Baxster threatened to send copies to our parents if we ever got questioned about them by cops or investigators."

"Wow," Logan muttered, feeling sorry for the kid.
Alex began to read again.

Alex's Journal, Entry 9
      *We surrounded him in the showers. Baxster was a
lean, naked eighteen-year-old kid, nicely formed with
pecs and abs to die for. The blond-haired kid did not
know how lucky he was to be sculpted so well. Like a
Michelangelo marble statue, Baxster stood there before
Bobby, Max, and I, the three of us dressed as members of
a football team. Slowly, we peeled off our blue jerseys and
skintight acrylic pants until we were all standing there
peering at Baxster with nothing on but our jock straps.
Once these came off, slowly and inch by inch, Baxster's
manhood rose straight up and then curved slightly back
into a perfect arch, his round head touching just beneath
his belly button.*
      *"You know you're going to enjoy this," Bobby said,
"don't you, tiger?"*
      *Baxster's eyes traveled down to our slowly rising
boners. "What are you going to do to me?" he asked,
hesitantly.*
      *Max and I moved forward, swiftly and without any
pretense, grabbing Baxster by his arms and pinning
him against the shower wall. Max grinned at him and
whispered, "Relax. We won't hurt you. We just want to
play with you for a while."*
      *With that, he bowed his head and ran his tongue all
over Baxster's left nipple, eliciting a whimper. He began
to writhe in their grasp. I moved in on his right, bowed
my head, and worked his right nipple with wet and noisy
slurps.*
      *Within seconds, Baxster's arms were spread wide on
the wall he was forced up against, and then using our legs,
Max and I spread his legs wide as well.*
      *Spread-eagled, with us two sucking on his tits,
Baxster watched as Bobby moved in front of him, a bottle
of lavender shampoo in his hand. He squirted the purple*

goo all up and down his protruding shaft and all over his pubic hair and dangling balls, then said, "Turn him around, boys. Let me wash his ass crack."

We raised Baxster's arms above his head, and with a renewed frenzy we sucked his nipples. Coming off and going down, then using quick flicks, we made sure Baxster was compliant. Keeping his hands and arms spread wide, we spun him around so that his face was pressed gently against the tiled wall in front of him. Once again, Max and I used our legs to nudge his legs apart, spreading them wide, opening his ass crack.

Bobby kneeled down, his eyes fastened on the tight little asshole revealed in a layer of fine hair.

He glopped on the sweet-smelling shampoo and coated the hole, the cheeks, the crack, and began running slick fingers down the crack and under Baxster's ball sack.

He washed all four areas for a long time. All the while, Baxster was writhing with pleasure and making little gasps as he rose up and down on his bare feet. He turned his head from side to side, his arms raised above him, his legs spread wide, and his ass being pleasured with incredible ministrations.

Just when he didn't think he could take any more, Baxster stopped turning his head, arched his back, and let out an explosive gasp, for Bobby suddenly went down open-mouthed on his asshole and began rimming him fiercely.

Max and I held Baxster against the wall, forcing him up a bit higher to give Bobby access or he would have slid down to the floor. He was squirming and bucking in our grasp, so overwhelmed with pleasure that he simply wilted into Bobby's grasp as he slid up behind him, pressing his cock against his butt crack. Bobby then reached around Baxster and ran both hands over his erect nipples, working them until he was mewling loudly.

Baxster was going wild with pleasure. "Ah! Ohhh! Mmmm! Uhnnhh!" echoed off the surrounding tile-covered walls, the muttered sounds never quite forming words.

Max and I released his wrists and ran our hands down to his extended pubic region. As Baxster's arms came down to the backs of our necks in a pleasure grab, we slowly caressed his cock and balls.

I, on his right side, ran my hand up and under his balls, cupping them and gently kneading them, using the tips of two fingers to flick the area between his sack and his ass crack.

Max, on his left, grabbed onto his hard shaft and jacked him for several seconds, working him into another frenzy before releasing him to watch with fascination as Baxter air-humped for long moments, stabbing his seven inches of hardened flesh at nothing as he was overwhelmed with the sensations rocking his entire lithe body. It looked like he was fucking an invisible fourth person as the three of us continued our play with him.

"Uhhh! Uhhh! Unnhhhh!" slipped out between Baxster's lips.

He grappled frantically with his fingers at the heads of me and Max holding him. He bent forward repeatedly as Bobby tit-flicked him. When that felt too good, Baxster air-humped some more, going into spastic little dances that caused the three of us to laugh.

Max gave him a hard grip on his dick and made him cum in his tight-fisted grip.

He released him only to find that Baxster continued to buck and squirm and writhe as if his cock needed his hand once more.

CHAPTER THIRTEEN

A lex made a hasty retreat to the bathroom and remained in there for quite some time. Logan could only guess what Alex was doing as he stepped outside.

The night air was chilly, and as he stood beneath the stars, closing his eyes, he imagined the horny eighteen-year-old performing rapid cock strokes inside the bathroom. Logan would have resisted him, he knew, but he wasn't taking any chances.

When he came back inside, he found Alex curled up on the couch, asleep. "Um," he said, "aren't your parents going to wonder where you are?"

Alex stirred slightly and mumbled, "Mom's out of town. I don't have a dad." He rolled over and went back to sleep.

Logan placed two blankets over him, then quietly padded down the hall to catch a few hours of sleep before the sun came up.

Four hours past sunrise, he was seated at his desk, amused by the soft snoring of Alex still sleeping the day away on the nearby couch. The leather-bound journal lay open on the desk beside his keyboard.

Logan wondered at the great detail Alex was capable of producing. Logan wished he knew who had sent him this journal. When asked, Alex had simply said, "Bobby stole it from me, gave it to Baxster. Baxster gave it to Brian Peters. Brian had it bound with the leather backing and embossed with that metal disk on front. I wanted it back after I saw how cool the cover was, but Brian said it was going in the archives. I never heard about it again until I learned you had it."

The leather-bound book had a rather cryptic feel to it. The words had a connection to these symbols, and Logan wanted to find out what that connection was. He began researching the symbols, which took him all the way through the rest of that morning.

He came up for air and left the cabin to take a walk. When he'd started, Logan had no idea he would soon find a constant theme linking the facts in a bizarre way. The Celtic knotwork that circled the Egyptian-looking lion and dragon seemed at first to tie these two symbols together. Druids came to mind immediately. And druids caused Logan to think of ancient religions that predated Christianity. Images of rune-carved stone monoliths drifted through his thoughts as he read up on the Celtic druids of Ireland, Scotland, and Wales.

And then his research took a different turn altogether. Logan discovered that Queen Scotta, whom Scotland was named after, had come from Egypt—and that the purest bloodline of the Celts came from Egypt when Scotta and her ships came to Scotland's shores.

"But where do they fit into this scheme?" he said out loud as he walked the trail winding through the hills above the river. "Ancient Sumer, the Summer Country, and the Greeks and their pederasty, man-boy love trickled down into Egypt, where temple prostitutes and fertility rites were performed. Temple prostitutes were often young males who had sex with those who paid tribute to the gods and planted their seed, in symbolic and physical ways. The worshiper was always the top, inserting his hard phallus into the soft rectum of a passive, willing young male in a fertility offering said to please the gods and ensure bountiful crops. So therefore, where Greeks were boy lovers to mentor, to teach, to nurture, and to educate young boys with their man-on-boy relationships, the Sumerians, Egyptians, and other tribes and races practiced this submissive sexual practice as part of their religion, connecting sex with boys with the worship of gods.

"What gave them the notion that gods were pleased with this type of sex? Or was this concocted from the tale of Ganymede, who was abducted by Zeus because of his rare, boyish beauty and made to be his submissive cupbearer and lover?"

When he returned to the cabin he found Alex still sound asleep, so he quickly scanned the notes he'd typed in earlier.

1. Why did the Greeks have young boys as lovers? Were they sexual partners or simply mentors to these boys?
2. Did these boys willingly participate with these older male suitors? Did they consider it natural to learn from them in all manner of things, both sexual and educational?
3. Were they ever forced? (*See previous notes on the abduction of Ganymede, which became sort of a play between the suitor and the boy he wanted to have relations with*)
4. Did these boys consider it abuse? Or were most honored to have the attention and affections of an older man?
5. Why has this continued throughout history? Male prostitutes are common in every country. Young boys actually go out to seek sex with older males. Male temple prostitutes were common in biblical days. It was not only common but simply part of life.
6. Why then were laws made to outlaw this practice? Even though laws were made and penalties stiff, boys and men still seek each other out and continue these encounters. It carries over to this day.
7. Define "boy." In most societies twelve or thirteen was considered a man. In the Jewish faith, a bar mitzvah is held for a boy of thirteen to celebrate his manhood.
8. So is there a difference between pedophile and ebophile. Ped would be men sexually attracted to any boy who is prepubescent. Ebo would mean being sexually attracted to young males who had reached puberty, aged thirteen to eighteen.
9. Separate both from the fact that neither of these acts are committed by homosexuals per se. Ten percent is what they claim. But the majority of gay men do not engage in or condone such sexual encounters with young boys or children. There is a sexual grid that each person has and that grid determines who they are attracted to. Saying that all gay men would engage

in sex with boys is like saying all heterosexual men would do the same with young girls.

10. Is there a reason? Is there a frozen, arrested, sexual drive that attracts these men to younger males? Is it in the genes? Is it trying to recapture that first sexual encounter? Some would say to connect with youth. Is it only about sex? Power and control over these younger males? Or is there any love involved? Is it possible that an older man can have great affection for a younger male?

11. Do any younger males seek this relationship out? Are they, too, attracted to an older man? A role reversal? Or is it that they enjoy having power over an older man by pleasing him?

12. To most married adults, gay and heterosexual, this man/boy encounter or relationship is appalling and they consider those who engage in such as sexual predators and sexual deviants who should be locked away and punished for their crimes.

13. But if this practice has been with mankind for all the years, in so many societies, is it right to consider a consensual encounter (age of consent in most states is sixteen) between two individuals regardless of age so very wrong? Are these people who engage in this behavior perverted? Not those who forcibly and sexually abuse children, but those who enter into a consensual sexual encounter with each other. Because there are millions out there.

14. If we prosecuted all folks who practice sodomy (in some cases, any sex outside the missionary position) we would be flooding the courts with all manner of folk, then labeling them as sexual offenders.

15. Sodomy is still on the books in the majority of states. Most believe it applies only to anal sex, but not so. It derives from the city of Sodom, which was destroyed, according to the Bible, for the many sins of its citizens, not homosexuality. But all lawmakers have associated

that word with any sex play outside of the norm. Anal as well as oral.

16. Answer these questions thoroughly, and I'll have the makings of a very pertinent book.

Chapter Fourteen

Brian Peters greeted Logan cordially at the door of the Judson mansion. "Please come in, Logan Walker. I have much to share with you."

He was small in frame and face, and in his early thirties. His hair was dark, his skin was tanned and smooth. Yet for all his good looks, Logan had a hard time imagining Brian Peters as the Boy Wonder who'd been Franklin Judson's right-hand man these past ten years.

Against his better judgment, he'd left Alex back at the cabin. Alex was too terrified to return to his home in Omaha. He'd practically begged Logan to let him stay longer. Logan had called Noah, asking him to fetch Alex's car and to keep on eye on his place, in case the two investigators came back.

"I know where your investigating is taking you," Brian Peters told Logan quietly. "Before you stumble further down the road you're on, perhaps I can give you a bit of direction."

Logan remained silent.

"I just want to make it clear to you," Brian said, "that Frankie is not the monster you assume he is. By now I'm sure you've heard rumors, and I want to set the record straight about Franklin Judson. Some call him the Gay King. I have been Franklin Judson's valet, courier, and private butler for the past ten years. I've also been in charge of filming and directing the films in his personal library. That's what prompted me to call you. I want to set the record straight."

"Why are you sharing this information with me?"

"Damage control," Brian said. "Trying to undo some of what

Baxster Crown has done to blackmail Frankie. It's not fair how this is playing out. There is a porn library. It's been removed from the mansion so there's nothing here to incriminate Franklin. I have it in a safe place. But I do have several DVDs here with me. I will show you."

But first Brian served him a tasty meal of seared shrimp and scallops. He offered him a drink, but Logan opted for a soda instead of alcohol, as he wanted to stay sharp. They sat in comfortable lawn chairs beneath the shade of massive twin elm trees. Brian made small talk as they ate, and when finished, he lit up a pipe.

"So far," Brian said, "I assumed you don't like what you hear about Frankie. Rich older gay man taking advantage of all these young gay boys. A monster who recruited hundreds of gay teens to service him and his friends. I know on the surface this doesn't look right, but all had a deep need to be loved."

Brian stood up and gestured for Logan to follow him back inside. He led him to a sunken living room at the back of the mansion, where they sat in two ample chairs. Brian picked up a remote control and began to talk.

"The films were produced using young street whores. We showed our little productions to individuals who Frankie invited to our parties. These men were all members of the Order of the Pagan Princes. Surely by now you've researched the symbols on the book that was sent to you. I am assuming you know of the order that stretches back into the depths of time and has ties in so many cultures with fertility rites, temple prostitutes, and the channels linking many souls with the Divine through acts of pure pleasure."

"The lion embracing the dragon on the leather-bound journal," Logan said. "I didn't find anything concrete. I concluded that the Celtic hoop, the Egyptian lion and dragon all symbolized something significant. I didn't have the time to follow those threads."

Brian said, "I sent you that book in hopes it would enlighten you to our plight."

"Your plight?" Logan asked. "Why send me writings of such graphic, sexual detail? Weren't you afraid it might disgust me to the point that I'd want to expose your employer? Didn't you consider the fact I might take such offense that I'd begin my own crusade to reveal to the world what Franklin Judson is all about?"

Brian stared directly at him. "Are you not gay?" he asked Logan, his eyes widening slightly.

"Whether I am gay or straight, what does that have to do with me accepting what I've read in this journal so far?"

"How much did you read? If those writings disgusted you," Brian said, "you would not have continued to read them, correct?

"I sent you that journal to help you to understand. To let you know the Gay King did not seduce any of them. You can't rape the willing. Seductions and enticements were not involved. All parties were more than willing. The fact is, there are boys who enjoy having sex with older men, and older men who are inclined to have sex with young boys. It has been happening since the dawn of time.

"We have the Greeks with their accepted and commonly practiced pederasty, but that is only one society where sex between men and boys took place frequently. All over the world, this takes place in each and every society, from tribal Africa to sophisticated Japanese bathhouses to the suppressed Chinese to Russian porter boys. The British had their urchin class, their boarding schools where male-on-male sex ran rampant amongst the 'fags,' younger boys who serviced the older boys most willingly and submissively." Brian smiled. "Surely you knew all of this, right?"

Logan nodded.

Brian raised the DVD controller and the film began. "In case there is any confusion, we have starring in this particular production Baxster Crown and the three young men from the journal you've been reading: Alex, Bobby, and Max. Consider it part of your research."

Brian Peters and Logan watched.

Alex juggled his balls slowly and with care, spreading his pubic hair out with more globs of shampoo until both orbs were shiny and slick with goo.

Bobby slipped back down and began rimming the spastic figure of the naked Baxster, sucking and driving his tongue deep, which sent Baxster into more spasms. As Bobby's tongue slid in and out in frantic motions, Baxster pushed his butt back into his face so as not to miss any inch of the tongue Bobby was slipping him.

"Uhhh! Ahhh! Ohhhh!" continued to slide between his lips. Finally Baxster cried out, "Oh, let me cum now! Let me shoot a gusher! Beat me off, one of you, please! Please, let me cum!"

Bobby ran his tongue up and through his extended butt crack, then slowly rose to stand behind him. He nodded at the other two, and they stopped playing with Baxster's balls and cock.

Bobby grabbed a handful of Baxster's wet hair and pulled him back into his embrace. Baxster was still air-humping even as Bobby ran his free hand down his chest, over his abs, and down to cup his balls. *"Do you think we have it churned enough, tiger?"* he whispered into his ear, the tip of his tongue swirling there for seconds. *"Do you think you will boil over and spew a great gooey load for us?"*

"Oh, yeah!" Baxster gasped. *"Foamy milk! Spurting geyser! Shooting my wad far! I will jizz a gusher! It is what you guys want to see, right? Me shooting my sperm, right?"*

Bobby laughed and said, *"Yes, to see you go white, buckling at your knees, crying out with a whimper, your eyes at half-mast while you drool for us. That should cover it. But first, we have something else in mind."*

Baxster leaned back into his embrace, his boner jutting up between his legs. Alex and Max stepped in on either side of him and used their hands to spread his legs. The three of them lifted him up slightly so that his cock was standing up between them, and then Bobby came around in front of Baxter and moved in between his spread legs. He lowered his head, opened his mouth wide, and slowly sucked his entire length into the warm, wet confines of his mouth.

As he swallowed his cock to the pubes, Bobby made little moaning sounds punctuated by the moans Baxster was making even as the other two snickered and watched with wide-eyed fascination as their teammate's nose rested in Baxster's thick pubic hair.

Deep-throating after all the tender ministrations caused Baxster to rise up in the air. He screwed his eyes closed, then opened them repeatedly as if he could not believe the feelings coursing through his squirming naked body. He rose and fell with each suck of his cock. He began a steady slow bucking motion, his legs held by the strong hands of Alex and Max on either side of him, while Bobby grasped him by the hips and held him in place while he feasted on his fully extended dick.

Baxster started to huff and puff, so turned on that he was fully prepared now to blow his wad.

And then the mouth came away from his dick.

Alex and Max slowly lowered him to the wet floor. Bobby followed him, remaining between his widely spread legs. He grinned at him like a hungry wolf as he poked the tip of his middle finger into just the rim of his ass.

Bobby used his shampoo bottle once more and squirted a great gob of soapy purple globs down around Baxster's crack and hole, swirling his middle finger around until he buried it to his knuckle.

He slid in two fingers and Baxster, without so much as a grunt, rose and met him. "Ram me full, boys!" he whispered seductively. "Slide those big cocks into me and fill me full of white milk! Hump your fucking brains out! Pin me to the floor and have your way with me!"

Alex and Max on either side of Baxster suddenly let out gasps of surprise as he grasped them firmly by their jutting boners. As he began to stroke them, holding them both at arm's length, he jacked his ass up until Bobby's cock slid into his hole. Baxster slowly worked his ass-glove down and over the full extent of Bobby's flesh rod.

Bobby could not take any more and he dove on top of Baxster, pinning him to the floor as he madly humped him like a rag doll, driving his cock in and out, in and out, like a jackhammer. Max stuck his own cock in Baxster's face, prodding his wet, gooey head across his lips. Baxster licked the head several times, ran the tip of his tongue across his sperm duct, and then turned his head to the side for Max to slide his dick into his mouth.

For long moments, all that could be heard there in the showers of the locker room were the moans and groans of the four as they grunted and puffed.

It was Bobby who came first. Rising halfway, his upper body arched above Baxster, he shot with force as his ass jiggled about, moving from side to side, then straight up and down in five last quick humps.

"I'm blowing inside him, boys! I'm coating his insides with my jizz!"

Even as he came, keeping his cock buried in Baxster's ass, he drooled all over Baxster's chest. Baxster was hardly aware of the spit bath, however, as he worked Max's cock back and forth in his mouth. To get a better angle on the warm mouth, the rimmer gently pushed the butt fucker out of his way, even as Bobby's dick came loose from Baxster's ass and he kneeled there over him.

Baxster broke off his lip lock and whispered, "I promise to finish you, but Alex is about to blow, so move aside. Give him room to pelt me with warm cum."

Max reluctantly removed his cock from Baxster's mouth, then moved so Alex could lean over Baxster's naked form and jizz freely. Spurts of milky cum, coaxed by a last frenzied pumping of Baxster's tight-fisted hands, shot all over his chest and nipples. Alex continued to cum, breathing heavily and rocking back and forth in Baxster's grip.

Baxster released him and used both hands to pull Max over his face to finish what he'd promised. Bobby and Alex looked on, totally drained as Max began a steady rising-and-falling motion over Baxster's face, burying his shaft all the way in his mouth.

The two marveled at how far down Baxster's throat Max appeared to be. And still Baxster was hungry for more, and his neck strained just beneath his chin as he gulped and slurped and took all seven inches down into his throat.

Max rose to his hands and knees and froze, looking like he was about to take it doggy-style. Baxster kept his sucking motions at a fevered pitch, then ran his middle finger up into Max's asshole. Max moaned and his head bobbed about and drool leaked from the corners of his mouth as Baxster sucked him off.

"Unnnn! Unnnn! Unnnn!" Max let out in short intervals, and then one long, low "Oooyah!" as he spasmed above Baxster, and spasmed and spasmed until he had spent his load.

Bobby rose then and stood over Baxster. "And now," he said, "pleasure yourself before us."

"What?" Baxster asked in disbelief. "Without any help from any of you?"

"Just beat off!" Bobby said with a small chuckle. "Who knows, you perform well enough, you might perk us up for a second go-around. Now, just beat your meat in your tight little fist."

Baxster lay sprawled at their feet, his eyes moving from soft dicks to their spent faces. He then slowly reached up, wiped cum off his chest, and used his sperm-coated fingers all over his rock-hard cock. He ran the goop all down the shaft, around both of his balls, then reached up and smeared some more off his chest to coat his head and sperm duct. He arched his back, causing his sperm-slick dick to protrude up toward them.

Baxster played while they watched. He sighed. He groaned. He began to breathe heavily, his nostrils distorted, his mouth slightly ajar. Baxster raised his legs, hoping one or two of them might grab onto them, and Max and Alex did. They held his legs a little apart while he writhed there, flicking their sperm all over his most sensitive sperm duct. He bucked backward, closed his eyes tightly, and was about to blow when Bobby commanded, "Stop!"

Baxster did so at once, panting breathlessly. "Okay," he asked, rather excitedly. "Now what?"

"Milk it," Bobby whispered. "Milk him, Alex. Make him blow white!"

Alex used one hand at first, running it up and down the length of his shaft. He worked it all over his glistening rod, rubbing sticky sperm all over it, until the head was shiny and looked ready to burst. Then he used both hands to cup Baxster's shaft and milk it slowly until Baxster was squirming around with pleasure once more.

"Stop!" commanded Bobby once more. "Stand up and turn around, with your boner jutting out before us."

Baxster did so, and Alex went right for his chest, slurping and licking both nipples. Baxster hugged his neck tightly and gave him free access. Bobby gently reached out and placed two fingers over and under Baxster's jutting boner.

Baxster went back into a little spastic dance, his lithe form shooting up and down between their naked bodies, his legs spread wide, his feet barely finding purchase on the floor, his arms wrapped tightly around Alex's shoulders, his ass air-humping like a madman. "I'm blowing!" he gasped.

The other three watched Baxster's pulsing cock as gobs of white cum spurted from his cock head. Bobby continued the gentle rubbing with only one finger and worked Baxster until he shot six more globby spurts, all the while crying out with tiny whimpers that caused the other three to laugh out loud.

CHAPTER FIFTEEN

B rian turned off the DVD player. He got up from his seat, crossed the room, and opened up the double doors of a rather large bookshelf recessed into the wall.

"Frankie's library," he told Logan, "is fairly extensive. I've actually compiled a list of the books it contains, and I would encourage you to read some of them for information pertinent to the book you are writing. You would be surprised at the many books of boys on boys, boys on men that have been written. A majority of people would call this the sexual abuse of boys, but read for yourself and decide if these writings depict abuse or consensual relationships."

Logan was still wrestling with the fact that Alex had made these pornographic films with Baxster willingly. Of course, he'd said he had done so on account of Baxster's threats to expose him after producing the first one. But Logan figured Alex had still had a choice. And Alex hadn't looked like he was too troubled about performing in the film he'd just seen. He joined Brian before Franklin Judson's extensive library. "All of these," he asked Brian, "are sexual in nature?"

"Yes," Brian said, handing him a list. "Does it surprise you that there are so many?"

"Quite frankly," Logan said, "yes. I had no idea."

Logan slowly read the list of books:

1.　*33 Snowfish* by Adam Rapp
2.　*The Abomination* by Paul Golding

3. *All American Boy* by William J. Mann
4. *Allan Stein* by Matthew Stadler
5. *The Asbestos Diary* by Casimir Dukahz
6. *Avoidance* by Michael Lowenthal
7. *Billy* by Whitley Strieber
8. *Boy O'Boy* by Brian Doyle
9. *A Boy's Own Story*, an autobiographical novel by Edmund White
10. *The Brothers Bishop* by Bart Yates
11. *The Coming Storm* by Paul Russell
12. *Counterfeit Son* by Elaine Marie Alphin
13. *The Culvert*, an autobiographical novel by Clint Adams
14. *Death in Venice* by Thomas Mann
15. *Dream Boy* by Jim Grimsley
16. *Enchanted Boy* by Richie McMullen
17. *Embrace* by Mark Behr
18. *Edinburgh* by Alexander Chee
19. *Fall from Grace* by Andrew Greeley
20. *Father of Lies* by Brian Evenson
21. *Flannelled Fool*, an autobiography by T. C. Worsley
22. *For a Lost Soldier* by Rudi van Dantzig
23. *The Fourth of June* by David Benedictus
24. *A Good Start, Considering* by Peter Ryde
25. *Happy Baby* by Stephen Elliott
26. *The Heart Is Deceitful Above All Things* by JT LeRoy
27. *Hey, Joe* by Ben Neihart
28. *An Honorable Profession* by John L'Heureux
29. *The Immoralist* by André Gide
30. *Jumping the Scratch* by Sarah Weeks
31. *A Kind of Hush*, an autobiographical novel by Richard Johnson
32. *The Lantern Bearers* by Ronald Frame
33. *Little Chicago* by Adam Rapp
34. *Lord Dismiss Us* by Michael Campbell
35. *Loving Sander* by Joseph Geraci
36. *Mac* by John MacLean
37. *The Man Without a Face* by Isabelle Holland
38. *The Moralist* by Rod Downey

39. *Morning Star, Volume I of the First Born of Egypt* by Simon Raven
40. *Mysterious Skin* by Scott Heim
41. *Mystic River* by Dennis Lehane
42. *The Priestly Sins* by Andrew Greeley
43. *Queer* by William S. Burroughs
44. *Return to Innocence* by Gary M. Frazier
45. *The Romance of a Choir Boy* by John Gambril Nicholson
46. *Sandel* by Angus Stewart
47. *Sarah* by JT LeRoy
48. *Savage Justice* by Ron Handberg
49. *Secret Friendships*, an autobiographical novel by Roger Peyrefitte
50. *The Sex Offender* by Matthew Stadler
51. *Shakespeare's Boy* by Casimir Dukahz
52. *Sleepers* by Lorenzo Carcaterra
53. *The Smell of Apples* by Mark Behr
54. *A Son Called Gabriel* by Damian McNicholl
55. *The Sorcerer's Apprentice* by François Augiéras
56. *Teardrops on My Drum*, an autobiography by Jack Robinson
57. *Terre Haute* by Will Aitken
58. *Time of Our Darkness by Stephen Gray*
59. *Touched* by Scott Campbell
60. *The Tricky Part: One Boy's Fall from Trespass into Grace*, an autobiography by Martin Moran
61. *What Happened to Mr. Forster?* by Gary W. Bargar
62. *When Jeff Comes Home* by Catherine Atkins
63. *When Jonathan Died* by Tony Duvert
64. *The World of Normal Boys* by Karl Soehnlein
65. *Altar Boy: A Story of Life After Abuse* by Andrew Madden
66. *Autobiography of an Englishman* by "Y"
67. *Beyond Closed Doors: Growing Beyond an Abused Childhood* by John Andrews
68. *Escape from the Shadows* by Robin Maugham
69. *Father's Touch* by Donald D'Haene
70. *Book Twelve of the Greek Anthology*, a memoir by Richard Hoffman

71. *If It Die* by André Gide
72. *Moab Is My Washpot* by Stephen Fry
73. *Out of Bounds* by Roy Simmons and Damon DiMarco
74. *The Quest For Corvo* by A. J. A. Symons
75. *Running with Scissors* by Augusten Burroughs
76. *Slayer of Innocence*, a biography by Jim Conover
77. *Some Boys* by Michael Davidson
78. *Strong at the Heart: How It Feels to Heal from Sexual Abuse* by Carolyn Lehman
79. *The World, The Flesh and Myself* by Michael Davidson
80. *Dares to Speak*, a 1997 anthology of essays on Boy-Love, edited by Joseph Geraci

Brian said, "Much of the literature describes pedophilia and ebophilia, but some are about love."

"Love?" Logan asked, in disbelief. "Men having sex with boys?"

Brian gave him a look of puzzlement. "Some are not about abuse of boys at all, but about love shared by both partners. Surely in your research you have discovered many of these consensual relationships have developed into very loving relationships. Or does that disgust you? That a boy could actually fall deeply in love with a man? Love has no bounds, as some writer once claimed. And it certainly does play a key role in many of these relationships.

"In our case, if you interviewed every man or boy involved, a deep emotional attachment developed between them and a strong bonding took place in eight out of ten cases. Yes, there are some who abuse boys, and I would like to weed them out, as they give the rest of us a bad name. But for the most part, there is a certain magic that takes place between boys and men. Deny it all you want, and leave that component out of your book. But if you were honest, after all that I share with you through these books, you will get a fuller, clearer picture of how things really are."

Logan simply stared at him.

"Despite the many men who actually love boys," Brian continued, "there are abusers, many in positions of authority. And this kind of sex has nothing to do with love."

He gestured at the shelves of books in the recessed alcove,

saying, "Cameron Miller in *Counterfeit Son* has been sexually abused all his life by his father. Nathan in *Dream Boy* is abused by his drunken father. Brown in *Little Chicago* is abused by his single mother's boyfriend. Jamie in *Jumping the Scratch* is abused by a caretaker at the trailer park where he lives. In *The Sorcerer's Apprentice*, a boy is sent to live with a priest who abuses him. In *Altar Boy: A Story of Life After Abuse*, Andrew Madden is molested by a priest. Martin O'Boy in *Boy O'Boy* is abused by a church organist. Gabriel in *A Son Called Gabriel* is abused at school by a priest. The abuser in *Father of Lies* is a lay provost from the Mormon church. Andrew Greeley's *The Priestly Sins* and *Fall from Grace* describe abuse in the Catholic Church. Robin Maugham describes the nighttime activities of pedophile prep schoolmasters in *Escape from the Shadows*. Mr. Rudge, one of the teachers, also abuses a boy while staying at his home as a tutor. James Moore in *The Abomination* is first seduced at a 1950s English prep school by a master, Mr. Wolfe, at age nine. At English public school, he is abused by his music teacher. David Rogers is a nineteen-year-old student when he falls in love with thirteen-year-old Antony in *Sandel*."

He paused. "So, yes in some cases there is no love involved, simply abuse. In some countries, it is a criminal offense to make sexual contact with a child. It is often described as child grooming. But child sexuality dominates most of these books. Of course, readers should also define in their own minds when exactly a boy is no longer considered a child. Seventeen-year-old Todd Spicer in *The World of Normal Boys* invites fourteen-year-old Robin to a party and then has sex with him. Robin then discovers that Todd had done the same thing with Scott when Scott was twelve and Todd aged fifteen. Nathan in *Dream Boy* has a sexual relationship with Roy, an older boy who lives next door. In *Lord Dismiss Us*, Carleton loves Allen, a much younger boy. Thirteen-year-old Karl De Man in *Embrace* has an affair with his best friend Dominic. Edmund White, in *A Boy's Own Story*, at fifteen had anal sex with his twelve-year-old friend Kevin. The younger boy took the lead. James Moore in *Abomination* is first abused at age nine, and he welcomes and encourages the master in his advances and the encounters are gentle and loving for the next four years. Matthew in *Allan Stein* falls for his hosts' very attractive fifteen-year-old son Stéphane, and the boy encourages the man. Ten-year-old Serge in *When Jonathan Died* is sexually very demanding, and Jonathan obliges his every whim.

"Tony in *Sandel* takes the initiative in developing an intimate relationship between himself and David Rogers. Tony leads him on, suggesting that David photograph him without his clothes on. Ruy in *Shakespeare's Boy* is portrayed as a willing participant in his sexual adventures. In *The Tricky Part*, Martin is initially passive, but then discovers he desperately needs the physical contact. Martin is ambivalent about the touching and other sexual acts: he wants them, but he is also ashamed.

"Robbie in *Touched* appears not to be deeply hurt by the abuse itself, though the police investigation, the court experience, and the reaction of his family all hurt him deeply. Martin Moran describes the long-lasting effect of his childhood abuse in *The Tricky Part*, his attendance at counseling sessions for adults who were sexually abused as children, and his eventual recovery. Theo in *Happy Baby* craves pain, and his desire to be hurt stems from the brutal treatment he received as a child in state custody and the memory of Mr. Gracie, a caseworker who raped him when he was age twelve.

"Dave in *Mystic River* remains deeply disturbed by his abuse all his life. He eventually cracks and murders a man he sees abusing a boy in a car. After two and a half years of captivity, Jeff in *When Jeff Comes Home* is released and returns home. Jeff narrates the story of his abuse and recovery and is affected by the shame of not having hated the sex. Jeff initially refuses to cooperate with investigators. His abuser is, however, eventually caught, and Jeff gradually comes out of denial."

Brian turned at the sound of the soft scraping of shoe leather on the hardwood floor just beyond the den.

Logan gasped when a dark figure appeared at the open French doors, a rather large, silenced pistol in his meaty grasp.

Ben Donovan raised the gun.

CHAPTER SIXTEEN

Ben blinked in surprise as he became aware of Logan standing there.

"You?" Ben said in astonishment. "You are certainly in the wrong place at the wrong time."

"I can see that," Logan said.

"They sent you, didn't they?" Brian said, his voice almost a whisper.

"No one sent me, you sorry son of a bitch! I came here on my own! You set me up, you sick bastard! And now, you die!"

Brian began to weep.

"Nothing personal," Ben said to Logan. "You're collateral damage."

"Wait a second," Logan said.

Ben lightly caressed the trigger of his pistol. "Why?" he asked.

But then something clicked inside Logan's head. "If," he said, "Brian went through all this trouble to send me Alex's journal, why have me killed?"

Ben raised his gun, pointing it at Logan's face. "This is Brian Peters, right? This is the man who contracted with me to put a hit on you, correct?"

Brian stammered, "N-nn-nnn-no! I have no idea what you're talking about."

"Liar!" snarled Ben, fiercely poking the tip of his silencer into Brian's right cheek.

"He might not be," Logan told Ben. "Something doesn't make

sense. Isn't it more likely Frankie would simply toss money at this to make it go away? Like he has done so many times in the past? Why is this time different?"

Ben thumbed back the hammer on his pistol. "I don't give a shit about the hows or whys. I just know this sad son of a bitch set me up." He placed his gun in the center of Brian's forehead.

Logan asked, "So, I ask you, Ben, would a smart businessman like Frankie Judson involve himself with a man like you?"

Ben snorted, "To keep from being toppled from his throne, damn right he would!"

"I think not," Logan argued. "Brian here is Frankie's right-hand man. He has only Frankie's best interests in mind, whether it's wrong or right. Brian Peters desperately wants to show the world that there is another side of these boy liaisons, Frankie's dealings with young men—"

"All the more reason," Ben growled, "for me to kill you both. Peters here for even suggesting it, and you for taking him up on it." Ben sneered at Brian. "You denying you made the phone call? The call that got this ball rolling?"

"Yes," Brian said. "I've never spoken to you in my life. Why do you think it was me?"

Ben hesitated. "Well, it was the name you gave me when you proposed the deal. You insisted that you were only trying to save Judson's empire from crumbling. All the stuff I told you out there at your cabin, Logan? It was stuff I found out before making my decision. I just figured I would be doing the world a big favor."

Brian leaned back on the balls of his heels. "I didn't hire you. I swear. I will admit I am a member of the Princes. But you're mistaken if you think any of our order posed a threat to anyone. Even those of the highest order are opposed to violence. If your caller claimed to belong to the Princes and hired you to kill Logan Walker, he lied to you. The Princes don't pose a threat to Mr. Walker. It was their suggestion that I sent him the material. It was the Princes who planned to finance the printing of his finished work."

Logan glanced sideways at Brian.

Ben laughed. "What? To promote their bizarre beliefs? To declare to the world that their man-boy love is based on an ancient religion? Might as well take my bullet now, writer. If your book ever sees the light of day, folks will crucify you for writing such trash."

He aimed at Brian's forehead. "Rest in peace."

❖

"Hold it!"

Ben didn't fire. The voice echoed throughout the den. Brian flinched and fell backward, arms thrown over his face.

Logan sighed in relief as Noah Standing Bear entered the den. He hadn't known Noah had followed him, but evidently, Noah was taking his guardian duty seriously. He stood there, a .45 caliber pistol in his grasp.

"Told you, Logan," Noah said, "you were being foolish. Instead of allowing Ben here to walk away last night, I advised you to allow me to deal with him outside the law. Now look at how ungrateful this big bastard is. Only one way to deal with a hired assassin sent out by this Gay King."

Noah's dark eyes remained fixed on Ben. "Put the gun down, Ben," he said.

Ben simply glared at him. He did, however, lower his gun. "How's this?" he asked.

"Drop it. On. The. Ground. Now," Noah demanded.

As Ben complied, Noah glanced back at the doorway to the den. "You can come in now, kid. The snake has been defanged."

An older blond-haired teen stepped into the den, a scowl etched on his rather handsome features. He looked first to Ben, then shifted his gaze to Logan.

Logan blurted, "Baxster Crown?"

"Yes," Baxster said. "You must be the writer Alex told me about. The little shit told me you were good-looking."

Baxster looked smugly at Ben. "You and I met out at Camp Lakewood when you gunned down Todd instead of me. Remember? Brian didn't send you out to Lakewood. He doesn't operate that way. You've been duped by Mike Carrol and Brad Helman. You were being taped the night out at Camp Lakewood. That tape is now in the hands of three terrified kids. Call off your hit on me and I can get that tape for you. But Carrol and Helman are searching for it, too. At the rate they're going, it'll just be a matter of time before they discover who has it. Then, Ben Donovan, your goose is cooked."

Baxster paused. "After you made the mistake of murdering Todd, his body was discovered near a soup kitchen on the lower east side of Omaha. It was front-page news in the *Herald*, too. Local golden boy found shot and killed. Todd's cover story was that he happened to be serving as a volunteer there at the soup kitchen. All kinds of wretched folks frequent the City Mission's kitchens. It made for a good story, too, leaving the public outraged that a kind, caring person like Todd, serving his community, was shot and killed.

"This story, which the *Herald* reporter evidently bought hook, line, and sinker, was a great cover for the fact Todd had been murdered shortly after starring in a porn flick. The tape these three boys confiscated from Lakewood's surveillance recorder has footage of not only you shooting Todd, but also the actual porn flick Todd was performing in. Carrol and Helman want to get their hands on it to sell to a very high roller. What father in his right mind would want the public to know his own son had been the star of a gay porn flick?"

He paused for effect. "Oh, by the way, Todd Guildman was the son of Nebraska Senator Douglas Guildman."

CHAPTER SEVENTEEN

Mike Carrol ordered, "Get naked. Prepare yourselves to pleasure us."

Brad Helman switched on the camera. Earlier that evening, Ridge Majors had approached the two young men as they worked the streets on the lower east side. He had forced them into his car at gunpoint and driven them to his studio. However, the moment they stepped in the door, Ridge turned them over to Carrol and Helman.

"They're yours now," Ridge had said. He left the studio, closing the door behind him.

Mike worked on getting Max and Bobby intoxicated, while Brad slipped a powdery substance into their drinks. As the drinks went down, Max and Bobby listened to Mike talk about the half a dozen videos they'd recorded. "Strip and get down on your hands and knees," Brad demanded.

The two did as ordered.

"Tell Brad you want your butt cheeks smacked!" Brad growled as he stripped behind them.

"What?" Bobby asked. "Ouch!" he cried out as Brad slapped him squarely on his upraised ass. The flesh of his palm struck Bobby's bare butt cheeks several times in rapid succession.

"Ow! Ouch! Ohhh!"

Max found Mike's cock thrust into his face. Mike ran his dick head slowly over Max's upturned face, smearing pre-cum all over his cheeks, his nose, and his chin.

"Take it in," Mike ordered. "Open wide and suck me inside, inch by fucking inch, my little fag."

Max had no choice to open his mouth wide. Mike grabbed him by the ears and directed his hardened flesh into Max's mouth.

"Ahhhh!" Mike moaned as Max went to work on him. "Oh, yeah, little bitch knows how to work that tongue! Flick! Flick! Flick! Deep-throat me good. Inhale me. Suck harder! Harder!"

Max froze, impaled through the mouth by Mike's nine inches. Tears came to his eyes, slowly rolling down his cheeks, but he kept going.

"Now," Mike ordered, grasping handfuls of Max's blond hair on both sides of his head, "ever so slowly, tongue your way down the length of my dick. Slow! Slower! Ah, that's it!"

"I want some of that, too," Brad said, grabbing Bobby's ass. Brad slapped his butt hard. Bobby started to lower himself into a more submissive position, but Brad grabbed him by his throat and forced him back against the wall. Mike did the same with Max.

"Okay," Brad growled, "on your knees. Both of you." Bobby used quick flicks of his pointy tongue on the most sensitive spot on Brad's dick. Once he got started, he got carried away, running the tip of his tongue up and around his head.

Max gently sucked one of his balls into his mouth, working it slowly with loud, wet smacks. Brad brought his hands down to rest on their heads.

"You," Brad breathed at Bobby, "work on my tits. Now."

Bobby planted his lips on Brad's left nipple. He tickled it with the tip of his tongue. Brad sighed, his hands locking behind Bobby's head. Again Bobby flicked his tongue, drawing back to watch Brad's nipple harden and rise to his gentle ministrations. "Suck my tits," Brad growled, forcefully moving Bobby's head and his mouth over to his right nipple, "right off my chest!"

Bobby tongued his right nipple, teasing it with slow lashes.

While Max continued a steady tonguing up and under Brad's balls, Bobby was force-fed Brad's wet nipples, spending thirty seconds or so on one before having his head shoved over to the other. Brad writhed in pleasure, arching back against the wall, going up and down on the balls of his feet.

Mike stood there grinning. "Okay, Brad, you've had your fun. Now let's move them to the bed. We need them fucking each other in order to finish up."

Brad reached down and grabbed the boys' erections firmly. He yanked a few times. Leading them by their cocks, he made his way toward the king-sized bed. Once there, he released Bobby. Still grasping Max, he turned him around and forced him to sit on the edge of the bed, then to lie back, spreading his legs wide.

"Here," he said to Bobby, handing him a tube of lotion. "Lube him up good."

When Bobby was done greasing him up, he lathered himself. Max's eyes never left Bobby's cock. Brad climbed onto the bed, grasping Max by both ankles. He held Max's legs high. Max gasped once Bobby entered him.

Brad commanded, "Impale this little pale white bitch all the way! Spear him! Ram him! Make this little bitch squeal!"

Max did squeal as Bobby shoved himself into his core. Max squealed again. To quiet him down, Brad leaned forward, placing his dick directly over his mouth, and smeared pre-cum all over Max's mouth, demanding, "Lick me! Suck me! Take me in!"

Max angled his head so he could slowly work his tongue all over Brad's sperm duct.

"I said gobble me up!"

Max opened his mouth wide. He began to suck in earnest when Brad released his legs and reached down and fingertipped his nipples. Bobby grabbed Max's legs to steady himself to get three good deep thrusts. Each time he withdrew, Max moaned around Brad's cock.

Max moaned when Bobby drove deep with one long thrust, then he began to writhe and whimper with wild abandon. His hands snaked up and latched onto Brad's ass cheeks, pulling him forward, burying his cock deeper into his mouth. He lifted his hips to meet Bobby's deep, steady thrusts. Each time Bobby pulled halfway out, Max stayed with him, tightening his cheeks. Soon, he was squirming and writhing and whimpering with pleasure.

Beside the bed, Mike grinned as he made sure the camera was angled correctly. He thought of their reaction when they came down and sat watching the replay.

Mike was certain they would give him anything he wanted.

When they finished, Max was driven back to the corner where Ridge had found them. "Go home and go to bed. Don't worry about your friend. He gets to go home as soon as we are finished with him."

Once Max disappeared down the street, Mike glanced over at Bobby. "Now, we drive you home so you can get us that tape. Either that, or we share your new video with your parents."

Bobby said nothing, slumped sullenly in his seat.

"Let's give him something more to remember us by, Brad," Mike said, reaching over to grab the crotch of Bobby's jeans. Brad reached over the seat, pinning Bobby's arms to his sides, and held him firmly in place while Mike stimulated him through his jeans.

"No," Bobby muttered, pitifully. "No more. I'm sore. I've had enough. Just leave me—"

"Alone?" Mike purred softly, leaning closer to him. "Now, what fun would that be? Just relax, because you have no choice."

Bobby lifted his hips off the seat, allowing Mike easier access to his balls and cock.

Hearing him moan, Brad lightened his grip on his upper arms and let Bobby stretch his arms above his head so that Brad could grasp him by both wrists. Mike brought Bobby to a writhing, bucking, squirming orgasm while Brad held him in place.

When he came, he sighed.

An hour later, showering and rinsing the spunk off, Bobby leaned his head against the shampoo rack, remembering handing the DVD over to Mike.

"Just remember, we can snatch you up anytime we want. We own you."

CHAPTER EIGHTEEN

L ogan stood there in the driveway, watching Noah Standing Bear
drive away down the street while Donovan drove off in the other
direction. Baxster approached, grinning broadly.

"Take me home with you," he said. "I need someplace to hide
until things cool down."

Logan shook his head. "Ben owes you one now. The fact he
made a big mistake in killing Todd Guildman had to make him feel
like a fool. Personally, I think I should turn your information in to
the police. Ben is a murderer, and I don't feel right about keeping
that secret."

Brian Peters stepped out of the mansion carrying a second
leather-bound journal. Overhearing Logan's last remark, he said,
"Carrol and Helman are dangerous men. One of them posed as
me to contract the hit on both of you. They want Baxster dead to
make the whole blackmail plot against Frankie go away. They have
been brokers for a long time, making tons of cash on rich men like
Frankie caught up in similar plots. To negotiate quiet deals with
boys like Baxster, brokers like Carrol and Helman are hired to clean
up the messes.

"At first, they appeared professional. But even Frankie began
to suspect they were not on the level when they suggested a more
permanent solution—that he should have a prearranged accident."

Baxster removed a pack of cigarettes from his shirt pocket.
"Mind if I smoke?"

"Go ahead," Logan said.

Baxster whipped out a lighter from his jeans pocket and lit his cigarette. Brian fanned the air in disgust and said, "Well, Frankie attempted to terminate their contract. He found out they have garnered millions from financially well-off clients.

"Logan? Here, take this journal. It belongs to Baxster. It will provide more material for the book you're writing. Any questions you wish to direct to me, my business card is tucked inside this journal. Don't hesitate to call."

He turned and walked back inside the mansion.

Logan gestured at Baxster to follow him to a cedar-made gazebo situated off to one side of the Judson driveway. "Sit with me," he said. "I may have some questions for you, as well."

Baxster joined him on the wooden bench at the center of the octagonal gazebo. "Sure, Logan. I'll tell you anything you want to know. I'll read you my journal." He smiled at him and placed one hand on his knee.

Logan pried his hand off. "Let's get something straight, Baxster. You aren't going to seduce me. If you're willing to talk about time you spent with Franklin Judson, that will be helpful. Are we clear?"

Baxster replied, "Crystal."

Logan handed the leather book to Baxster, saying, "Go ahead, read it to me."

Baxster removed his shoes and tucked his bare feet under him. Adjusting himself, he grinned impishly at Logan. "It all began with a boy named Morgan Brock. He was sent my way to seduce me, to invite me into Frankie's bed."

He began to read:

Baxster's Journal, Entry 1

Morgan approached me at school. He was seventeen, a cross between a jock and an honor-role student. I had just turned thirteen. In contrast to the hunky Morgan, I was one of those floppy-haired emo kids, scrawny and scraggly as a scarecrow. He invited me over to his house under the pretense that he wanted to play video games with me. He stripped me the moment we got in the door.

"Let's shower," he said, with a sly wink. "It will make you all the more horny. Suds up really good, wash in all the hot spots to prepare for my moist lips and lashing tongue. My mom is at work for the rest of the night, so we have until morning to do things to each other up in my room."

We were both freshly showered when we entered his room ten minutes later. He closed the door behind me and switched off the lights.

I stood naked before him in the dark, my boner jutting out before me. Morgan's hands came down on my shoulders and he lowered me to my knees in front of him.

He then placed a blindfold over my eyes, gently tying the cloth at the back of my head. I then felt the same cloth material, silky soft as he ran it lightly down my shoulders, whispering, "Raise your hands above your head."

I did so, wondering if he was really going to tie me up. This was new to me. I had never done this before, but I complied and soon he had lengths of silky cloth wrapped around both of my wrists.

He moved in front of me, tugging me over to his bed. He gently lowered me onto my face, shoving two pillows beneath my pelvic region to raise my ass in the air. I felt two firm tugs on my wrists and allowed him to spread my arms above my head and tie me to the twin bedposts. Once he had me securely in place, he got up and I heard him rummaging beside the bed.

"Spread your legs wide," Morgan commanded. "Give me room to play with you."

I slid both legs over so that my toes were curled up on either side of his twin mattress.

"I warmed this in the microwave," he said as he squirted globs of sweet-smelling gel onto my upraised butt cheeks. "It's Dr Pepper–flavored Motion Lotion. It should taste really good."

Morgan worked the gel down into my butt crack, swirled it around my clean hole, and smeared some on my ball sack. Very gently and slowly, he reached beneath me and pulled my boner back so that it was bent back toward him. Once he had the full length stretched out down the pillows, he began slow twists around my head and shaft, coating both with the lotion.

When I thought he was through, I tried to lift myself to allow my cock to slap back into a better position, but Morgan placed one hand on my butt and kept me pinned to the pillows. He lowered his head and slurped the shiny length of my shaft, making tiny swirls over my sperm duct. He kept my cock in place with one hand, then slipped his other hand up and over my crack and cheeks. He sucked just the head of my cock into the warm, wet confines of his mouth and lashed it thoroughly with his tongue until I was going into a spastic frenzy, whimpering with delight.

Then he stopped. He used both hands to raise my hips, and my cock slapped back into place with a meaty thwack. Settling me back down onto the pillows, he rubbed the lotion all up and down my crack, fingertipping my tight hole, constantly but barely penetrating. He grabbed ample folds of my butt cheeks and massaged them, then ran his fingers down to cup my inner thighs.

He withdrew from me for a moment, then lowered his head and tickled my balls with the tip of his tongue, lapping and flicking, swirling, and making little lip sucks, treating me to a whole array of feelings that made me tingle all over.

He squirted more warm lotion all up and down my back. I could feel his rock-hard cock prodding my butthole even as he leaned over me and worked the gel into my flesh. For long minutes, Morgan simply massaged my shoulders and neck, his dick plopping down on various places on my back as he worked.

The fact that his ministrations had ceased to be sexual added to my desire to have him continue to play with me. But I knew this was a tease, that he was doing this on purpose.

Morgan got up from the bed. I heard a slight flicking noise and then he removed my blindfold. As he did, he turned my head slightly to one side so that I could see his white bedroom wall. The small, bright light he had turned on sent its rays toward Morgan standing above me with a massive hard-on and cast incredible shadows on the wall. I could see his well-defined eight-inch cock protruding up from between his legs.

Morgan turned completely to the side and struck a pose, his boner clearly revealed as a black, shadowy love muscle that started with his mushroom head, ran down his shaft, and ended at his bush and balls.

He raised me by both hips, and my butt protruded in the air and was well defined on the bedroom wall, as well. He raised me higher, and my cock looked enormous as it stood straight up and pointed up toward my belly button, displayed on the wall across the room.

Morgan then pushed me back down, lowered himself between my legs, and began a steady prodding motion, his plump head barely grazing my cheeks and my hole.

We watched Morgan dry-humping the space between my cock and my ass for long moments. Just the anticipation of what he was about to do nearly sent me over the edge. Seeing the image of his prodding hard cock moving in and out of my crack turned me on considerably.

I gasped as he finally made perfect contact, his head sliding into the rim of my hole. We looked at the wall, both of us pleased by the sight of how we were connected, going to be further connected, as Morgan was about to be buried deep in me and I was about to be impaled by his long, hard shaft.

We both watched in fascination as I arched my back, pressed my butt into him, and he began to slide his manhood inch by inch into my waiting rectum.

He was buried in me all the way to his balls before I knew it. When he pulled out, he did so slowly, so that we got to watch him slide out of me inch by inch again. Morgan stopped just before his head came free of my hole. *He gyrated around a bit, making me squirm beneath him. He then aimed himself by grabbing onto my hips and slowly shoved himself all the way inside me again.*

Buried this way, his own ass looked perfectly curved as he began to perform tiny pelvic thrusts. He shoved in and pulled out, shoved in and pulled out, all the while watching his long, dark shaft's shadow on the wall, attaching me to him in a cock butt lock.

Morgan withdrew all the way and I gasped as I looked to his bulbous head an inch from my butthole. He drove into me again, this time with such force he buried my face in the pillow. I turned my head to one side to watch his long, lithe body buck up and come down, ramming me as he began to breathe and gasp like a madman. He humped me ruthlessly, so far gone with pleasure that all I could feel was his drool dribbling down my shoulder each time he drove forward.

In the midst of shoving me into the bed, Morgan latched onto my hips, drew me up into a doggy-style position, and slid one hand down to grab onto my boner. As if caught by the sight, he slowed his spastic humping and jacked me off as we both watched our shadows fucking on the wall.

It was clearly a sight as I shot a load of cum, the splash of sperm jetting out as a tiny dark shadow from my cock as Morgan furiously beat me. He then went back into the frantic, mad hump and sighed continually as he drove in and pulled out, and finally flattened me out on the bed beneath him as he churned out cum butter up into my ass, his drool running down my shoulder.

I collapsed on the bed. My arms still stretched out above my head, my wrists still attached to the bedposts, all I could do was lie there while Morgan slowly drew his softening cock out of my hole.

We looked to the wall as he rose above me, his dick arching down at an angle over his hairy nut sack. Morgan simply sniggered. "How about a double shooter tonight, kid? Think I can work you up for that?"

I glanced back over one shoulder, and that's when I saw him holding up a hand-held vibrator.

"This is going to feel good," he said.

I sighed and arched my back like a cat doing a lazy stretch.

Morgan was right. It felt great.

Chapter Nineteen

Baxster stretched and yawned. "Does this turn you on?" he asked, a seductive smile on his lips. "Does my journal get you hot and horny?"

Logan ignored his question, asking one of his own. "Is this leading to how you finally met Frankie?"

Baxster nodded. "Yes, of course. I'm getting to that next."

Baxster's Journal, Entry 2

Morgan held three more sessions with me before he got around to asking me if I wanted to make some real money by selling myself to an older man.

I wasn't opposed to the idea, as I had many fantasies by then of a father figure who came into my life and swept me off my feet, making my life so much better. I even went so far in my head that I often envisioned myself becoming a boy lover to a rich sugar daddy who would take me in every position possible and take care of me for the rest of my life.

Morgan's grooming led me to the man of my dreams. I fell deeply in love with Frankie the night that I met him.

He was not a tall man, nor was he built like a hunk. But he was handsome in his own way, having short dark hair, a clean-shaven smooth face, and dark blue eyes that held such a warmth in them that I was on fire within the first hour we sat and talked to each other.

I got lost in those blue eyes of his. Frankie was sincerely interested in learning everything about me.

Asking me where I was born. Who my parents were. What they did for a living. Whether they knew I was gay. Whether or not they accepted me. What I wanted to do with my life. Whether I was sad or happy by then in that chapter of my life.

Frankie was unlike any man I had ever met before.

He was not a pretender either. He was for real, and immediately took great interest in me.

In fact, that first week, he never even suggested that we go to bed together. He really wanted to get to know me first, as if sex was to be reserved for a later time. And we talked together about everything under the sun.

He shared with me stories about his own boyhood. About how he grew up gay in a small town where everyone knew everyone else's business. Where he had to keep his secret to himself or be shunned by his parents and the entire community. He told me about tinkering around with his grandpa, how they worked on a design in his old garage he'd converted into a workshop. Together they came up with a device that would allow mechanics or anyone working on farm machinery to grip onto bolts and nuts and screws. They called it the "Iron Wrench."

Frankie spent those hot, sweaty days tinkering in his grandpa's garage, and eventually, he obtained a patent for his tool, and thus Judson Machinery was born. One sale led to another, and then deal after deal was brokered, and slowly Frankie's empire was established, with plants that produced his simple tool all over the world. He became a multimillionaire by the time he was thirty, and twenty years later, at the age of fifty, he sold Judson Machinery to Strong Motors for a whopping 450 million.

I met him just five years before he sold his family business to Strong Built.

Even then, Frankie was rich by anyone's standards.

But only I knew how conflicted he was.

One summer night after making love to me, Frankie broke down and cried.

I was terrified, thinking he was about to tell me I had

*to go, that his love for me had run its course and that I was
soon to be turned out on the streets, no longer welcome in
his bed, in his life. And so I was relieved and surprised as
Frankie shared with me a very personal part of his life.*

*There he was, a gay man who had built an empire
much like a king, having spent the first years of his
boyhood working in the gritty, dirty, hot, humid confines
of his grandfather's garage. At the end of his boyhood, he
had created a device that would change the world of tools
needed to make machinery run efficiently. In the eyes of
most mechanics, Frankie's creation was a flash of genius.*

*Frankie believed the original seed for his creation
came directly from God.*

Which confused him greatly.

*Why would God gift him, a gay man, with the
inspiration and the knowledge to create such a tool?*

*He became even more confused when his success
netted him such kingly wealth.*

*The real conflict he faced, however, was that he found
himself attracted not to gay men, but to gay boys. In the
eyes of the world, he was a pedophile, a dirty old man
who dithered with a boy's nether regions. Yet in the eyes of
the business community, he was a corporate magnate who
had made millions on his simple, creative product. His
attraction to young boys seemed to be quite a contradiction
to his success in the business world.*

*Frankie broke down and cried in my arms, telling me
how he hoped he had never inflicted psychological harm
on me with all the sex we shared. He was a man and I was
just a boy.*

*I tried to comfort him by telling him that in some parts
of the world, a boy of thirteen was considered a man. I
even told him that my friend, a Jewish boy, had recently
turned thirteen and his parents held a bar mitzvah for him
to celebrate his transition from boyhood into manhood.*

*I swore to him that I wanted to have sex with him.
That I loved him deeply. That it was not just about the
sex between us. Frankie still cried, feeling wretched that*

*he'd subjected me, and dozens of other young boys, to the
world of man-boy love.*

*After that night, however, Frankie's conflicted feelings
on the matter must have taken a backseat.*

*Or maybe my permission had been given for Frankie
to do whatever he pleased with me.*

*Because my training in the art of sexual play began
in earnest one day later.*

Baxster Crown removed his cigarette pack from his shirt
pocket. Logan watched him casually blow three perfect smoke rings.
"Turned on yet?" Baxster asked, his brows raised.

Logan asked, "Sexual training?"

"Oh, yes," Baxster said.

Logan shook his head.

"So," Baxster said, "how about I tell you the rest of the story
while we're having sex?"

"No, thank you," Logan told him. "I just don't roll that way,
Baxster."

Baxster placed a hand on top of Logan's.

"I'll pass," Logan said, prying Baxster's hand off.

Logan ended up dropping Baxster off at a rather expensive
house in the Northwoods district of east Omaha. He claimed it was
owned by his new friend, the one who had replaced Frankie. He told
Logan that he still loved Frankie.

"Sure didn't consider me a harasser when I was giving Frankie
bed service. Now they claim I am a nuisance."

Logan studied the three-story house with its well-manicured
lawn. "You didn't blackmail Franklin, demanding he pay you hush
money to keep you quiet about his former relationship with you?"

"Oh, that?" Baxster chuckled. "That was just to get Frankie's
attention. He hurt me by wanting nothing more to do with me. Hell,
I would have stayed with Frankie the rest of my days. I loved him
that much."

"So," Logan said, "you were genuinely attached to Frankie?
You do realize there was a big age gap between you two, right?"

"Age shouldn't restrict love," Baxster said. "If you really love
someone, why should age even be considered a factor? That's a

fucked-up law, that because an older man like Frankie loved me, he could spend the rest of his days in prison."

"Those laws," Logan argued, "are in place to protect kids like you from predators who—"

"Frankie isn't a predator," Baxster contended. "You condemn him for showing me love when no one else ever did in my fucked-up, rotten life? Do you know how dark it is in my world? Do you know what being loved by Frankie, an older man, did for me? It changed my life."

"Changed your life and led you to what?"

Baxster studied him. "Frankie didn't burn me, if that's what you mean."

"You claimed he did," Logan said. "Rumor has it that he infected you and began paying for your treatments with money from his nonprofit corporation. You deny this?"

"Frankie did not infect me," Baxster said. "I just said that to get—"

"Frankie's attention."

The kid looked sad. "Yes," he said, "to get his attention. I thought he would take me back in and tell me he loved me, and we could continue being lovers."

"I just don't see how a man twenty or thirty years older than you can be that attached to you, physically or emotionally."

Baxster stood up then, moving away from the vehicle. He looked off down the street, shook his head sadly, and said, "Sorry, Logan, I don't think someone like you would ever understand."

He walked toward the house.

CHAPTER TWENTY

A lex was waiting for him at the cabin.
Logan had hoped the kid would be gone. He didn't want to rescue anyone, let alone a gay teenager who had floundered his way into such a mess. He was mildly surprised and somewhat amused by the effort Alex had put into making his return home special.

He had the dining room table set, illuminated by candlelight. A bottle of wine sat in a large bowl filled with ice. A steaming roast on a platter was at the center of the table, heaped on both sides by carrots, potatoes, peas, and a scattering of small white onions.

The table was set for two. Alex pulled out a chair, offering it to Logan with a warm smile.

"I started culinary school," he said, stepping away as Logan seated himself, "a year ago. I'm not that good yet, but I want to own my own restaurant one day. I hope you like what I cooked for you, Logan."

And there it was, his name coming out of Alex's mouth with a slight bit of affection.

"While you were gone," Alex said, cutting him a hefty slice, "Brian Peters called. He left me a message for you."

Logan poured them both a glass of chilled blackberry wine, raising his brows to indicate Alex should continue.

Alex picked up his glass and said, "Brian said in order for you to see another side of what goes on behind the scenes in regard to the man-boy thing, he wants you to attend a court hearing. In three days, Max is testifying against his former pimp in court. The pimp is Ridge Majors, the same guy Baxster and Max hooked me up with when I started hooking. Cops have been trying to nail Majors for several years. He doesn't use hush money to keep his boys from coming out against him. He has most of them on film to keep them quiet. Rumor is there are three dead boys down at the bottom of the Missouri River. Majors dumped them there when they made too much noise about some kind of sex scandal between them and a state senator."

"Unlike Frankie," Logan said, trying not to sound too sarcastic, "who also has this problem that follows these boy-lovers around. Boys who can't keep quiet create quite a dilemma for the man."

Alex nodded. "Well, that's one way to look at it. But Brian thought you should know that Frankie never used force, never threatened harm, never resorted to violence when it came to his boys."

Logan sipped at his wine. "What's the kid's story? This Max?"

"Max opened his mouth and talked about Majors abusing him in juvenile court. He got himself into trouble by stealing a car, and to get the car theft reduced to joyriding, he cut a deal. He confessed to his probation officer that he had been selling himself to some clients under the guidance of Ridge Majors. His testimony is going to sink Majors and a dozen other prominent citizens."

"This is good," Logan said, taking a bit of the roast. "Very good."

"Thanks," Alex said. "I borrowed beer from your neighbor, the big guy down the road. I invited him to dinner, but he told me he had other things to attend to, so he took a pass. But he did share his Guinness with me. Said he'd never heard of marinating beef with it. I told him I would save him a slice."

"Noah had beer at his place?" Logan asked. "A man who swore off alcohol ten years ago?"

Alex shrugged. "He said it was well aged, that he had an entire twelve-pack set aside just to prove he was superior to the brew, that he had more power over it than the other way around."

Logan grinned. "Noah has his reasons for the things he does. I stopped questioning him years ago."

"Does he know you're gay? How does he feel about that?"

Logan said, "He's gay himself. We met during a crisis intervention one winter night years ago." He stared off out the nearby window, where he could barely see the stars dotting the sky just above the distant river. He cleared his throat.

Logan still felt the raw pain even seven years later. He still missed his former lover, Jimmy West. "I was in crisis over my lover leaving me that winter night. I was drunk and wandering down the road toward the lake, not caring if I lived or died. When I reached the half-frozen lake, I was determined to throw myself in and end it all. Noah was standing there, contemplating the same thing. We startled each other, both of us beyond drunk, both of us at the very end of our rope. We must have looked pathetic, both of us stumbling around the snowy shore line of the icy lake.

"Noah launched into drunken babble about why the All Father, the great Wakan Tanka, had placed such a burden on him. He was a warrior. Had been to the Gulf. Came back with awards and medals. Was a medicine man of his People, a holy man of the Lakota, supposed to be blessed by the All Father, not cursed as he deemed himself to be. He spoke of the Berdache, Sioux warriors who took on the mannerisms of women. He talked about how Crazy Horse never had a wife, how he was still the mightiest of the Lakota warriors, just like him, Noah Standing Bear, who had fought like a warrior from long ago and gave a good accounting of himself in his service as a Marine of the United States.

"Noah wanted to die that night because at thirty years of age he came to the realization that he was gay, that try as he had over the years to suppress it, to change it, to make it all go away, he could not. He came to the sad conclusion that the All Father had placed a gay spirit inside him, and to remedy such a situation, he thought suicide was the final and only solution.

"I have never liked fighting. Hell, back in high school, I had one fight that sent a terrible bully to the nurse's office with a bloody nose. Several of my classmates led me there ten minutes after him, to have the nurse use smelling salts to bring me out of my daze. I punched him, yes, but the nausea that overcame me afterward had me fainting three times before I was carried to the nurse's office.

"To stop Noah from throwing himself in the lake that night, I ended up placing a direct shot to his nose. The blow staggered Noah and sobered him enough to watch me faint and fall forward into the icy-cold waters of that lake. He dove in and rescued me. Later that night, seated before his wood stove, we shared our stories, and we've been friends ever since. We share a bond. Noah thinks he's my guardian angel."

Alex reached out and placed a warm hand on Logan's forearm. "An awesome story, Logan," he said, his eyes conveying that he was moved by him sharing such a personal part of his life. "I'm glad you didn't succeed that night. The world would be an emptier place without you. Besides, who would rescue me?"

Logan gently removed Alex's hand from his forearm. "Look," he said, "don't get any ideas here, Alex. I'm not seeking a relationship at this point in my life, not that I could ever have one with you."

Alex softly asked, "Because of my age?"

Logan nodded. "I'm thirty-five, kid, and you are barely nineteen. Let me ask you a question. Fair?"

Alex said, "Fair. I think. Depends on what you want to ask me, Logan."

"What lover finds it necessary to ask his partner this question—have you checked in with your mother lately?"

Alex muttered, "You certainly know how to spoil the mood."

CHAPTER TWENTY-ONE

The next morning, Alex picked up Baxster's journal, offering to read it aloud to Logan.

"Sure," Logan told him. "Start on entry three, if you will, Alex."

Alex flipped through the pages.

Baxter's Journal, Entry 3

The moment we exited the plane in Saudi Arabia the hot, sultry air engulfed me, causing the light clothes I wore to stick to my sweaty body in more than a dozen uncomfortable places. As instructed by Frankie I wore no underwear, and my silky, loose-fitting pants crept slowly up my ass crack as we walked across the tarmac. We were greeted cordially by four Arab bodyguards stationed before a sleek black limo.

The heat of the desert was unbearable. My red T-shirt clung to me like a second skin. The sweat-drenched fabric left little to the imagination. The limo driver silently appraised me, turned up the air, and drove us slowly away from the plane.

When we arrived at our destination, our driver stopped before a large iron gate situated at the center of a long driveway. On either side of the closed gate, twelve-foot-high stucco walls formed a perimeter around the palace. I sat there, gawking like a young boy discovering his first pubic hair as I took in a dozen domed towers standing out against a startling bright skyline. The entire three-story structure looked like a palace straight out of the Arabian Nights. The iron gate opened and the driver drove us toward the sprawling green lawn beyond. There in the middle of the Saudi Arabian desert, such greenery was complemented by nude statues and a large fountain, clear water spewing out of the mouth of a stone lion situated at the center of its wide bowl.

Frankie and I were greeted at the door of the palace by a young Arab boy dressed in white silk pants and a blue dress shirt. He was handsome with raven hair, and by the smooth complexion of his face, I guessed him to be about fourteen years old.

As he approached us, he had a confident smile on his face. "Welcome to the palace of my brother, Prince Abdul Tarik Sikk," he said. "Frankie? I am at your service this night. Baxster? You will proceed down this hallway to begin your service to the prince and...his friends."

I felt envious of this grinning Arab imp as he led my man Frankie away to the stairs at the end of the large entry alcove. As they reached the top of the stairs, Frankie gave me one last look and winked at me, as if to say, "Enjoy yourself here tonight."

As I reached the end of the long hallway leading away from the entryway, I was greeted by two naked Arab boys, who I guessed to be around sixteen years old. They were stunningly handsome twins, their faces framed by tangles of wild black hair. Both were well-proportioned, with deep clefts between their pecs and defined six-pack abs, their sleek skin tanned from many hours spent beneath the desert sun.

My eyes drifted down to their circumcised cocks, standing at full attention. Both had eight inches of hardened flesh protruding in a slight curve upward from thick patches of black pubic bushes. I was amazed at their identical dick heads, looking like two shiny mushrooms perfectly formed on two long, slender shafts. My mouth watered just to see these two finely sculpted specimens of Arab boys displayed before me.

"Baxster," the boy on my left said, "I am Ali. This is Farik. We are childhood friends of Prince Abdul, and tonight we have hours of fun times before us. But first..."

"You must wear this." Farik finished his sentence, producing a black cloth seemingly out of nowhere.

"Uh, kinky," I said, "but I can deal with—"

"Silence!" Farik snapped. "You must speak only when given permission to do so. You are here tonight to do one thing: Give our prince pleasure."

He slipped the black silk cloth over my eyes and tied it with a gentle tug behind my head. He then commanded, "Strip. Take off all of your clothes, but do it slowly, for the prince is watching. He likes to see American boys get naked before him. He likes to relish these last few moments when your lean body is still your own."

Ali stiffly said, "Because very soon, it will be his to do with as he pleases."

I was hard before I unzipped my pants.

I performed a slow striptease. The second I stepped out of my silky pants, Ali and Farik gripped me firmly by both wrists and I was led forward, at their mercy because of the blindfold.

Ahead of us I could hear several showers spraying water at once. As they led me into the warm spray, which hit me from several directions, the sweet scent of mint filled the air and I took several deep breaths of the heady smell. I realized it must be body wash or Motion Lotion.

"Lift your hands above your head," Ali ordered me. "Comply at once to please the prince."

I quickly raised my hands and felt leather straps placed around my wrists. They tightened a bit and caused me to raise onto my toes. Ali and Farik used their legs to spread mine farther apart, both running soapy hands in between my tender thighs. I expected straps to be placed around my ankles, too, but they simply kept me spread out while applying great gobs of mint lotion all over me. My thighs. My balls. My cock. Both of my ass cheeks. In the crack of my ass. Up my back and into the long blond curls of my hair.

Ali and Farik really knew how to give a boy a proper shower. "Bend forward," Farik said. I did so at once, exposing my ass to whatever they had planned for it. Ali spread my left cheek while Farik spread my right cheek, and then more gloopy lotion was squirted all over my butt ring. Ali teasingly flicked my ass ring again and again. I rose onto my toes, sighing. He twirled the tips of two fingers around and inside my butt ring. Farik helped him by using both hands to spread my butt cheeks. Ali slowly snaked his two fingers into my ass chute, going knuckle deep. When he was sure I was comfortable with that, he slowly snaked deeper. The moment he hit my prostate, I groaned softly. He ran his prodding fingers around inside me, teasingly touching my pleasure spot, firing me up. This went on for quite some time. Somewhere in the middle of his light fingering, Farik removed his hands from my butt, embraced me, and planted his open mouth over my left nipple. I had the urge to return his embrace, but with my hands held so firmly by the leather straps above my head, I could only hang there, waiting for his tongue to strike.

Ali began a three-finger fucking method, each time swirling fingertips over my prostate. Farik positioned his wet mouth over my super-sensitive nipple, simply breathing warm air on it for long moments. When he finally flicked his tongue over it, my nipple went erect and surges of pleasure traveled from deep within my butt to my chest in undulating waves.

I writhed and squirmed. I groaned and moaned. I gasped with pure pleasure as the two Arab boys played with me, performing their separate moves over and over. I never wanted it to stop. And yet, when it did, when Ali removed his fingers from my ass quite suddenly and Farik ceased to suck on my nipple and pulled away from me, I squirmed around, arching my back, raising my butt, making maddeningly little thrusts with my pelvis. I wanted the feelings their gentle ministrations had elicited in me to continue. Not to stop. Not ever to stop.

Prince Abdul then gave a command. "Ali? Farik? Remove the clasps from his wrists. It is time to play with our sex slave."

I felt the two brothers reach up and remove the leather straps from my wrists.

The prince moved up behind me, using one finger on my ass cheeks to turn me one way and then another as he inspected me. "Very nice," he said, in admiration. "You shall prove to be much fun."

As I was led away from the jets of spraying water, I felt carpeting beneath my bare feet. Prince Abdul rested both hands on my shoulders and instructed me to kneel, facing away from him. I did so. "Now lean forward, placing your head and arms in Ali's lap."

Ali was suddenly before me and he cradled my head in his crotch. As I wrapped my arms around his waist, Abdul reached down and grabbed me by both ankles and slowly raised my lower body so that my upper body was angled downward. Farik moved up behind Abdul, latching onto my legs and forcing them to wrap around Abdul's slender waist. With a firm grip he locked me in place so that I basically hung suspended there, my ass vulnerable to the prince's planned invasion.

I felt him squirt lotion up and down my butt crack. I sighed, my open mouth just inches from Ali's ramrod-straight boner sticking in my face. I licked the slick mushroom head, then buried my nose in Ali's thick black bush, smelling the mint and the heated musk emanating from his groin. Ali ran his lotion-covered hands up my arched back, sensually slithering like twin snakes up to my butt cheeks. Gripping each of my meaty cheeks firmly, he spread them.

Abdul drove two fingers into my ass, deep, without stopping.

I grunted one second with pain. The next, I was

groaning with pleasure as he forcefully finger-fucked me. Surges of pleasure engulfed my nipples as Ali ran his hands beneath my chest and began speedy little tit flicks. I gasped and muttered, almost saying words; but remembering no words were allowed, I mewled with pleasure.

Farik released my legs, which were now hooked tightly about Abdul's torso, and dropped to the floor behind the prince. In this position, he reached between Abdul's legs and firmly grasped my rock-hard cock. I practically screamed, throwing my head from side to side in Ali's crotch as Farik milked me furiously, his lotion-coated hand turning and twisting as he ran it up and down my seven-inch shaft.

It greatly turned me on to be hanging upside down, the three Arab boys working me over in a mad flurry. I gasped. I whimpered. I bucked up into Abdul's plunging fingers. I gyrated around in Farik's strong grip. I arched my back and made my tits more accessible to Ali's flicking.

The whole three-way workover was driving me crazy. I loved it. I embraced it. I was really throwing myself into being the sex slave they desired me to be.

Just as I was about to cum, Abdul said, "Farik? Stop now, before he spurts his seed."

Abdul withdrew his fingers as if drawing a knife from a sheath, his fingers curved like an Arab scimitar. He had a clear passage into my chute, worked over so unmercifully by his rapid, repeated jamming. His fingers curved, he drove in deep several more times, striking my prostate with precise taps that sent garbled muttering from my lips.

Again, I came close to cumming, and Abdul knew it. He felt my legs clench around his waist, saw my back arching in a deep curve, and he stopped finger-fucking me with such heated passion.

"Turn him over," Prince Abdul commanded.

At once, Farik grabbed my ankles, unhooking my legs from around the prince. Ali took hold of both of my arms, *and in sync with Farik, placed me on a cushion on my back. Farik spread my legs wide. Ali raised my hands and arms above my head. In this way, I was splayed, spread-eagled, before the prince.*

I wanted so badly to see him. But the blindfold remained in place. I could only wonder what he had planned for me. My ass, balls, and cock were his for the taking.

He sat there, I imagined, gazing down at my naked body, admiring my slick and hard cock, my walnut-sized balls, and my light blond pubic hairs. Ali and Farik moved to a kneeling position at my head. They drew my legs up and spread them wide. I felt Abdul's bulbous head seeking entrance to my ass. I sucked in a breath, holding it as his lotion-slicked dick head slowly entered my already loosened ass ring. I realized all of the fingering was to prepare me for the prince's royal fuck.

He slid into me inch by inch, and just when I thought he had his hardened manhood planted inside me to its full extent, Abdul laughed and said, "There is more!"

With a gentle thrust, he impaled me with all nine inches of his royal cock.

Ali and Farik, sensing me tense up, began noisy, wet slurpings on my nipples, still holding my legs high in the air and wide apart. Abdul then slowly withdrew, taking all but two inches of his rock-hard penis out of my butthole.

I let out my breath and sucked in another as he rammed me hard, plunging his nine-inch love muscle all the way inside me. He was relentless in seeking and giving pleasure.

We breathed and gasped together, definitely sharing the feelings of intense pleasure as he fucked me brutally. I lay sprawled there, held in place by Ali and Farik, the prince's fuck boy.

"Turn him," the prince commanded, pulling out of me with a swift withdrawal that left me wanting him deep back inside me.

Immediately, Ali and Farik released my legs, one

grabbing me by the wrists, the other latching onto my hips, forcing me up onto my hands and knees. So I was prepared to take the prince's cock doggy-style.

I felt a dick slapping against my face as Ali reached over me to grasp my ass cheeks. He had no sooner spread them than the prince manically drove his hard rod into me and fucked me furiously. I grunted. I gasped. I whimpered. I opened my mouth to say, "Fuck me like a rabid dog!" when I felt Ali shove his cock directly between my lips.

"Take your pleasure with him!" Prince Abdul breathed heavily, continuing to ram and plunge and drive deeply inside the tight confines of my ass.

Ali fed me his entire eight inches. I relaxed my throat muscles and inhaled him into my throat. So turned on by then by the fact that the prince was taking his pleasure plunging into my asshole, I tongued Ali furiously.

Neither he nor the prince lasted long. Abdul stopped, frozen in mid-fuck, and then with a savage growl he went crazy on me. Firm fingers locked around my ass and hips, he drove and plowed and plunged, and at last exploded inside me. I counted all seven massive spurts of royal spunk he planted in me.

A second later, Ali cried out and his creamy splooge gushed past my tongue and down my throat. He continued quick little thrusts until he was drained.

Farik's cock filled my rectum as I remained up on my hands and knees, but by the time he finished ramming me furiously, I was sprawled on the mattress, my head turned to one side so that I could suck air in and out of my open mouth.

I was just about to say, "What about me?" when the prince reached beneath me and grasped my cock and balls. With a little force, he made me stand before them. My hands were then placed back in the straps, and they continued to toy with me for the next three hours.

I came four times before the sun rose in the desert skies that next morning.

CHAPTER TWENTY-TWO

Alex left Logan's cabin early the next morning. Dejected and morose, he drove to his home in north Omaha. He just didn't want to live anymore.

"Make a Wish?" Alex read the words before him on his computer screen. He stared, realizing he had surfed his way to a site that offered hope to terminal kids. He leaned forward, his slender frame hunched over his keyboard as he mockingly read the rest of the text: "Make-a-Wish Foundation, dedicated to helping kids see their dreams come true!"

Blowing his long, scraggly bangs out of his eyes, he scowled. "As though making a wish will get you what you want!"

Viciously jabbing the left button on his mouse with his right index finger, Alex closed the site. "Wish. Hope. Pray. Dream. And good fortune will smile upon you. Biggest crock of shit I've ever heard!"

Alex spun about in his chair, focusing on the photo taped to his bedroom wall ten feet away. Narrowing his eyes, he slowly plucked six metal-tipped throwing darts from the corkboard memo pad situated beside him on his desk. As he picked up each dart, he glared angrily at the black-and-white photo on the wall. Alex growled, "Shouldn't have done it. Shouldn't have pushed me so far. No one knows what's really hidden just below the surface. Should have left this one alone!"

He seethed with pent-up rage as he heaved the missiles across the room, one by one, at the face staring back at him. Tears trailed down his narrow face. His vision blurred, and he shook his head. He grinned sadly, pleased his darts had struck true.

Ridge Majors stared back at him, darts piercing his forehead.

Alex hiked up his baggy jeans, shrugged out of his overlarge flannel shirt, readjusted his sleeveless T-shirt, and wheeled around in a tight circle, executing a combination of moves he'd seen in some martial arts flick. Flexing his skinny arms, bulking up his slender shoulders, sucking in his gut, and puffing out his small chest, Alex launched into a series of chops and punches and roundhouse blows. He stopped only after losing his balance and banging into his half-open closet door. His knuckles slammed into hard wood and Alex slid dizzily to the floor.

Reality struck him. As he used the closet door to pull himself to his feet, Alex caught a glimpse of Ridge on his wall. He heard snide laughter washing over him. Even when he averted his eyes, Alex could not shake the dreadful feelings.

"Why are people so mean?" he railed as he launched himself back across the room and snatched the darts from the photo. "Why did he use me like that? Why did he use all of us the way he did?"

Max had called soon after Alex had arrived home. He told Alex how Ridge abducted him and Bobby, forcing them at gunpoint to return to his studio. "Those two guys now have the video of Todd Guildman getting shot and killed out at Lakewood. Things just go from bad to worse, don't they?"

Max had hung up, leaving Alex in an even sadder state. The room began to spin. Alex felt his stomach doing flip-flops, his knees weakening, and he found himself seated on the floor beside his bed. The eyes from the photo on the wall leered at him. Alex began moaning, "No. No. No. No."

He climbed to his feet. "One day you're gonna be sorry you messed with me. One day you're gonna reap the whirlwind!"

Alex tapped his mouse button several times as he traveled to a different site. In the Search box, the word "BEACON" appeared and Alex hit the Enter key.

He smiled as the familiar image of a lighthouse appeared on the screen. Within a deep, dark blue background, where the vague images of a shoreline and ocean waves could barely be seen, the brilliantly bright, white lighthouse stood out in sharp contrast. Alex's eyes were drawn to the undulating red flames burning in what appeared to be a lantern set atop the lighthouse. The flames danced wildly in the wind for brief moments, and a tiny speck appeared beyond the shoreline, out among the white-capped ocean waves.

Alex looked from the lighthouse to the speck, which became a ship, complete with torn sails and battered hull. The waves played havoc with the vessel. With violent force, the ship was hurled between monstrous waves. Sounds of cracking timbers and ripping cloth came blasting out of the speakers. The sea flung it through the stormy winds, skimming it across the waves. When the badly battered ship emerged on the other side of the massive swell, the flames atop the lighthouse burned brighter. Alex's eyes darted from ship to beacon and back in rapid succession. Slowly he let out his breath, sighing in relief when the ship at last cut a steady course toward the lighthouse on the shoreline.

Alex never seemed to tire of watching and waiting as the ship with torn sails and battered hull sailed into the small cove at the lower left side of his screen. He sat and watched until the bright red flames atop the lighthouse ever so gently faded as an amber spark appeared on the distant horizon and day broke upon the ocean.

The site had been appropriately named *The Beacon*. But instead of standing out clear and bright against the dark so that ships sailed safely into a haven, it was set up to guide and help people who found themselves lost and adrift.

It was by coming to the site that Alex had made an odd connection in his young life.

It was there he had met Maxwell Broadstone.

Maxwell Broadstone, scheduled to testify against Ridge Majors.

Two things connected them, creating a bond. They were both gay, and they had stumbled into street prostitution at almost the same time. Alex's own mom ended up being Max's probation officer. Alex's mom Jenna, a thirteen-year veteran of the juvenile justice system, had no idea her son knew Max, let alone had established a relationship with him. She also had no clue Alex was gay or that her son sold himself on the streets.

Alex had heard Jenna speaking on the phone about Max. The way she spoke of what Max had been doing, selling himself to older men, the disgust and contempt she displayed during numerous phone conversations she held with her colleagues, sent Alex into severe depression. If his mom ever found out that he was just as involved in the sex trade as Max was, she would disown him in a heartbeat.

If Jenna ever learned that, he would just want to die.

❖

Logan ended his phone call with Brian Peters on an angry note. He had asked him to set up an interview with him and Franklin Judson. Brian adamantly refused to comply. If Logan was expected to thoroughly research this book, he wanted to meet the man responsible.

Logan assured Brian he would not incriminate him and even promised to allow Frankie to remain anonymous. He just wanted to meet the man.

Frankie Judson was an enigma. He had gone from inheriting his grandfather's tool business to becoming an international success. Logan had to admit that Frankie was a beyond-successful businessman who appeared to have the power of a magic Norse ring that produced gold. And yet he was also a man who had sexual relations with young boys.

He somewhat reluctantly agreed to track down this Maxwell Broadstone to interview him about his upcoming court case. Brian had assured Logan that despite the case against Ridge, Max was still selling himself. Brian was certain he would find him somewhere in the Old Market.

Before leaving the cabin, Logan picked up Baxster's journal, taking it with him.

CHAPTER TWENTY-THREE

After cruising up and down the lower district of Omaha's north side for two hours, Logan did not find Max in the Old Market.

He did learn from several of the boys he encountered that there were three other hot spots for cruising. He drove to each of them, ready to give up at the third location, in Radley Park by the river.

He had just asked a fourth boy if he knew Maxwell when he'd spotted a police cruiser driving slowly through the park. Logan decided to return to the Market, have an espresso, and put in a phone call to Brian to let him know his lead didn't pan out.

He fished Baxster's journal out of his backpack and decided to read more of the kid's racy writing.

Baxster's Journal, Entry 4

Frankie and I landed in Tokyo. It was raining slightly as we drove away from the airport there. It was a welcome relief compared to the desert heat of Arabia.

Frankie had made prior arrangements, and our limo driver drove us to a secluded monastery high in some forested hills. Frankie and I were greeted by a black-haired, black-eyed Japanese man who seemed to know exactly why we were there.

He escorted Frankie up a set of stone steps and into a lamplit pagoda. The last sight I caught of Frankie was him waving at me as I was surrounded by four rather good-looking Japanese boys, all between the ages of sixteen and nineteen.

Greeting me with warm, pleasant smiles, they led

me beneath two large pine trees overlooking a large blue lake.

"To play the Hare and the Hounds," the oldest boy, named Kenji, said, "you must reach the lake before we do, then we become your sex slaves for as long as you want to play with us, Baxster."

"Sex slaves?" I asked, looking all wide-eyed and innocent. "You mean do things to you? Sex things?"

"Yes," said Taki, the second oldest. "But if any of us make it to the lake ahead of you, you get passed around between us for a long, long while."

I looked to the other two boys moving up on either side of me. "Chan? Nari?" Kenji said. "Grab onto the Hare to prepare him for his run, will you?"

The moment the two dark-haired boys grabbed my arms, I put up a brief struggle, pretending that I was trying to wrench free.

"Taki?" Kenji said to the other boy. "Latch onto his legs. Hold him still while we undress him."

Taki, leaner than the other three, was stronger than he looked. He grabbed me by both legs, pulling them apart while Kenji reached down and unzipped my zipper.

"What are you doing?" I asked, faking disbelief. "Why are you—"

"Ah, look at this white boy." Kenji laughed as he produced my semi-hard penis from my open fly. "He likes this. He is already getting an erect penis!"

I threw myself forward, but the four Japanese boys quickly picked me up and pinned me to the picnic table behind us. They spread-eagled me, pulling my arms and legs wide. Taki took hold of two of my belt loops and slowly worked my pants and underwear down to my ankles. "Shoes and socks," Kenji said, and immediately Nari and Chan removed both as I squirmed and writhed on the table, my bare butt making squelching sounds as I slid back and forth between the four boys.

Kenji yanked my underwear and my pants down over my feet and tossed them over his shoulder.

For long moments, everyone, including me, stared down at my rising boner as it grew rock hard and stood seven inches tall, jutting up from the hairy patch above my large, round balls.

"May I touch it?" Chan asked, his hand reaching out to grab my meaty boner wavering in the air.

"No," Kenji said. "You know the rules, Chan. Not until the Hare either loses or wins the race. But there is something we can do."

Kenji reached down into a pack at his feet and withdrew six long feathers. He grinned at the other three boys. "Finish stripping him," he ordered.

I tried but failed to break free as Chan, Nari, and Taki removed all of my clothes, leaving me sprawled on the table between them, my boner still the center of attention.

Kenji handed out the feathers. "Gently, boys. We want to coax tingling feelings up through his balls. Work him over nice and slowly."

I stopped struggling the moment Taki ran the tip of his feather across my left tit. They all watched it stiffen and get hard. Chan, on my right side, used his feather to tickle my right nipple. This time, even I watched my tit rise up.

Chan and Nari seemed to get lost in their actions, flicking and rubbing the tips of their feathers across the tips of my tits. I relaxed in their grasp and settled back with all of them leaning over me, spread-eagled before them.

"Let him go now," Kenji softly said. "I think he likes this enough to lie still for it."

They did and I simply lay there, watching the feathers skimming my tits. I began to make little puffing sounds, which turned the four boys on even more. Taki and Nari, both holding my legs down, began running their feathers up and down my ball sack and into my crack. I lifted my hips to make my ass and balls more available to their play.

When Kenji lightly caressed my dick head, I sighed

out loud. Kenji ran the feather down my shaft, teasing the sensitive sperm duct with the tip of the feather. He flicked it back and forth over this spot until I began to whimper and moan.

I muttered, "This feels so good."

They all laughed. Chan and Nari continued to feather my tits. Taki skimmed my ball sack and my crack. Kenji continued to slide his feather across my shiny head, now slick with pre-cum. I began breathing steadily and letting out little moans. Just as it appeared I was about to cum, Kenji ordered, "Turn him over!"

I did not fight them as they flipped me over on my stomach, Kenji holding my boner protectively so that it did not rub against the table. "On your hands and knees," he said.

They helped me to get into doggy-style position, on my hands and knees before them, while they all shucked off their clothes. "Are you guys all going to fuck me?" I asked as I studied their rigid cocks bouncing around between their hairy crotches.

"Depends," Kenji said, "who wins the race to the lake. But that won't happen for a while yet. We want to play with you."

I then rose as Taki took two feathers and ran one up under my slick boner and his balls and the other one up and down my ass crack. I didn't know whether to rise or fall, and so I did both, making little bucking motions with my hips and ass. Chan and Nari laughed as I air-humped frantically before them, my eyes wide, my mouth letting out little puffs of air, my nostrils distorted.

Taki worked me over this way for five minutes while the others pulled at their own boners as they watched me gyrating before them. Finally, Chan and Nari went back to tit-flicks, which made me look like I was going into spastic convulsions. I was bucking up now wildly, getting lightly touched in five places at once. The tit flicking combined with the ass swipes and the cock switches were driving me absolutely nuts. I made sounds that caused them all to gaze at me in wonder, for I was madly humping and humming at the same time.

"Mmmm! Mmmm! Uhnnnn! Mmmmunh!" slipped out between my lips, my half-lidded eyes fixing on each of their faces, then traveling down to their rock-hard shafts.

"He's going crazy!" Chan whispered.

"He is drooling," Nari said, watching tiny trails of saliva dripping down my chin.

I lay sprawled there, looking up at the boners standing so stiff and straight before my face.

"Now," Kenji said, "Run to the lake."

Chan and Nari reached down and helped pull me to my feet. Taki gave me a playful slap on the ass. I took one look at the lake thirty yards away and took off running. The four Japanese boys gave chase, the meaty thwacks of their boners slapping against their pubic regions as they ran.

I ran naked on the beach before the lake, my arms pumping wildly, my head thrown back, my cheeks puffing out, my wavering, bobbing boner slapping my stomach above my madly jiggling balls.

Behind me, four naked and horny Asian boys closed quickly on my heels.

When I finally stumbled and fell, three feet short of the lake, my four pursuers dog-piled on top of me, all prodding me in various places with their full erections. Kenji took a hold of me by one arm and led me forward to two inner tubes tied together in the water near the shore. Chan and Nari ducked beneath the water and came up with their dark hair slicked back on the sides of their heads. Each boy was positioned with his head in the center of an inner tube, both peering hungrily and eagerly at my naked body as Kenji and Taki helped lower me on top of the inner tubes.

The moment I was sprawled atop the tubes, Chan began sucking my nipples within the first inner tube, while Nari sucked on my cock from within in the second.

By the time Taki kneeled down on the sandy shore,

I was moaning with pleasure and willingly opened my mouth wide to take in his stiff cock jutting up into my face. By gently moving the inner tube, Taki was able to slide his erect dick in and out of my wide-open mouth even as the other two worked me from below each tube.

Kenji produced a small jar of Vaseline from somewhere along the shore. He undid the cap, globbed a large dab on his seven-inch cock, rubbing it up and down until it was a shiny pole standing straight up at attention. He then reached into the jar and swabbed out another dab of the sticky, slick goo and ran it up and down my butt crack, swirling his little finger into my hole. Slowly, he slipped his two little fingers into my greased hole, opening me slightly.

Beneath him, I was writhing uncontrollably in pleasure. The combination of tit sucking and cocksucking was proving to be overwhelming, and I was so far gone with the thrills and tingles passing through my body, I barely noticed the two-finger penetration of my asshole.

Kenji gestured at Taki to join him. When he removed his cock from my mouth, Kenji steadied the two inner tubes to allow Taki to climb up and over my convulsing body spread beneath him. Kenji even helped guide Taki's fleshy rod into my hole.

I gagged on Kenji's seven-inch cock stuffing my mouth, but raised my hips to open myself up for Taki's hard cock. I groaned as Chan and Nari sucked me with renewed vigor. Chan was obviously switching tits as he sucked for I was bucking to one side then the other, and Nari was sucking fervently at my cock, for I started doing little pelvic thrusts to bury my dick deeper inside his mouth.

Kenji continued to slide his dick in and out of my open mouth, both hands locked on the inner tube. I reached around and grasped Kenji's hips to keep a firmer grip on him as I gave so much pleasure.

I suddenly stiffened as Taki impaled me with one long thrust. Beneath me, sensing my tenseness, Chan licked furiously at my left nipple, then switched sides and slurped all over my right nipple. Nari deep-throated my seven-inch cock, and soon I relaxed as Taki thrust deep inside me.

Once I began whimpering, Taki reared up slightly and then drove deep, plunging in with an up-and-down motion that caused the inner tubes to bob in the water. So with my mouth filled with Kenji's hardened flesh, and Chan sucking on my nipples, while Nari sucked on my cock, I began to writhe, whimper, groan, and hum.

Kenji came first, flooding my mouth with white creamy cum. He moved the inner tube in and out, in and out, furiously pumping my mouth around his sperming cock. He cried out, humping my face until he had emptied his balls.

As he slowly pulled out, sliding his slick cock out of my mouth, cum dribbled down my chin. Kenji lovingly reached down and wiped it off, then gently patted me on the head, saying, "You were wonderful! A few more sessions between us, and you are going to be a professional cocksucker."

I simply moaned, my hands still clamped onto Kenji's hips and buttocks as the other three continued to suck and fuck me. I glanced back at Taki riding me from behind. He went to say something but instead shuddered as convulsive humping motions overtook him. I made my cock and my tits more accessible to the two boys beneath me, but also performed tiny bucking moves as Taki ran his cock into me with wild abandon.

"I am coming!" Taki gasped. "I am—unhhhh! Ohhh! Mmmm! Oh, oh, oh, baby!"

Chan and Nari came out from under the tubes, both stroking their boners furiously. They stood directly over my forehead and cheeks, shooting thick loads onto my face.

Taki slowly pulled out of me, sighing as he did so.

I was so relaxed I just stuck my cum-slick ass in the air, wiggled it at the four of them, and said, "Any more training today, because I don't know if you noticed it, but I have not cum yet. So which one of you wants to get me off?"

In the end, it was Kenji who gave me a long and slow blow job, artfully using his tongue and lips to bring me to a nice climax.

Taki, Chan, and Nari stood over us, watching until Kenji's head stopped bobbing and I stopped writhing and squirming and gasping as I came and came.

Chapter Twenty-four

Logan had just finished reading when Alex stopped in front of the glassed-in gazebo of the Grind coffeehouse. The kid peered in and hesitantly raised his hand to wave at him.

Logan nodded.

Alex entered the coffeehouse.

Logan surveyed the Grind's clientele. Everyone present appeared to be going about their own business.

"Hi, Logan," Alex said. "How's the book coming?"

"Fine," Logan said. "How's things for you, Alex?"

Alex slid into the booth, shrugging. "Things for me?" he asked. "Funny you should ask. I don't want to bother you."

Logan took a few moments to assess the kid's solemn demeanor. "That serious, huh?"

Alex sighed, tears filling his eyes. "Yeah, that serious."

Logan bought Alex a cup of hot chocolate. He sensed the boy was deeply troubled and in a way felt responsible. He figured he owed it to him to see him on his way in a better state of mind.

When Alex was finished with his drink, he asked, "Could I tell you something, Logan? Something personal?"

"Sure, Alex." He looked around the crowd, trying to determine if anyone there even noticed the street kid talking to him in the corner. "Yes," Logan told Alex, "I'll listen to you. Do me a favor, will you? Give me ten minutes to join you two blocks down the street from here. I'll pick you up in front of the Emporium Bookstore. I don't want to call any attention to us. No offense."

Alex agreed. Logan scribbled some more on a notepad. He

drank the remainder of his coffee and casually put pen and paper into his weathered leather shoulder case.

Ten minutes later, he and Alex sat at a picnic table on a high bluff at the edge of Donner Park, overlooking the dark waters of the Missouri River. Alex began speaking.

"I liked being dominated," he said, cringing as he said it. "I liked others having their way with me. I liked getting fucked and made to do all kinds of things."

He sighed. "At first, I thought about reincarnation. You know, like maybe I had the soul of some slave boy from ancient Rome. Like maybe in another life, I'd been violated by a savage master who commanded his other slave boys to do things to me. I even looked up 'Conscious Rivers of Thought' on the Internet and wondered if those weird snippets from long-ago lifetimes were real. It struck a chord with me. I began fantasizing about being a slave boy standing naked on an auction block, having many men examining me, checking me out to see if I would service them properly.

"I played through that scenario many times in my jack-off sessions. I was bought and paid for by my master, taken home and thrown into a mass of writhing naked bodies of six or seven slave boys. They played with me for hours, just like Baxster and Maxwell did. It was like a dream come true. I got hard just thinking about being dominated. Controlled. Told to do things with my mouth, my tongue, my lips. Made to do things."

Logan said, "I studied on the Internet about dominance. Playful dominance is encouraged. Rough play is okay, as long as there are safewords. Not very nice things have happened to victims of a dominance game gone wrong."

Alex stared at Logan. "So you don't think I'm strange, then? That I'm some kind of pervert for what I like?"

Logan hesitated.

Alex lowered his eyes, crossing his arms before his thin chest. "You think I'm twisted, right?"

Logan told him, "I can understand what those boys were doing to you, getting you addicted to sex. And I can understand you getting to like it, being dominated and fulfilling your fantasies. But crossing the line into unsafe sex with so many partners and engaging in street prostitution? How can I convince you that you need to stop this behavior? How can I help you to stop putting yourself in danger?"

Alex said, "Take me home and let me be your boy, and I'll never sell myself to anyone else again. I'd like that."

"I studied the 'sugar daddy' affairs many boys seek. Some of these arrangements make both partners happy. But—"

"But," Alex said, his bottom lip protruding, "you aren't attracted to me. I'm good enough for a one-night stand."

"You're very good-looking," Logan said. "Downright handsome. But I don't roll that way, Alex. I'm just not wired for that kind of relationship."

"I wish," Alex said. "You would make the perfect lover. Hell, I'd give up all of my street trade—"

"Lover?" Logan said. "Lovers are on equal levels. Lovers usually have a lot in common. For example, if you came to live with me and we had a computer to share, what would you use it for?"

"Looking up porn to beat off to," Alex said. "Or playing online games."

"Exactly," Logan said. "You're on an entirely different level than me."

Alex shrugged. "Once I knew you loved me, I would be all yours forever. I just need someone to be there for me."

Logan thought, *That's what Baxster said to me, too. Soul mate. Everyone, at any age, in any gender, in any walk of life, is searching for that one true soul mate. But what happens when someone finds a soul mate who is ten or twenty or even thirty years younger than them? How can the two ever hope to have an uncomplicated relationship? With laws forbidding it, and one word to the wrong person sending the older companion to prison and the younger one to years of forced therapy? Is this the minefield Frankie walks into every time he starts a relationship with his young charges? And why? Why risk his entire career, his entire life, on these sexual flings? What drives him to take such risks? Is he that desperate to love or be loved?*

CHAPTER TWENTY-FIVE

The cool night wind drifted in through the open door. Laced with faint traces of wood smoke from some neighbor's chimney, the gentle breeze ruffled the lace curtains.

Jenna McGuire lay watching them from her bed across the room. She took a deep breath of burning wood and stretched, feeling a tightness in her muscles. She chided herself for the three-hour workout at the dojo, aware that age and time were creeping up on her. She felt a dull pain in her lower back and knew that though she remained devoted to the martial arts she practiced on a weekly basis, she was pushing herself too hard.

Slowly working the kinks out of her back, Jenna snuggled deeper beneath her freshly washed, lemon-scented sheets. She recalled the conversation she'd overheard the other day. The words had trickled in from the den where her eighteen-year-old son, Alex, played Nintendo with his friend Bobby.

"Your mom's hot," declared Bobby. "She reminds me of Lara Croft."

Reading her weekly reports in the kitchen, Jenna had sat silent, waiting for Alex to respond. Jenna heard her son say, "Lara Croft? Get real, Bobby! Her boobs ain't *that* big!"

Bobby laughed. "Yeah, but you gotta admit she's quite a hottie, don't you?"

"Shut up!" responded Alex. "You're talking about my mom, for Jesus sakes! I don't make observations about *your* mom's boobs!"

"Yeah," Bobby had chuckled, "because *my* mom's nothing to look at!"

Later, Jenna discovered through one of her juvenile clients exactly who Lara Croft was. Max Broadstone had looked at her like she was from some other planet as he said in astonishment, "Probation officer to a whole slew of delinquents! Mother of a teenage son! And you've never heard of *Tomb Raider*? Geez, ain't you in touch with your boy?"

Jenna had assured Max she would pay more attention to what games her son was playing. She went out at the end of work that afternoon and rented the *Tomb Raider* movie.

Lara Croft, played in the movie by Angelina Jolie, was an action/adventure heroine. Her only resemblance to Jenna was the thick French braid and her fit and trim body. Jenna only wished she looked half as good as Angelina.

Jenna tossed and turned, attempting to get comfortable. Jenna sat straight up in bed. Her heart pounding wildly, she looked at the open sliding door ten feet from her bed, sensing at once that something was not right.

She quickly scanned the large bedroom. Moonlight bathed one half of the room. Her roll-top desk, dresser, and vanity table appeared to be glowing in the incandescent light. But ominous shadows dominated the other half of the room. She peered into the blackness.

Jenna blinked rapidly. There appeared to be a cloud of blackness lingering in the deeper recess of the corner. Jenna looked to the half-open door. The lace curtains on either side of the door now hung lifeless. Strangely, the comforting sounds of night were muted. Chirping crickets. An occasional car passing down the street. The soft hooting of the barn owl that lived beneath her eaves. The tinkling of wind chimes hanging above her patio. The gentle splashing of cascading water from the fountain in her garden. And a bark from the dog down the street.

Jenna's eyes were drawn back to the curtains. When she had opened the sliding door, she had left merely a six-inch gap.

Now it was wide open.

Who opened that door? And why?

She heard the whisper of polyester-covered legs or arms moving ever so slightly, as if someone shifted position in the shadowy mass across the room.

Jenna's bare feet made tiny slapping sounds as they hit the polished wooden floor. In her black sweats and overlarge T-shirt, she prepared to fight. Jenna steadied herself. Slowly, she curled her fingertips inward so that each one connected with the palms of her hands as she extended her knuckles.

Her eyes focused on a man standing there staring at her. Instinctively, she moved one leg behind the other, taking a defensive stance.

Picked the wrong house, you stupid schmuck, she thought. *Bet you never figured on your victim holding a black belt, did you, asshole?*

The tall, broad-shouldered man moved out of the shadows. He had a long, angular face, and he grinned at Jenna. Slowly and silently, he raised his glove-covered hands, curling his fingers like claws.

Clawing at the air, the man's movements became more frenzied. The man took two steps forward, stopped, performing a complete spin as he lowered his arms to his sides. Staring at her with a glazed look in his dark eyes, he bent his knees and dropped to a crouch, spreading his legs wide. His hands came up and he began furiously chopping at the air. He charged across the room.

Jenna waited and forcefully drove the heel of her hand directly into the man's nose. Bones shattered. Blood spurted. And the intruder cried out as he sailed backward, his arms flailing wildly.

❖

Logan escorted Alex up the long driveway to his house. The kid tucked his chin against his chest, slid both hands into his front pockets, and slouched like a badly made scarecrow.

Logan tried to think of something to say, but nothing came to mind. "This is as far as I go," he announced quietly, trying one last time to make eye contact with Alex.

Alex kept his eyes glued to the shadowy alcove of the doorway, refusing to even glance in his direction.

Logan could only guess what was now going through the kid's head. "Alex, thanks for sharing with me. I swear, your secret is safe with me."

Alex stumbled and froze, his eyes narrowing in concern as he stared at the open back door in front of them. "Something's wrong!" he hissed. "Mom would never leave the door like that!"

He swiftly entered the house.

❖

Jenna stood there, staring in concern as the injured intruder clambered to his knees before her.

"Jesus, lady!" Brad Helman gasped. "Okay! Back the hell off! All I wanna do is talk."

"Just who the hell are you?" asked Jenna. "And what the hell are you doing in my house?"

"Jesus!" Brad moaned. "Where did you learn to hit like that? I think you broke my nose!"

"I could have done worse. Now answer me, what do you want?"

"All I want is to talk. Oh, Gawd, my nose is on fire. Do you got an ice pack?"

"Damn your nose!" Jenna snapped. "You broke into my house because you needed someone to talk to? In about two seconds, I'm going to hit you again. So hard this time, you won't wake up until the cops get here to haul your sorry ass away!"

"Ah," Brad said, "don't do that. You do, and you won't hear what I have to say."

Jenna fired back, "I don't need to hear any bullshit from you. I'm calling nine-one-one."

"Miss McGuire?" Mike Carrol stepped from the hallway into her room. "Put the phone down, please."

"Go fuck yourself!" Jenna snapped.

"Put the goddamned phone down!" Mike demanded, a solid *click* following his words. He aimed the pistol he'd just cocked at Jenna. "There," he said, "that's better. Now we can talk."

Mike used his free hand to remove a handkerchief from inside his suit jacket. He tossed it to Brad, who was still bleeding from his broken nose. Mike rolled his eyes as Brad gingerly swiped at the blood flowing from his nostrils. "You done clowning around, moron?" He chuckled dryly. "Told you we should have just cut to the chase. Now look at you."

Plastering the bloody handkerchief to his nose, Brad peered up at Jenna with bleary eyes. "Jesus, lady, there was no need to use excessive force. We didn't come here to hurt you. We just came to—"

"Talk?" Jenna said. "You've both said that before."

Mike lowered the hammer on his pistol and pointed it down at the floor. "Sit down there on your bed. Listen."

Jenna remained standing.

Brad staggered up from the floor and stumbled past Jenna to seat himself on her bed.

"Jenna McGuire," Mike said, "juvenile probation officer—let's just make this simple."

"Simple is good," Brad mumbled through the blood-soaked handkerchief.

"Maxwell Broadstone is scheduled to testify in court this coming Thursday. As his probation officer, you are going to recommend drug treatment for the troubled young boy."

Jenna asked, "Max? This is about Maxwell Broadstone? You broke into my home to stop Maxwell testifying against Ridge Majors."

Mike said, "Mr. Majors is a prominent businessman in the Omaha community, and this problem child, Maxwell, with all his slander, nearly ruined his business career—"

"Career?" Jenna interrupted him. "A pimp? For God's sake, do you know how much damage he's done? Majors has been selling young boys for the past twenty years!"

"How many of those young boys sold themselves willingly? Majors simply provided them an avenue to market themselves to well-paying clients."

"Allegations have been taken down," Jenna reminded him, "in a court deposition. Max Broadstone is to be the star witness against Majors."

"Star witness?" Mike chuckled. "A good defense lawyer would shoot holes in the testimony. Not a lot of credence could be given to the poor, abused victim if his drug history is made known to the jury. During his review hearing tomorrow, you are to put in a recommendation for treatment. This case needs to be derailed now. This goes to trial in three days. Just do what we've asked you to do, and no harm will come to…"

He let the words hang there a moment.

Jenna said nothing.

"Recommend treatment during the review hearing of Max Broadstone," Mike said, "or we may implicate your young son Alex. We have a client who cannot afford to be associated with this pornographer. If this case goes to trial, who knows what Max may say?"

"Fuck you!" Jenna snapped. "Leave my son out of this!"

"Oh," Mike said, "we would have, but Alex's been involved with—"

Logan pawed at Alex as he lunged past him out in the hallway. The slender kid darted past him. "Mom!" Alex yelled.

Logan entered the room two steps behind the agitated kid. Brad growled, "What the hell are you doing here, Writer Man?"

Mike gestured at Brad. "Hold off there, Killer Dog." He slipped his gun in a holster beneath his jacket.

Jenna turned to face Logan.

Alex said, "He's with me, Mom. He's a writer. His name is Logan Walker."

"A writer?" Jenna said, more confused than before.

Alex said, "He's cool. He's on our side. He's not with these guys, if that's what you're thinking."

Jenna met Logan's concerned look. "At this point, I don't know what to think." She glared heatedly at the two men. "Get the hell outta of my house!" she snapped.

Mike latched onto Brad's left arm. "We delivered our message. It's time we leave." He ushered his partner out through the sliding glass door, then turned to deliver his parting words.

"Alex," he said, "I will keep your secret. At least tonight. Convince your mom to cooperate."

Jenna snapped, "Just how do you know my son?"

"Save yourself and your kid from definite grief. Strongly recommend drug treatment for Maxwell during that review hearing tomorrow. A whole world of hurt is going to descend on this family if you don't do as I asked."

He turned and walked out through the lacy curtains covering the sliding glass door.

CHAPTER TWENTY-SIX

L ogan closed and locked the sliding door. "Alex?" he said, "turn the light off a minute, please."

Alex did as he was told, and two minutes later, Logan stood back from the door. "They're gone. They climbed over that fence out back and disappeared down the alley."

Jenna snatched up her house robe from a chair beside the bed. She slipped into it. "Alex?" she said. "Show Mr. Walker to the kitchen. I'll join you in a minute."

As Logan crossed the room to join a forlorn-looking Alex at the shadowy bedroom door, Jenna slid a slender stick into the slot of the sliding glass door, securing it in place. She then followed the other two down the hallway and into the kitchen.

Logan took the seat she offered him. Jenna busied herself making coffee. Alex remained standing, looking like he might bolt any second.

"How do you like your coffee?" Jenna asked Logan.

"Black would be fine," he answered her.

"Alex?" Jenna said.

Alex pulled the back door closed and locked it. He stood there, his eyes fixed on the wall beside the door.

If she starts to question him, he thought, *he'll be gone with the wind in the next few seconds. Maybe I should distract her long enough to settle the kid down so he doesn't run right out the door.*

"Alex?" Jenna said, placing her hands on her slender hips. She leaned back against the stove. "Do you know these two men?"

Alex turned, his eyes narrowed. Logan decided to throw him a lifeline. "I know them," he told Jenna, fighting not to flinch as she turned her inquisitive gaze on him. "They're private investigators, though shady. I suspect they're not legitimate."

Jenna nodded. "Private investigators who break into my home to threaten me? I should call the police and report this."

"Perhaps," Logan agreed with her.

But Alex said, "You do that, and things will just get worse."

She looked up once more at Alex. "Alex? How do you know these men?"

Alex stood there.

Logan was just about to intervene when there came a knock on the back door.

"Logan?" came a familiar voice. "Logan, you in there?"

Jenna and Alex both looked to Logan in surprise. He smiled back at them. "It's friend, not foe," he said. He unlocked the door, pulling it open. Noah Standing Bear stood there.

"Can't leave you alone for a moment," Noah said, gruffly, "without you stumbling your way into way more trouble than you're prepared to deal with."

Logan stood there, baffled. Noah smiled. "Told you God told me to watch over you, Logan. Everyone has to have a guardian angel. Even if God in all His wisdom couldn't have found someone better than a big Indian like me."

Noah chuckled, and Logan turned to Jenna. "Can he come in?" he asked. "He's a friend of mine."

"Yes," Jenna said. "Sensei Bear is welcome in my home."

"You know him?" Logan asked, surprised.

"Yes," Noah told him. "Jenna is one of my most experienced students. But I am as surprised as you that this trail led me here to her doorstep. I wasn't actually shadowing you tonight, I was trailing those two crooked investigators. I even know why they came here."

"As if this night couldn't have gotten any more bizarre," Jenna said.

Alex yawned and wandered off down the hallway, mumbling that he was heading for bed.

"We still need to talk about this," Jenna said as he disappeared into his room at the end of the hall. "I want a full explanation in the morning, Alex."

Noah said, "Those two are working for State Senator Guildman, father of the young man Ben Donovan shot and killed out at Lakewood summer camp. To keep his name out of the press, they're trying to quash this case before it goes to trial. If the press find outs the senator's troubled son was doing gay porn, it would damage Senator Guildman's career."

Back at his cabin, Logan thumbed through Baxster's journal, almost certain he'd seen the name Ridge Majors somewhere. Finding his name at last, he placed the book in his lap and began to read:

Baxster's Journal, Entry 5

The thing about sucking an extra-big, extra-long cock is you have to take it slow. Ridge Majors had a giant schlong, one that was five inches soft, and nine inches hard. For any man to be that well-endowed is a small miracle, but one that presents two major problems for someone like me trying to pleasure him. First is taking it in my mouth and throat. The second is taking it all the way up my ass.

I first simply sucked on his massive, round head. It was shaped like a Shitake mushroom, a long, thick helmet that first gained entry into my mouth as a fit of passion overcame both of us.

The moment he had me in his studio, Ridge frenched me, keeping a lip lock on my mouth even as his stripped me out of my clothes.

I continued to suck on his tongue as I did the same favor for him, practically ripping his T-shirt and underwear off him.

I then went down on him, sinking to my knees before him.

Ridge ran his hands through my hair, grasping me

by both ears. He guided me forward, but I already had my mouth open wide, prepared to suck him inside.

Until I saw the giant, protruding rock-hard boner wavering before my face.

I gasped in wonder and disbelief. I had never seen such an enormous cock before.

Ridge forced my head into his crotch, but allowed me to position my mouth for the invasion of his long tube of pulsating meat. "One inch at a time," he said, grinning down at me.

At first, there was a lot of "Occch! Arggggg! Occchhh! Arggg! Occchh!" as his bulbous head struck repeatedly at the entrance to my throat.

My gag reflex kicked in and I could not help myself, making all kinds of disgusting choking sounds.

Ridge clamped his hands a bit roughly over my ears, whispering, "Deep-throat it, Baxster. Let it slide and glide over your tongue and rest at the back of your throat. Breathe through your nose. Suck and swallow my cock inch by fucking inch. Just go slowly."

I again made odd sounds. "Acccck! Accck! Occccc! Occcchhhh! Accck!"

"I said," he instructed me firmly, "to take it slow. Your throat needs to stretch some to get used to my big, thick head. Let that rest there for several minutes."

I felt his dick sliding out of my mouth, away from my suctioning lips. I gobbled him back up, slowly sucking his head in. It prodded at my throat, once more poking at my gag reflex muscle.

Finally, I was stretched wide open for him.

His cock head and five inches of his shaft were all the way down my throat.

Ridge's thick, long, hard cock was filling me up, and I was linked to him in some strange sense of connectivity. I felt like I was an extension of him; his cock and my throat were making us one.

I took him deeper into my throat, kneading his ass

cheeks with mad passion. I ran my fingers up his back, down around his mounds, up and into his crack. Ridge had no choice then but to fall forward, embedded deep inside me, his hands planted on the wall behind us to hold himself up.

Pleased that I was pleasing him so thoroughly, I began to hum around his cock buried so deeply down my throat.

"Oh, my fucking God!" Ridge cried, arching his back and rising up on his toes. "Unfuckingunbelievable! Hum away, baby! Hum away!"

I did so, repeating several rhythms that elicited more groans of pleasure from him, writhing around over my face. Inch by inch, I spat him from my mouth, slobbering all over his length as his cock slid out of me. We froze for several moments. Me on my knees, my open, wet mouth just inches from his slick and shiny dick head. I jacked him several times, squeezing and pulling on his shaft. Running my hand over his head, under his pleasure spot, fingering it, while I rested my mouth.

"More," Ridge commanded. "Hum louder. Suck harder. Use more of your tongue."

I opened wider than before. Using my hands on his butt cheeks, I forced him forward. His cock slid slowly past my lips, over my tongue, and deep down into my throat.

"OCCCCH!" I gagged only once this time, and then I relaxed. He was planted all the way down my throat. My nose was resting in his pubes.

I hummed loudly. "Hhhmmm! Mmmmmm! Ahhmmmmmmm! Mmmmm! Mnnnnnnn!"

Ridge went crazy above me. Grabbing me by both sides of my head, he began to fiercely fuck my face. His cock was ramming deeper, driving in and poking my throat.

"Acccck! Arrrrgh! Oooommphf!" I could not help but respond.

Still, I tried to hum at the same time. "Mmmmmm! Mnnnnnnn! Ooohpmhmmmmmmm!"

I then took full control. Grasping him firmly about his left butt cheek with my right hand, I drove my left middle finger directly up into his asshole. He froze, perched on the tips of his toes, his hands locked around the back of my head. He began to mewl.

I wriggled my finger deeper, striking repeatedly at his prostate gland, firing off such amazing feelings inside him that Ridge mumbled, "I love you, boy! I love your sweet mouth! Your probing finger! Your masterful tongue wagging! Oh, suck! Oh, finger-fuck! Oh, suck the juices right out of me!" I did so, now working him over furiously. I dug deep inside his ass cavity first with two fingers, then switched to three. I sucked him all the way down my throat, my eyes wide, tears streaking my cheeks. Slobber and drool ran down and over my chin. Still I continued to inhale his length, wind whistling through my distorted nostrils, my head bobbing, my mouth and tongue working feverishly.

I sucked him for five long, intense minutes, until his knees buckled and he locked his hands behind my head, holding me in place. He bucked up wildly, slamming his dick down into my throat.

Ridge whispered, "Ah, yeah! Ah, yeah! Cumming! Spurting like a motherfucker!"

I felt one tremendous warm blast hit the back of my throat. Then a second gob, a third, and a fourth and fifth, each blast all gooey and sliding down into my stomach.

Ridge shot three more lighter loads into my mouth, then attempted to pull out.

"Mmmmm! Mmmmmmmn! Mmmmmmmmmmnnnn!" I repeated over and over, and he stayed put for just a while longer, trying to decide if his super-sensitive cock could take any more sensations.

"Stop!" he growled. "Stop! Let me go! No more sucking!"

I froze, my lips wrapped around at least five inches of his cock.

"Mmmmmmmm! Mmmmmmmnnnnn!" I teased him.

I forced his cock all the way to the back of my throat, again and again, my gag reflex causing me to make disgusting sounds. "Occccc! Acccccck! Occcccccchhh!"

Ridge clamped down on the top of my head, pulling his dick out of my mouth.

"Stop!" he ordered. "Stop it, goddamn you! You'll get some of this later, you greedy little cocksucker!"

I slipped my finger out of his hole. I fell backward, my legs spread wide, my own boner standing at full attention there before him.

"Watch me," I whispered up at him. "Watch me cum, please!"

Ridge stood there panting, his eyes locked on my cock sliding in and out of my fast-moving hand. I began to whimper. It was not going to take long. I was so horned up from such a strenuous suck session, I was going to shoot any second.

My legs spread wider, my feet planted flat on the ground. I raised my hips with each whack of my cock. My hand was a blur as I ran it up and over, up and over, up and over.

I screamed as I came.

Ridge stood there amazed. "All seven blasts hit you in the face!" he said.

"Camera-friendly." He laughed. "You are going to be camera-friendly, Baxster."

CHAPTER TWENTY-SEVEN

The next morning, Logan took a seat in the back row of Juvenile Courtroom 3. Court had been in session for nearly thirty minutes, Honorable Judge Naylor presiding over the review hearing of Maxwell Broadstone.

It was an informal hearing, so Judge Naylor sat at the head of a long rectangular table. Naylor, in his late fifties, was tall and angular. His short-cropped black hair was thinning and turning gray. He smiled warmly at those gathered around the table.

There were six others sharing the table with Judge Naylor. Three sat to his left, three to his right. Jenna McGuire was seated close to Naylor on the right. She was speaking quietly to Maxwell Broadstone, seated to her right.

Logan studied the young man. He was a handsome kid, with a clean-shaven face, high cheekbones, and blue eyes staring a hole in the table between his long-fingered hands. If Max was listening to whatever Jenna was saying, he didn't indicate it.

His public defender, a rather hefty lady with a mass of poofy red hair, sat on his other side. Her attention was on the judge.

Across from them were the three out to prosecute Max.

The city prosecutor was a severe-looking, middle-aged lady with short-black hair. Her nose was sharp. She wore circular glasses, causing her dark eyes to appear overlarge behind the thick lenses.

Two men likely associated with the court in some capacity or other sat on her side of the table.

Judge Naylor asked Miss Van Horn, the prosecutor, for her recommendations for Max. She stated he hadn't complied with several of his probation stipulations and urged the court to either confine him to an institution or make him a ward of the state.

Judge Naylor scribbled notes while she was speaking. He turned to Jenna. She glanced to the entryway of the courtroom.

Logan turned his head to see Mike Carrol and Brad Helman stepping into the room and taking seats in the back row. Since the court hearing was open to the public, only the county deputy paid them any attention before reassuming his bored expression.

"Your Honor," Jenna said, "despite the truancies Miss Van Horn cited, I don't see any reason to make him a ward of the state. I strongly urge the court to sentence him to Horizon's Treatment program. Max has a substance abuse problem, and an evaluation and subsequent treatment are needed."

"Treatment?" Judge Naylor asked.

"Yes. During our last visit, Max shared about his addictions with me and how they are impacting his life. I see treatment as a positive option."

Van Horn argued then, and the public defender argued back. The man from Social Services spoke as well.

Max just sat there, zoned out in his own little world.

Logan wondered if maybe the kid really did have an addiction problem. What kid wouldn't self-medicate if he was so deeply involved in the sex trade?

Max suddenly came out of his stupor. "I know I'm not supposed to talk during this hearing, but I have something to say. It no longer matters where I end up. Last night my dad found out about me. The way I am. What I've been doing. Someone sent him that sworn deposition that was supposed to be kept secret. My dad read it. He knows what I am. What I've done. My dad hates me now. Wishes I'd never been born. Wishes I was dead."

Sneering at Van Horn, Max sprang up and out of his chair, snarling, "I'm gonna snap your neck, you ugly bitch!" He launched himself across the table, both hands latching onto her neck.

Van Horn screamed.

"Max!" Jenna shouted. "Max, please!"

Max saw the bailiff coming toward them. He swung off the table to his feet. Waiting until the bailiff grasped one of his wrists, Max reached down and drew the bailiff's revolver from its holster.

He wrenched his wrist free of the bailiff's grasp and brought the pistol up to his own head. Time seemed to freeze.

He wheeled around, keeping the muzzle of the pistol tight to one side of his head. "Do you know what I've been through since I confessed? All the hours a therapist drilled me over and over about my sex life? Do I fucking identify as gay? Do I feel like all these men were abusing me? Am I addicted to sexual pleasure? Do I think I might be infected with HIV? Have I ever had syphilis or gonorrhea? How many times did you use a condom? And now my dad knows! And despises me!" Max tightened his grip on the gun. "Now, there's only one way out."

He began to slowly squeeze the trigger.

"Max?" Jenna said calmly but firmly. "Please don't do this. We can work this out. I promise."

"Too late," Max said, his tone flat.

Jenna shoved the table, hard. The edge caught Max directly in his groin. He cried out, and the gun slipped away from the side of his head.

Jenna dove over the table, grabbing Max's wrists. A moment later, the bailiff clamped his huge hands down onto Max's slender shoulders, nearly forcing him to his knees.

Jenna whipped Max around so swiftly that the bailiff let him go and the gun came loose from his grip. The bailiff picked up the gun up, eased the hammer back down, and holstered the weapon.

Max squirmed in Jenna's grip, but she maintained just enough pressure on his bent wrist to keep him in place beneath her.

When Logan looked away from all the commotion at the front of the room, he caught just a glimpse of Mike's backside as he exited the courtroom a step behind Brad.

Logan stood and followed.

❖

Brad smirked and said, when he noticed Logan following them, "That's one fucked-up kid."

Logan had to restrain himself from punching the guy in the mouth.

Mike said, "Turn it down a notch, cowboy. It's not us you

should direct your anger toward. What you witnessed in there is something we've seen time and again. There's no telling the damage inflicted on these poor kids who thought playing naked was so much fun. Who knows what's more damaging? Doing the deed, or talking about it later?"

Logan snapped, "How do you live with yourselves? Preying on kids and the men they serviced? How can you capitalize on either party's miseries? You speak of hush money like it's a magic wand. As if money will sweep all these deeds away. Don't you two have a conscience?"

Brad snorted, "What about you? Writing a book about this perversion? Do you think anything you say will fix the problem? Make people aware? Make it all go away?"

"I'm just giving an honest look into the..." Logan stopped himself, for he did not know exactly what he meant to say.

Brad leered at him. "Instead of judging us, judge yourself. We're a cleanup crew. How are you going to portray these men? These boys? These illegal relationships? You going to justify them? Condemn them? Explain why they happen? Just how are you going to serve this up?"

Before Logan could answer, Mike and Brad walked away.

Chapter Twenty-Eight

L ogan drove home to his cabin.
He needed a drink.

When he sat down at his desk, Crown and Coke in hand, he noticed the blinking light on his answering machine. He hit Play. Jenna said, "Quite tragic what happened in court, right? Max has been sent to the Fairview Springs mental institution for an evaluation. If my drug treatment recommendation didn't derail Ridge Major's hearing, Max pretty well sank that ship himself today. Desperate kid. In a desperate situation. Please contact me later. I still need to know how Alex fits into this. If you know anything, please share it with me."

Logan sat there for a long while.

He recalled what Max had shouted in court. Max certainly didn't think talking to a counselor had been worth it. And his dad? The poor guy could have probably gone to his grave quite happily never knowing about his son.

He just wasn't sure it was up to him to share Alex's secrets with Jenna.

❖

After typing an entire chapter of his book, Logan came up for air four hours later. He picked up Baxster Crown's journal and stretched the kinks out of his shoulders.

Baxster's Journal, Entry 6

I was startled, having just been woken by something prodding my face.

When I opened my eyes I saw Lucas straddling my chest, a leg on either side, his hard round knob repeatedly tapping my face. He held himself upright against the wall behind us and made little humping motions. Prod. Prod. Prod. He tapped my left eye. My right eye. My nose. My chin. My wet, slightly open lips. This time when he pulled away with a gyration of his lean hips, a string of pre-cum connected us, stretching from his cock head to my lips in one long, rather thick strand.

"Lick your lips and swallow," Lucas said, softly.

I did so at once. The taste was nice, a bit salty but very satisfying all the same as I rolled it around inside my mouth and swallowed the tiny glob of sperm down my throat.

Lucas smiled in approval. He soon had a tube of lube in his hand and was coating his seven inches of hard manhood with the slick, shiny substance. I lay there beneath him, watching him slowly work the greasy solution all over his cock head, down his shaft, and then back up again in long, gentle motions.

"What are you doing?" I asked, my eyes glued to the rock-hard, slick shaft and large purple head just inches from my face.

Lucas did not answer at first. He simply scooted back, his bare ass sliding over my chest, my belly and, for a moment, forcing my own erection to bend at a slightly awkward angle. When his ass passed over it, my springy dick made a loud whapping sound as it struck my pelvic region with sudden force.

Lucas gave a small laugh.

He peered up at me, his eyes locking with mine. Slowly, ever so slowly he lowered his head, his chin coming to rest on my ball sack. He licked his lips, working up a fair amount of saliva for what he was about to do next.

Again I asked, "What are you doing?"

Lucas remained silent. His chin grazed my balls as he lowered it between my legs. I spread them to give him better access. His chin came to rest on the bed, but his tongue darted out, flicking my gooch, the space between my balls and my asshole. It was extremely sensitive and I gasped and lifted my ass up, allowing him to invade this touchy spot of soft flesh.

Lucas licked at me, firing off all my nerve endings down there between my legs. He tongue-tipped me at first, causing me to rise and fall with each flickering he administered. We had no sooner got a rhythm going than Lucas switched to slow, warm and wet lickings, using the entire front of his tongue to snake down over my gooch and slide in and out of my crack. He flicked my ass ring, creating a tingling feeling that shot through my butthole and seemed to connect with my sperm duct. Pre-cum soon slicked my dick head with gooey gobs of sperm.

Lucas continued to rim me with long, slow tongue-lashings, while at the same time he reached up and smeared my pre-cum all over my head. I was gasping and soon moaning with the two feelings racking my body as he worked my rim and my sensitive trigger just beneath my dick head.

He stopped suddenly, and I looked up at him in disappointment, curious as to what he was going to do next in this sex play between us.

He raised my left leg, placing it over his shoulder. He did the same with my right leg so that I lay there sprawled beneath him, my legs spread wide, my ass undefended.

"What are you doing?" I asked for the third time.

"Going to fuck you," Lucas at last answered.

I felt warm lube squirting into my ass. He used one hand to squeeze the bottle of sweet herbal gel and the other to lather and plaster my crack and my hole. He fingertipped me a few brief moments, driving in, pulling out, driving in, pulling out. I felt little resistance from my hole as he worked his pinkie inside me. Once he had thoroughly run his little finger in and out of me, he started barely penetrating my ass ring with his index finger. He teased me a while, dipping in with shallow jabs. He finally went knuckle-deep, and then all the way up inside me. Once he loosened me with his index finger, he gently worked a second finger in, so that his index and middle finger formed a dick-like penetration, with both fingertips grazing my prostate, causing me to moan with great pleasure. He twirled and swirled his two fingers, performing graceful twists that went round and round inside me, driving me over the edge. I was whimpering without even realizing it, and we looked at each other and froze.

We both smiled at the same time.

A third finger slipped into the relaxed confines of my ass. Lucas repeatedly jabbed very gently deep inside me, firing off such feelings that I was muttering, mumbling, and occasionally swearing, dirty words that seemed to inspire him to finger-fuck me with a rapid jab—jam—jab—jam— jab—jam motions. He worked me over very thoroughly, all the while lowering his head to lick at my sperm duct just beneath my dick head.

When he stopped quite suddenly, withdrawing his tongue from my cock, his fingers from my ass, I continued to make little bucking motions with my hips.

He giggled at my antics. He then scooted up so that his greased and lathered dick head rested in my ass crack, just in contact with my hole.

"Go slow," I begged him. "Just push the head inside and let it stretch a bit first, okay?"

Without a word, Lucas poked his plum-sized dick head into my asshole.

I gasped and latched onto his shoulders. He repositioned my legs, forcing them up higher on his shoulders, forcing me to angle my ass upward for him to get a full frontal thrust when the time came for such.

I gasped, "Slow. Slow. Let me stretch," as his bulbous head stretched me out, and then Lucas slowly began to worm his seven-inch shaft in past my sphincter and deeper, deeper, deeper into my bowels.

The thorough finger-fucking helped prepare me for insertion of the full seven inches of hardened, greasy cock as it slid all the way inside me. In fact, I wanted more.

"Deeper!" I cried out, whimpering a bit.

Lucas grunted as he drove himself deeper into the warm confines of my ass. Again he drove in, barely pulling out. And just when I was totally impaled by his long, hard shaft, he withdrew all the way to the head. Leaving this inside me, he gazed into my expectant eyes, and then with a swiftness I did not expect, he rammed his cock into me with great force.

I cried out with pure pleasure, and Lucas went wild, driving in, pulling out, driving in, pulling out, jackrabbit-fucking me as he, too, cried out with each forward thrust.

"Oh, fuck!" he moaned.

"Oh, fuck me! Fuck me! Fuck me!" I groaned.

Driving his dick into me furiously, Lucas muttered, "Unh! Unh! Uhhhh! Fuck! Fuck! Fuck!"

I found his open mouth directly above mine, and so I raised my head and slithered my tongue between his lips. Lucas responded immediately, entwining his tongue with mine. We licked each other's tongues wildly and with mad passion. He formed an O with his lips and sucked my tongue into his mouth, working it over as if it were a cock. As we kissed, his fucking turned to a slow grinding that sent his cock deep in, swirled it around, and nearly set it free, and yet the head stayed inside.

I formed my tongue like a slender projectile and drove it up inside his mouth, holding it firm and straight. He licked the entire length, taking it into the warm, wet confines of his mouth, sucking and slurping at it as if trying to swallow it. We were connected not only by his dick buried deep in my ass, we were lip-locked and performing a tongue dance that was graceful and wild at the same time.

After several minutes of hot kissing, Lucas pulled away to breathe and turned his attention back to the bucking motions he'd been performing before the kissing began. He withdrew, grasping me firmly by my hips to lift me so that I could meet him halfway, my ass up and opened for his rapidly pounding dick.

I felt his dangling balls jiggling around between my legs, felt the friction from his pubic hair joined with mine, and definitely felt the long, yet quick thrusts of his cock as he worked himself into a frenzy.

He was grunting with a savage, feral sound erupting from his lips. "Ahhh! Ugh! Ugh! Ahhh! Unnhh!" kept steadily ringing in my left ear as his head came to rest against mine.

He was sledgehammering me with a ferocity I did not think possible. The normally gentle Lucas had turned into a horned-up wild beast with a take-it-all intensity. I turned my head to look into his eyes and was on the verge of alarm when I saw how far gone he was, his eyes half-open, his tongue drooling saliva onto my shoulder, his face contorted into an almost ugly mask.

"Ahhh! Ahhhh! Unnh! Unnh!" kept exploding from his mouth, rising in volume as he became even more furious in his fucking. He was a man on fire. He would not stop. Could not stop. Driven to the point of no return. His cock obviously tingling with a thousand and one feelings. His cock head led the charge into my anal cavity, ramming my prostate, firing off sensations inside me that had me squirming and writhing and moaning beneath him.

He grabbed me by both ankles and began to plow me. I tried, yet failed to latch onto his shoulders, my fingers slipping and sliding off him as he pounded me into the bed.

I gasped, "Oh, Gawd! Oh, dear Gawd! Oh, Jesus! Oh, sweet Jesus!" suddenly turning our lovemaking into a religious experience.

When overcome by such powerful sexual feelings, how can anyone say there is no God?

*It felt...tremendous. It felt...great. It felt...wonderful.
It felt so fucking good, words just could not describe it.
My nerves tingled and cried for it never to stop, to go on
forever, to build and build until I exploded and burst.*

*I lay there suddenly knowing why orgasms lasted
mere seconds. If they lasted any longer, we would pass out
from the pure ecstasy of the moment, driven unconscious
by the pulsing, throbbing feel-goods that spread through
our entire being when we came. If those few short bursts
of sperm went over the normal five- or six-shot limit,
we would go insane, and become a writhing mass of
jangled nerves on the bed where we fucked or sucked or
masturbated, or had all three done to us. This sexual high
was addictive and more powerful than any drug, drawing
us inside/outside of ourselves, alternating between the
two, filling us with so much pleasure we never want it to
end.*

*Sex, I concluded as I lay there getting my ass fucked
raw, getting my brains fucked out, was the most powerful
force on this planet.*

*I think when I came, I shouted out the name "Lucas!"
but I couldn't be sure.*

*It felt so fucking good when the orgasm finally hit me,
all I could do was lie there, my ankles even with my head,
impaled by his driving shaft, which was going in and out
of me at ninety miles per hour as he bucked and squirmed
and drove in and pulled out and, at last, did a rapid pump
into my ass cavity.*

*"Ohhhhhhhhhh!" burst from Lucas as he spurted
seven powerful blasts of sperm inside me.*

*"Ahhhhhhhh!" I followed up with a second later as I
blasted thick gobs of cum up between us, coating my chest
and his as he came down to sprawl on top of me.*

*"Oh. My. God!" he cried out, his head coming to rest
on my shoulder, his saliva spilling out between his lips to
drizzle all down my back. He could not help himself, and
I thought it was one of the sexiest moments I had ever
experienced in bed. Lucas felt so good inside me; he had*

no control over his own slobber, it simply leaked out from his mouth as he was overcome by the powerful orgasm that rendered him almost unconscious. I felt his spit running down my shoulder and dribbling down my back.

Lucas, as an afterthought, spotted the puddle of drool between my shoulder and my collarbone, and with an embarrassed mumble, he reached up to wipe it off me.

"No," I said, firmly as I gently grasped his wrist. "Let it stay. Let it stay there until we are completely done. I like it. I like the feeling of your spit coating my shoulder, knowing it leaked out when you lost complete control inside me. It is fucking sexy, Lucas. Fucking adorable!"

Slowly, very gently, Lucas pulled his cock out of my ass. Even more slowly, he lowered my ankles, lowered my legs. Soon he was kneeling over me as I lay there panting from exertion, my eyes still glazed over from the best fucking I had ever had.

"Are you okay?" he hesitantly asked, as if he might like the answer on account of how rough he'd become in the last few seconds of our fuck. "Did I hurt you in any way?"

I laughed and said, "No, you were wonderful. Very caught up in the moment. I love you for taking me like you did. And if you don't do it again very soon, I will just have to spin you over and bury my bone up inside you."

Lucas studied my face for long moments.

I looked back, exhausted but expectant.

As spent as we both were, the moment I grinned, Lucas grabbed me by my hips, spun me over onto my face, and pulled me into a doggy-style position.

"Ready for some more?" he asked, with a slight chuckle.

In response, I pushed my butt back into him and nearly purred as he embraced me from behind.

The phone rang as Logan finished reading the entry. He reached over and picked up the receiver.

"Hello?" he said.

Brian Peters asked, "Would you like to meet an HIV positive boy Frankie's taking care of?"

"Taking care of?" Logan asked. "Because he infected him? Is this one of the boys Frankie misappropriated funds from his nonprofit corporation for?"

Brian released his breath slowly. "No, Logan, those were only rumors. Never proven true. No, this boy came to Frankie's attention quite by accident. I just wanted it on the record, as testimony to a goodwill gesture on Frankie's part."

Logan frowned. "How do I write about this particular goodwill gesture when I'm having a hard time buying this 'quite by accident' meeting between the two? Why would Franklin bother with a simple acquaintance?"

"Ask the boy yourself, Logan. St. John's Hospital. Room 404. He will not live beyond this week. His name is Lucas. Lucas Black."

CHAPTER TWENTY-NINE

Logan teared up at the sight of the wasted young man before him.

Lucas Black lay there in a hospital bed, a skinny waif who once had silky blond hair. His mass of curls now lay in sweaty tangles, knotted on his head. His once bright blue eyes were now deep, dark pools.

Logan meant to ask the kid several questions, but seeing Lucas sprawled there sick and dying, he did not have the heart. No, he would allow the young man to die in peace.

As Logan turned to exit the room, Lucas's eyes fluttered open. In a dry, raspy voice, he croaked, "Who are you?"

"Hello," Logan said, mustering up a warm smile and extending his hand, "my name is Logan Walker. I'm working on a book about," he paused, "about Franklin Judson."

Lucas softly said, "He's a good man."

"You don't blame him," Logan asked, genuinely surprised, "for your condition?"

Lucas stared at him, puzzled. "Frankie? No, Frankie didn't do this to me." He coughed and wheezed, "Frankie came to me like an angel of mercy. He's a good man."

That's entirely up for debate, thought Logan. *What gives here? Is it possible Brian was telling the truth? Could Frankie simply be using his money to ease this kid's last days? Could this kid have never had a sexual relationship with the Gay King? Is Frankie extending mercy, making up for all the other boys he infected by providing care for this one? In order to redeem himself? To prepare for his own death? This is confusing, to say the least.*

A rather gruff gray-haired nurse stepped into the room. Lucas cringed at the sight of her. Logan read the name tag pinned to the left shoulder of her hospital wear: *Annie Bundy.*

She glared at Logan. Lucas lay there peering up at her helplessly.

"For the wages of sin," Nurse Bundy declared, "is death. But God so loved the world that He gave His only begotten son, so that they who believe in Him might have everlasting life." Her thin lips crooked into a slight smile, one that did not reach her cold, distant eyes. "Are you prepared to accept Jesus now, Lucas? If so, I am prepared to lead you to Him."

Lucas opened his cracked lips but Logan spoke first, saying, "Good Lord, lady, don't you think pushing this at this point in his life is extremely rude?"

Nurse Bundy turned her cold gaze on him. "Rude? His soul is not saved. He has lived a terrible, sinful life, doing God knows what with his body. I, as a true child of the Lord, am trying to provide a means for his salvation. Do you know Jesus?"

Logan took a deep breath and said, "The Jesus I know doesn't appreciate pompous asses like you representing God. You need to leave this boy to die in peace."

Annie Bundy smiled. "You're definitely headed to hell, sir. I was giving Lucas one last chance to save his soul. I see I was wasting my time." She turned her gaze upon Lucas. "You will not live past morning, dear. If you change your mind between now and then, press the buzzer and I will come back and pray with you. Surely you would want your soul to be saved."

She moved across the room. When she reached the door, she glanced back and said, "The Devil's child, are you? Only Satan would thwart the well-meaning work of God's servant. Do you even realize the lifestyle that Lucas has led? The iniquities for which the Heavenly Father is now punishing him?" Annie started to walk away, then glanced back one last time, a sad smile on her face. "I forgive you, son. As God would want me to do. I will pray for your soul, as well. Just remember, it is never too late to ask Jesus into your heart."

Go to hell! thought Logan. *Just get your self-righteous ass out of here.*

Lucas lay there, his eyes closed, his breathing shallow and coming and going in short gasps. Logan reached out and placed his hand on the kid's shoulder.

"You going to use my story," Lucas startled him with his words, "in your...book?"

Logan peered down into his sad eyes. "I don't know," he answered, hesitantly. "I guess that would be up to you. Would you like me to?"

"Of course," Lucas replied, his eyes glazed, his chest rising and falling with each labored breath he took.

Logan waited patiently, wishing he could do something to ease his pain. *Dying of AIDS complications,* he thought, sadly, *is a terrible way to die.*

Lucas kept his eyes closed, as if summoning up enough strength to speak. "No one should have to," he said, in a feathery whisper, "to die like this." He fell silent then, drifting off to sleep.

Logan placed his hand on the dying kid's forehead, and then walked out of the room.

Chapter Thirty

Logan walked past the hospital chapel. The sooner he was out of there, the better.

He slowed his pace when he spotted two men inside. One had a head of thick white hair and was seated in a pew. The other man, lean with coal-black hair, was standing in the aisle, making the sign of the cross. As he turned, Logan saw the white collar he wore. A Catholic priest.

"May you find light at the end of your dark night of the soul, Frankie," he said, as he patted the white-haired man on one shoulder. "May God be with you."

Logan froze.

The white-haired man responded, "Thank you for coming, Father Murphy. Thanks for everything."

Father Murphy? Logan thought and he spotted the priest's black cane in his hand. *Murph. Ridge Majors called him the night he saved me from an ass whipping in the hotel parking garage.*

Father Murphy saw Logan standing there and offered him a kindly smile. Logan forced himself to smile back and nod. Father Murphy moved on down the hall with the support of his black cane. Franklin Judson was inside the chapel, praying.

Would God listen to the prayers of a pedophile? Logan stood there for several long moments, staring hard at the back of Frankie's head. *I wonder,* he mused, *what God is thinking, especially when a boy-lover like Frankie is talking to Him? Most of the world figures there's a special hell reserved for those who molest boys. Most of the world considers it an unforgivable sin to seduce, molest, and take indecent sexual liberties with innocent boys.*

Franklin Judson turned and looked back at Logan, curiously. His thick white hair was parted on one side, his bangs lightly feathered across his forehead. He wore wire-rimmed glasses with perfectly round lenses, and his light blue eyes held wit and intelligence. His suntanned face was clean-shaven. His was an old face, weathered and finely chiseled.

Frankie smiled. Boyish charm appeared in the flash of his white teeth, a softening in the hard lines of his sixty-year-old face. A slight twinkle came to the eyes of the Gay King.

"You remind me," he said, "of a little boy I once knew, who was so terrified that God might smite him that he refused to enter the sanctuary of the church his mother took him to one Easter Sunday morning." Frankie gestured down at Logan's shoe tips. He asked, "Are you afraid of God, Logan Walker?"

Logan was a bit surprised Frankie knew he was. He was also surprised Frankie was perceptive enough to recognize his reluctance to set foot in a so-called holy place.

"Would I be right to assume," Logan said, stepping inside the chapel, "you were that little boy?"

Frankie stood up. "Yes, that was me fifty years ago. My dear mother, bless her soul, had no clue her only son was one of those cursed homosexuals the small town of Beatrice, Nebraska, would not tolerate. Attending Sunday school with all my saved and righteous sisters and brothers, I was overcome with fear so overwhelming that I trembled at the fact that God not only hated me that I dared enter His house, I just knew he wanted me to die so he could severely punish me for being a young queer."

Frankie removed his wire-rimmed glasses and peered directly into Logan's eyes, his stare so intense that Logan stood there, mesmerized.

"You know I didn't ask to be born this way, Logan," Frankie said. "I didn't choose to start loving young boys. It was simply a facet of my sexual grid that attracted me to pubescent youth.

"You know those gay rights activists who have been trying to convince anyone who will listen that being gay is not a matter of preference, not a choice they make? Well, their claim is that they were born gay, not a choice, but an orientation assigned to them before they were even born. As Jesus once said in the book of Matthew, 'Not everyone can accept this teaching, but only those to whom it is given. For there are eunuchs who have been so from birth, and there are eunuchs who have been made eunuchs by others, and there are eunuchs who have made themselves eunuchs for the sake of the kingdom of heaven. Let anyone accept this who can.'"

He paused. "What if I told you this attraction to boys was part of my sexual orientation? Certainly not something that I chose to do, but a strong desire I was born with? Early on, during my childhood years, I experimented with peers my own age. But as I became an adult, I found myself longing to love boys, and longing to be loved by boys. Not prepubescent boys, but boys between fourteen and seventeen. At first I thought it was arrested development, that in my mind I was sexually stuck. My first sexual experience happened when I was fourteen, and so maybe I had tripped off something that kept me locked in place, leaving me with a strong attraction to boys that age.

"I struggled with it for several years before acting on my feelings. I was nineteen when I first took my thirteen-year-old friend to bed. It felt right. It felt natural. He was as into it as I was. In fact, all the boys since whom I have taken to my bed went willingly. I've never seduced a boy. They've had just as much passion as I have under the circumstances. The boys I have known sexually have all desired to be loved by an older man."

He paused and made a sour face. "Child abuser? Child molester? Pedophile? Sick and twisted pervert? But one night at twenty-four, I was sharing my bed with a fifteen-year-old boy when everything changed. That blond-haired, blue-eyed beautiful boy actually made love to me. Slow, passionate love. Love that extinguished the damaging labels. I then knew what Lord Douglas meant when he wrote *The Love that dare not speak its name*."

He slowly withdrew a silk handkerchief from inside his suit jacket and proceeded to clean his glasses. "After that night, I decided I was going to share the same kind of love with any boy who came to me willingly. And there have been hundreds of needy boys aching to be loved, to be held."

Logan began to really listen to what the man had to say.

Not that he understood or agreed with it.

"Twenty years ago, the majority of the civilized world sided with the sexual preference argument. Now it is a smaller minority who claim it is a matter of choice. The majority has shifted their view in that twenty-year span." He gave a sad smile. "You and I know in our hearts that being gay is just who we are. No choice. No preference. We just are, and there's no reason to change."

Frankie actually teared up as he delivered his last comments on the subject. "Contrary to popular belief, that pedophilia or ebophilia is a sickness, I firmly believe it is just who I am. Part of my orientation. However, a practice once accepted in ancient Greece, which actually enhanced the lives of young boys and the men who loved them, has now been banned. Outlawed. Labeled as deviant. Laws make this a punishable crime.

"I know some cross a line into abuse rather than simply a relationship with a young boy. But for the most part, the majority of the 'offenders' are productive members of our society. They are men looking to be loved.

"Do you know how many boys out there need the empowerment and attachment of an older man in their lives? Juvenile detention centers, drug treatment, and thousands of institutions are filled with lonely boys who would greatly benefit from this. The Greeks got it right. The older men of their society were teachers and mentors as well as lovers, who connected with their young suitors, positively influencing their lives and helping them ease into a productive future. Now, we've made it a major crime. But why? There are boys out there seeking these relationships. Boys trying to fulfill a deep need to be loved."

Frankie sighed. "No, Logan, I did not ask to be born this way, but here I am, prone to love boys. I love because I was born to love. I take a chance each time, yes, but I leave behind me boys positively impacted by my involvement in their lives."

Logan left Frankie his cell number. He told him he would have many questions for him later, and Frankie agreed to answer them as much as he could without incriminating himself.

That next morning, Frankie phoned him to inform him that Lucas Black had passed away just before sunrise. Frankie assured him that Lucas did not die alone.

The Gay King then extended an invitation for Logan to attend a performance that evening at the Temple of the Pagan Princes. A performance, Frankie assured him, that would be most memorable.

Logan agreed to meet the man there.

CHAPTER THIRTY-ONE

The Pagan Temple

It was an ancient-looking theater. Stone walls surrounded the seats and the rather large stage. The seats, situated in a semicircle, were made from stone as well, gray slate with veins of green matching the walls. They were fashioned with thick padding. High along the two opposite walls were twin balconies, where a large crowd of shadowy figures sat.

Logan wished he could sit up there, blending with the shadows to remain inconspicuous, but Frankie insisted that he have a ringside seat. So he sat in the middle row, close to the stage, to witness what Frankie assured him would be a spectacular performance.

The temple was packed. Logan almost laughed as the word "congregation" came to mind. But once inside the temple, he felt a church-like ambience that reminded him of his own boyhood days seated in the back row of the First Methodist Church.

He watched as a brightly illuminated, giant penis slowly rose behind the stage. The ten-foot phallus rose to its full height, its perfectly shaped form radiant with glowing inner lights that intermittently changed to all colors of a rainbow, pulsing colored lights that ran up and down the length.

The lights slowly faded, and the entire stage was plunged into darkness. The audience remained silent. A white-robed figure appeared to one side of the giant white penis, his hands raised in supplication, his head thrown back in silent prayer, a golden crown resting on his snowy white head. It was Frankie Judson, the Gay King.

"We of the Pride of Princes," he said, "recognize the symbol of Life. In honor of this Phallus that you have so perfectly created, we give thanks to you, O Lord, for the seed it spews, for the life it produces. As it was placed by you at the center of our being, so it remains at the center of the universe. It is as always an instrument of pleasure that connects us to you, emanating invisible threads through time and space to allow us to commune with you. The Phallus is ancient. It is holy. It is a divine conduit, pulsing with your Life, your Light, your Love."

He paused, and whispered, "Amen."

Logan could hardly believe what he was hearing and seeing. *These folks are seriously thinking the cock is a means to communicate and connect with God?*

"In the beginning," Frankie said, "God created Man."

A light shone down directly from above center stage, bathing him in a golden aura.

"Or in the beginning," he amended, "perhaps Man created God?" Frankie smiled. "There are hundreds of religions and belief systems out there, and yet how many of them are simply Man's attempt to connect with a Supreme Being? Who did people of the ancient world worship in those thousands of years before the God of the Old Testament appeared? Most assume Judaism was the one true religion among idol-worshiping nations. And out of Judaism came Christianity. But what about the Greek gods and goddesses? The Norse gods? The Roman gods? The Native Americans? The Celts? The Asians?"

Dancers appeared on both sides of the stage, male and female, all naked. They cavorted, leaping high and spinning round in crazy circles, each one gracefully moving past the white-robed king. In a sudden wash of black light spilling down from above, glittering silken scarves appeared in each of their hands, glowing in multicolored brilliance. As the nude dancers glided toward the giant penis situated behind the priest, they whipped their glowing scarves directly at the smooth white shape, caressing it as they danced past it.

"Phallus worship," Frankie said, "was one of the first universal religions, a belief system taken up by thousands of tribes and nations in every part of the ancient world. It pre-dated every religion known to mankind."

The king paused while the dancers worked themselves into a frenzy, their fluttering scarves lightly skimming the now-glowing white shape of the giant penis. It began to pulsate with an inner light, going from white to light blue to a deeper sapphire to a brilliant violet so bright that several members of the audience placed their hands over their eyes to shield them.

One by one, the dancers spun, whirled, and leaped. The women and men lashed their scarves up and down the length of the purple penis. As one, all of the dancers turned, raising their scarves high above their heads, their faces turned toward the enormous phallus.

The king whirled round and placed both of his palms high on the glowing, pulsating purple penis. He spread his legs wide, arched his back, and began to rub the giant cock.

The music stopped. The dancers released their scarves, which drifted down, fluttering to the stage at their bare feet.

A single bright light emanated from the cock.

It pulsed. It died. It pulsed again. It died again. Over and over. Radiating and extinguishing light. Until finally a rhythm began, steady and sure, pulsing and dying, pulsing and dying. A sudden explosion took place on the bulbous head of the giant cock.

A burst of glitter exploded from the head of the phallus, raining down on the king and dancers.

A second spurt of multicolored glitter erupted from the head of the giant phallus. A third, a fourth, and a fifth followed.

Slowly the violet of the illuminated penis began to fade.

The glittering dust stopped spurting from the head.

The stage lights, the black lights, and the inner light of the penis faded to black.

The naked dancers spun and whirled their way offstage, leaving the king to stand facing the audience alone.

A single shaft of lemony-yellow light bathed Frankie's upraised face, causing his eyes to sparkle.

He said, "Phallic worship is a religion, the oldest religion in existence. Fundamentally, the Creator or Life Giver is the phallic worshiper's god. Evidence this worship prevailed is found in many countries."

A gigantic world map appeared on the wall behind the phallus as it slowly descended back into the stage, its long shaft still dimly lit, its rounded head giving off a faint light.

The king held up a handful of glitter and sprinkled it through his fingers onto the stage. As it drifted down to his bare feet, he said, "This symbolizes the creative spirit of the Life Giver, transfused through matter. The worship paid to the phallus in the early ages was considered not indecent, but reverential."

Bright spots appeared on the world map as he spoke of each location. "This worship occurred in ancient Egypt, India, Syria, Babylon, Assyria, Persia, Greece, Italy, Spain, Germany, Scandinavia. In these places, the phallus is represented as the symbol of generation. The act of generation was considered nature contributing to the reproduction of the species, and looked upon as a solemn duty consecrated to the Deity, a solemn sacrament in honor of the Creator.

"Phallic rites and observances entered into the religion of the Assyrians and can be traced back to the religion of the ancient Sumerians, the root stock from which the Chaldeans had their origin. Abraham instituted the rite of circumcision in remembrance of the Chaldean genital worship. Abraham in Genesis asks his servant to take a solemn oath, makes him lay his hand under his thigh as a token of sincerity. Jacob, when dying, makes his son Joseph perform the same act. Even among modern-day Arabs, a man will take an oath by placing his hand upon his member in attestation of his sincerity.

"And some say time began when the Anunnaki came to earth in ancient Sumer. Though this debate is waged among believers and nonbelievers alike, this is one take on how all life began: Enter the gym of the god Anu, and witness the meeting between him and his two sons, Enki and Enlil."

The stage revolved then, the new set displaying a makeshift gymnasium with trapeze, high bar, and weight bench.

Anu appeared there onstage, golden hair cascading to his broad shoulders, golden beard reaching to the middle of his well-proportioned chest. He was naked, with six-pack abs, a deep chest, long sinewy legs, muscular arms.

He had a golden mass of pubic hair with a half-hardened penis hanging low over massive balls. He turned around, his perfectly round, bare ass to the audience. He bent at the waist, lowering his barbell to the stage floor.

He turned to face two naked boys appearing on either side of the stage. Both boys appeared to be around thirteen or fourteen years of age. They performed separate actions, one leaping up to the high bar and the other swinging high over the stage on the trapeze. Their long, thin cocks could be seen along with faint shadows of pubic hair.

The blond youth grasped the high bar with both hands, swung himself up to perform a perfect pullover, and dropped to the stage. He stood there, his smooth, sleek body like a Greek statue. He leaped back up, grabbed the high bar, and slowly performed a half dozen pull-ups.

The dark-haired boy swung out above the stage several times, building momentum. The muscles beneath his glistening skin roiled. He brought his legs up each time on the forward swing, his feet stretched out before him, suspended above Anu and the other youth.

Finally, he released the trapeze. He skillfully tucked and rolled in midair, performing three complete flips before coming down to center stage, landing barely a foot away from the blond boy, standing there with his arms crossed before his chest.

The two boys glared at each other.

Anu smiled at his young sons, saying, "We of the Anunnaki, of the pure blood, come down from the skies to establish ourselves here upon the earth. Enlil the elder? What shall be your symbol of office?"

The blond-haired Enlil pirouetted and danced past his father and brother, raising his right hand in the air. He snapped the fingers of his upraised hand and a shadowy shape descended from above the stage. A spotlight illuminated the token of power the moment Enlil grasped its hilt. He whirled and twirled it, tossing the short sword back and forth from his right hand to his left. It began to glow with a bright golden light.

"I," the boy declared, "Enlil son of Anu, proclaim my symbol to be a sword of war! For I am a warrior! A conqueror! A master of savage slaughter!"

Anu smiled and said, "Very well, Enlil, a sword shall be your symbol of office. A fine token of power for a warrior to carry."

He turned his head and looked at the dark-haired boy. "Enki? And what shall you choose as your symbol, your token of office?"

Enki spun and whirled, launching himself past his father and brother. He performed a wild dance, springing up. He touched down at center stage, his right hand raised. He snapped his fingers and a dark shape descended from above his head. He grasped it as the spotlight illuminated the long, smooth shape.

"I," the dark-haired boy declared, "Enki son of Anu, proclaim my symbol to be a phallus of love! For I am a lover! A soul mate! A master of pure pleasure!" The two-foot-long phallus in his hand lit up with a deep blue light.

The stage lights faded to black, and both boys began to twirl their tokens around in dazzling maneuvers, trailing swirls of luminescent gold and blue light.

The boys danced toward each other and ended up crossing sword and phallus together at center stage.

In the shadows behind the two boys, Anu said, "I wonder which token of power shall prove to be the most potent, the most everlasting, the one to most impact the lives upon Earth?"

"Time shall tell, Father," said Enki, as his phallus-shaped token dimmed in his grasp.

Blond-haired Enlil swung his golden sword above his head and performed an overhand strike, directed at the unprotected head of his brother. But Enki performed a swift counteraction, whirling his phallus up and stopping his brother's descending blade with an expert parry. One last time his two-foot phallus lit up with a bright blue light, and locked together above the heads of both boys, the sword and phallus slowly dimmed, until gold and blue light faded to black.

The stage revolved and a chamber appeared with whitewashed stucco. It looked very Romanesque, with thick green vines hanging from a latticework roof. The entire center stage was framed by a trellis that arched over the figure of a dark-haired young man working behind a stone table with beakers, burners, and other laboratory equipment on a stone table.

Anu, dressed in a lavish blue robe, stepped into a shaft of light to one side of this laboratory. He said, "My one son, warlike in his ways, brought to Earth wrath, slaughter, and destruction, for Enlil was most violent in his dealings with Mankind. My other son, peace-loving, brought to Earth love, pleasure, and long-lasting life, for Enki was most loving in his ways. Time measured by human standards is like vapor to those who live forever. And yet, to formulate Man as we know him today, Enki designed him with the DNA, the cells, the emotions, and aspirations made available to him at ancient Sumer."

The light shifted from the tall, lean form of Anu and drifted to center stage where Enki was bent over the table, carefully pouring a bright green liquid from one lab beaker into another. He set the empty beaker down, held up the sparkling green substance swirling around inside the second beaker, smiling at the warm glow. He closed his eyes as if in prayer, raising the green concoction above his head.

"Soul of Man," he intoned, "DNA. Intellect. Knowledge. Emotions. Sexual drive of heterosexuals and homosexuals alike. All the makings of Creation. May Anu bless this making by my hand."

He began to lower the beaker, opening his eyes when his brother Enlil stormed in from left stage. He was dressed in armor resembling a Roman centurion. His metal armor was molded to his muscular, well-defined upper body. With one hand he removed his plumed helm, revealing long, sweat-streaked locks of golden hair. In the other hand, he carried a bloody sword.

He angrily flung the helmet down at Enki's feet and whipped his sword around so that the red blood coating his blade flew off and splattered the whitewashed wall directly behind his calm-looking brother.

"Haven't you finished creating this new Man yet?" he snarled. "I am tired of savagely slaying these weak, ill-bred, low-functioning hybrids! Give me a challenge, brother! Or you waste your time, designing and developing yet another subspecies of this Human race! Make for me a man of destiny and purpose! Make for me a man to challenge gods!"

The house lights dimmed. The stage turned black.

Chapter Thirty-two

Frankie sat across the table from Logan at the riverside tavern.

"So," the Gay King said, "now that much information has passed your way in a short time, can you sort it out?"

Logan took a drink of his third Crown and Coke, feeling a bit tipsy. "Do you really want me to finish this book? Even though it may incriminate you and all of your associates?"

Frankie shrugged. "Quite frankly, by the time it is published I'll be dead, Logan. It won't matter what you say about me. Tell the truth. Tell it all."

Logan took a long swallow of his drink. "You appear live and well to me," he said. "Have you had bouts with your HIV?"

Frankie said, "Two close calls so far."

"How candid do you want me to be?" Logan asked. "Your past with boys will never be accepted as normal by society."

Frankie took a sip of his own drink. "I know there are thousands who are less fortunate than me. If I could readjust the thinking of society, I would design an institution for men who love boys."

Logan took another drink. He almost laughed. "And if I had a magic wand, I would correct the inclinations of these men who abuse young boys. Don't you get what you are saying, Frankie? You wholeheartedly condone these relations. You've no doubt they are right."

Frankie frowned. "But, Logan, you've never met the boys I've bedded. Do you know what it's like to hold, to embrace, a boy who actually weeps when he is loved?"

Logan shook his head. "No, I don't. But, Frankie, is such a thing truly right? A grown man loving a boy?"

Frankie grinned, sadly. "I was born this way. As I see it, I have three choices. Put a bullet in my head. Refrain from ever touching another boy. Or continue to love them as I have."

Logan said, "What about seeking help?"

Frankie said, "I've been safe ever since I found I tested positive. God forbid I add an extra burden to some boy's life." Frankie looked Logan in the eye as he finished, saying, "It's bad enough that I got this. Do you really think I would spread it to others?"

CHAPTER THIRTY-THREE

The first snowfall in Nebraska that year came in late October. It fell steadily throughout November, and the deep drifts and cold spells that came with such weather had been conducive to Logan's writing. He finished the book the first week of December.

Ironically, that evening as he sat staring at the finished manuscript stacked neatly before him on his desk, he received a phone call from Brian Peters. He sounded very subdued, and it took a few minutes for him to inform Logan that Franklin Judson had died that morning of AIDS complications.

The Gay King was no more.

Logan offered Brian condolences and informed him he had finished the book.

Brian fell silent. Logan thought that perhaps with Frankie gone, it would no longer matter whether the book was ever published. He almost wished Brian would cancel his contract and scrap the project. Logan still wasn't sure how the majority of readers were going to react to the things he had written.

The story about the secret life of the Gay King wasn't going to be the next *Fifty Shades of Grey* or the next *Da Vinci Code*. It would certainly not be accepted in most bookstores either. Of course, it would find an audience on the Internet, an underground network of readers who would read it either as porn or to better understand these forbidden relationships.

"I'm sorry," Brian finally said. "This is going to take some getting used to. Frankie was a major part of my life. You said you'd finished the book?"

"Yes," Logan said. "I can send you a copy via email. Or I can deliver it in person sometime later this week. When is the funeral?"

Brian blew his nose and sighed. "Friday, the end of this week. Grace Methodist on Howard Street. The time will be in the *Herald*. You could bring me a copy then, Logan. I won't have time to read it until after the funeral. Fear not, all your hard work is appreciated, and Frankie left a substantial check for you."

Logan was a bit stunned. *Substantial?* he almost asked. *How much?* would have been his next words.

He'd thought his only payment would be the ten thousand already deposited in his PayPal account.

Logan said simply, "Sorry for your loss, Brian. I'll see you on Friday."

❖

Logan was awakened by a thunderous banging. He was out of bed in seconds. He grabbed his gun. By the time he reached the front door, the banging had stopped.

Opening the door he found Alex crumpled up on the porch, sobbing quietly.

"Oh, my God, Logan!" he cried, scrambling to his feet. "You've got to help him! You've just got to help him!"

Logan guided the distraught kid through the door. Alex plopped himself down clumsily on the couch, his breath reeking of vodka.

"Baxster is gonna die," Alex said, tears running down his cheeks. "Mike and Brad have him. They also have the DVD of Todd's murder. They're using Baxster and the DVD as bait to set up that hit man guy. They're meeting at the north end of High Meadows Park, along the river. Baxster told me, and went with them willingly, but the dumb bastard doesn't know how this will end. Those guys plan to for sure to kill that Donovan guy. And where will that leave Baxster?"

Logan saw it coming then. Alex was going to be sick. The copious amount of alcohol he'd consumed was going to take its toll on his system. Snatching him up by his parka, Logan hastily guided the drunken kid to the bathroom.

Alex was puking in the next few seconds. He dropped to his knees, draped over the bowl of the toilet.

Logan removed his coat and patted him sympathetically. "Get it out of your system, kid," he told him. "I'll see what I can do about Baxster."

Logan drove down the road to Noah Standing Bear's cabin.

Noah and Mountain sat there in his large backyard, basking in the warmth of an enormous campfire. The big Lakota listened thoughtfully as his writer friend shared what Alex had told him.

"Shoot the heartless bastards," Noah said at last. "Only one way to deal with mad dogs. Put them out of their misery."

Seated beside the crackling blaze there in his backyard, Noah told Logan what he had told no one else. "As a Marine, I served my country well. The first time I went into battle, I thought visions would flash through my head. When I opened fire on enemy combatants with a fifty cal, I figured I would see Crazy Horse riding into battle, bullets whizzing past him as he wore his magic bulletproof long shirt, for he was an Ogle Takan Un, a Shirt Wearer. I also thought I would hear the mantra in my head, 'Today is a good day to die!' But sadly, neither the vision nor the mantra came to mind. Actually, I was just plain scared shitless, killing only because I didn't want to be killed. Later, when the Marine colonel handed me the Medal of Honor, I came to the conclusion that I acted not bravely, but foolishly. Standing up in a hail of bullets whizzing round me like mad hornets. Firing round after round after round, for the fifty is one pissed-off beast in the heat of battle. Instead of Crazy Horse riding his spirited horse into battle, my mind went blank. Adrenaline kicked in. Survival instinct went on override. I killed only because I did not want to be killed. That is how I survived that battle and every battle thereafter."

Noah wouldn't hesitate to meet violence with violence.

Logan did not want his friend to be placed in that situation. But if anyone was capable of handling the two rogue investigators or Ben Donovan, it would be Noah. All three men were way out of Logan's element, and he knew it.

Noah gave Logan a thoughtful look. "You are determined to rescue this kid?" he asked.

Logan nodded.

Noah reached inside his parka and drew a .38 caliber Smith & Wesson from a shoulder holster. "Take this. You may have to use it. If so, don't hesitate. Worry about the consequences later. If you cannot do that, stay here while I take care of this."

Logan took the short-barreled pistol and chambered a round.

❖

They drove to High Meadows in Logan's Pathfinder, reaching the north end parking lot in less than thirty minutes. A vehicle was parked there already, and Noah felt its hood.

"The engine is still warm. I'd say fifteen minutes ahead of us." Stepping past the car, he moved across the parking lot and into the shadows beneath the surrounding trees. He bent down to examine the snow.

"Three sets of prints," Noah said. "One person walking in front of the other two, possibly Baxster at gunpoint. He leads them by at least three or four feet. They headed deeper into the park, possibly toward the high grounds or the gully near the river. We shall see when we come to the cross trail."

The big Lakota plowed a path through the knee-deep snow for the next several minutes, barely breaking a sweat. Twice during their trek through the deep snow, Logan stopped to catch his breath.

Noah pressed on.

He stopped, peering over the lip of a small rise. Voices drifted up from the gully below.

"Put the goddamned DVD down!"

"Fuck you! Fuck you and the horse you rode in on!"

"Do it, Baxster! Drop the DVD now or I will blow your head off!"

"What did you think to accomplish by using this little whore to be the messenger? You two assholes call yourselves professional? Both of you are a joke!"

"Settle down, Mr. Donovan. Put your gun away. We don't have to do this the hard way."

"Hell with that! If this fucker wants to dance, I am ready to make that happen!"

"Brad? Stop playing cowboy here! We came to make money off this deal! Turn it down a notch, partner!"

Logan and Noah peered down into the snowy gully. Standing before an Adirondack shelter were four figures illuminated by a haze of blue moonlight. Mike Carrol and Brad Helman stood facing Ben Donovan and Baxster Crown, who were on the opposite side of a dying campfire.

Towering above the blond-haired Baxster, Ben reached out to snatch the black case he was holding.

Baxster swatted Ben's hand away and took off running down the trail behind the shelter.

Ben fired his gun. A belch of smoke billowed from the muzzle. He fired off a second hasty shot, then ran after Baxster.

"Let's circle around this hill!" Mike told Brad, pulling him toward the trail on the far side of the clearing. "These trails all snake their way down to the Missouri. If we hurry, we can cut them off!"

Noah said, "I will follow those two clowns, Logan. You follow Ben and Baxster."

With that, the big Lakota raced off.

CHAPTER THIRTY-FOUR

As he stumbled clumsily down the riverside trail, Logan didn't feel like much of a hero. Trudging through drifts that were at times thigh-deep was slow going, giving him plenty of time to doubt himself.

He had to react sooner than he expected when he rounded the next bend on the snowy trail. As he came around the bole of a massive oak tree, he found himself standing face-to-face with Ben Donovan.

Surprise registered on Ben's face. His pistol was aimed down at Baxster, crumpled in the snow before him.

"You?" Ben shifted his gun to aim it at Logan.

"Me," Logan said. He raised his pistol and fired.

Ben shouted in alarm as the bullet struck his gun, ripping it from his grasp. "I'll be goddamned!"

Logan stood there. He had meant to shoot Ben.

"That," Ben said, "was a fine shot, writer."

"That," Logan told him, "was a lucky shot."

Mike and Brad came charging around the bend at the opposite end of the trail. Both had their guns drawn.

"This," Ben said, "is not going to end well."

"Toss that over to me," Brad ordered Logan. "Then both of you get on your knees. Hands behind your head."

Ben gave Brad a sour look. "Make me, asshole."

Logan tossed his gun, watching as it vanished in the snow at Brad's feet.

"Smart move," Brad said, scooping up the pistol and slipping it into the pocket of his jacket.

"Brad," Mike said, "shooting them execution style will not serve our best interests." He gestured at the snowy ground with his free hand. "Dumping the bodies in the river is our best option."

Logan shivered at the cold, flat tone of his voice. "Are you serious?" he asked, more than a little alarmed.

"They are," Ben said. "They've done this before, Writer Man. Many times before."

Baxster staggered to his feet, holding the DVD case up before him. "Come on, guys," he pleaded. "You don't have to kill me. Let me live and I'll do whatever you want. I could continue to be your go-between for passing messages to the senator. I can get you more money from him for this tape. I could threaten to go public with the shooting of his son. We could work as partners. We could make lots and lots of money working together."

Logan stared at the kid in disbelief.

There in the deeper shadows beneath the trees, his one last hope stood still and silent, partially concealed by the blackness.

And Logan tried not to smile as Brad and Mike herded the three of them down the trail, to the banks of the Missouri River.

❖

Ben stepped up onto the snowy embankment, shuddering at the sight of the freezing black waters. He exchanged a worried look with Logan. They were at the riverbank. They were about to be shot. And dead or alive, they were about to be thrown into those deep, dark waters. It was a scary prospect.

"Oh, shit," Baxster muttered. "This doesn't have to happen, guys. You don't have to do this."

"Yes," Brad said, stepping up to him. "I'll take that now," he added as he plucked the DVD case out of Baxster's grasp.

A thunderous roar erupted from the trail directly behind them.

Mike wheeled around. Something big and black smashed into him. With a sudden cry of pain, he went sailing into a nearby tree. He smashed into it face first and crumpled to the ground.

Noah raised his rather large pistol, aiming the .44 Magnum directly at Brad. "Drop the gun," he said, firmly.

Brad snarled, "Fuck you, Tonto!" He turned his gun on Noah.

But Logan was already moving toward him. He latched onto his gun hand, placed his wrist in a lock, and wrenched his arm down and around so that the rest of his body followed. As Logan swung Brad down to the ground, his legs struck Baxster and sent him flying off the embankment into the icy-cold river six feet below.

Noah performed a well-placed palm strike, breaking Brad's nose. Logan felt the give go out of Brad. He released him to fall on the ground in a heap.

"Ben?" Noah ordered firmly. "Find a stick and help the kid out of the river."

"Fuck that!" Ben said. "Let the bastard freeze to death!"

Baxster grappled at roots and clawed at the muddy bank, but the current was so strong it plucked him away from the relative safety of the bank. Crying out in alarm, he went spinning out toward center stream.

Noah placed his gun back in his shoulder holster. "Stick," he told Logan. "Find a long stick."

Logan began searching. Noah joined him and they hastily dug beneath the thick snow until Logan pried a long tree limb from the frozen ground.

"Got one!" he crowed triumphantly, swinging it up and around his head.

Noah ripped it out of his grasp. "It's up to you to save yourself!" he said, his deep voice carrying out over the water to Baxster, who was struggling to swim back to the bank. "Stop fighting the current. Go with the flow. I will move down the bank here twenty-some yards, but you will have to do all the work to draw close enough to the bank for me to snag you out."

Baxster righted himself, watching Noah sprinting downstream, the long limb in his hands. He began to stroke for the bank. The icy water was taking its toll.

Logan joined Noah on the bank some thirty feet downstream, watching Baxster's progress as he weakly dog-paddled toward the stick Noah held out to him.

"Got it!" Noah said, grunting as Baxster latched onto the end of the stick. "Now, hold on while I reel you in." He gave a mighty heave backward and drew Baxster to shore.

Baxster managed to snag onto the rocks lining the riverbank. His fingers scrabbled for purchase. He held on.

Click! echoed through the frosty air.

Logan and Noah glanced back to see Ben Donovan holding Brad's gun. He aimed it at Noah. "Shove him back in!" he growled. "Let the fucker drown!"

Noah's dark eyes met Ben's. "Logan?" he casually said. "Your call."

Logan gave Noah a perplexed look. "What do you mean?"

"Save him?" Noah said. "Or let him drown? Up to you."

Logan glanced back at Ben. "You know my answer, Noah. If you know me at all."

"Thought so," Noah responded. "I just wanted to be sure." With that, he gave Ben one last defiant glare and pulled Baxster up onto the shore.

Click! The sound of Ben lowering the hammer of Brad's gun back in place filled the air.

When they returned to the prone bodies of the two investigators, Noah guided a noisily chattering Baxster over beside them. He produced a set of handcuffs. "I'm cuffing these two together," he said. "We'll get you to a warm vehicle as soon as these two are ready for the long walk out of here."

Shivering violently, Baxster rummaged around in Brad's jacket and withdrew both the DVD case and Noah's pistol from the pocket. Handing the gun to Logan, he said, "For all the trouble this DVD has caused, I should toss it in the river."

Logan plucked it out of Baxster's shaking hands. "No, destroying this is not an option."

"Hey," Ben growled, "that needs to be destroyed, writer. If that is indeed the tape confiscated from Lakewood's security system, hand it over. That DVD incriminates me."

"Exactly," Logan said.

The big Lakota shrugged. "I suppose your moral compass is guiding you on this, right?"

"Yes," Logan told him. "My moral compass or the Great Spirit. I just can't walk away from this without making things right. Sorry,

Ben, but you killed Todd Guildman. The career of Ben Donovan ends tonight. Sorry, nothing personal."

Ben glared at him. "You would do that?" he growled. "You would turn this DVD in to the cops?"

Noah answered him, saying, "He would. And he will, Ben. Shouldn't have shot that kid."

Ben rounded on Logan, looming up in front of him. "Fuck you, Writer Man! Might as well shoot me! I'm not going to serve the rest of my days in prison!"

Logan raised the gun.

He took a two-handed grip, steeling himself for what he was about to do.

Ben lunged. Logan pivoted and spun out of his path. Ben careened off the trail and plowed into the frozen branches of a nearby tree, which snapped and cracked as he struggled to keep his balance. He spun back around to charge at Logan again.

Logan took aim and fired, directing his shot down at Ben's feet. Ben skidded to a stop.

Logan fired the gun three more times, kicking up snow at Ben's feet.

"You'll pay for this, asshole!" Ben thundered. He launched himself off the high embankment into the freezing-cold waters of the Missouri.

Noah drew his pistol, looking quizzically at Logan. "Your prisoner is getting away, Logan."

Logan said, "Let the river deal with him. No matter what, we turn this DVD in to one of your cop friends. Agreed?"

"Sure," Noah said, watching Ben make strong strokes out to midstream, where he latched onto a pile of floating debris and clung to it.

Logan, Noah, and Baxster watched as the strong currents carried him around a bend in the river and out of sight.

CHAPTER THIRTY-FIVE

By the time they made it back to the parking lot, Brad was in great pain from his shattered nose and Mike was staggering.

Shivering uncontrollably from his time in the river, Baxster talked in a low voice to Logan. "So," he asked, "are you really going to turn the DVD in to the cops?"

"Yes," Logan said. "Noah trains more than a dozen of Omaha's finest at his dojo. I'm sure he'll find one he can trust to do the right thing with this DVD."

"Got one in mind," Noah said, ushering Mike and Brad into the backseat of their vehicle. "Old Jake Mason, retired for the past ten years. I trust Jake will know what to do. Will that suit you, Logan?"

"Sounds like a plan," Logan said.

Baxster peered at Logan with alarm. "What about me? I'm on that DVD. Is there any way you can edit out our sex scene? If the cops see that, they might arrest me as an accessory or tie me into the murder. Besides, Senator Guildman would pay a lot of money to have that DVD."

"To what?" Logan asked. "Destroy it? Trust me, you'll be okay."

Noah stood beside the open door of the car of the two investigators. "What about these two?"

Logan said, "Can you call this retired cop tonight, Noah? Have him meet you down at the dojo? You could turn these two over to him. After all, they're the ones who contracted Ben to put a hit on Baxster, which got Todd Guildman killed."

Noah stared at Logan.

"What?" he asked. "Something doesn't sit right with you?"

Noah shrugged his beefy shoulders. "This all started with a threat made by the kid. Aren't you thinking this will all lead back to him?"

"Doesn't matter now," Logan said. "Frankie died this morning. Investigators may trace this all back to his corporation, but none of this will ever touch Frankie. He's gone now."

Baxster began to softly weep.

CHAPTER THIRTY-SIX

Logan attended Franklin Judson's funeral that Friday morning. It was snowing fiercely as the large crowd filled up the church. Logan was surprised so many were in attendance. He had to admit Frankie was well loved.

During the service, he was joined by Alex and a slender, raven-haired kid whose long, shaggy locks barely concealed the small silver hoops in both of his ears. *Bobby. It has to be Bobby, the boy I read about so often in Alex's journal.*

He studied him briefly and determined he was the same dark-haired kid who had starred in the porn flick he had watched at the Judson mansion when he interviewed Brian Peters. *Alex was right,* he thought. *This kid does resemble a Gypsy rogue or an Egyptian prince, and he also has the sleek, dark look of a panther.*

By the time the service ended, a blizzard swept in from the north. Visibility was poor during the drive out to the Fair Haven Cemetery located in the hills south of Omaha, and only a few funeral goers braved the elements to hear the last words spoken over Frankie beside his grave site.

Logan, Alex, and Bobby stood some distance from the tent where close family and friends gathered.

"Nice," Bobby said, his words muffled by the long black scarf partially covering his face. "It's Murph saying the final farewell to Frankie. How appropriate."

Logan narrowed his eyes, peering through the falling snow to the tall, lean priest beside Frankie's coffin. It was indeed Father Murphy. And the priest appeared to be sharing heartfelt words with those gathered there beneath the dark green awning of the tent. Logan could not hear what was being said, but he could detect sincerity in Father Murphy's facial expressions.

When the service ended, Logan and Alex returned to his Pathfinder parked at the end of the line of cars. "Where's Bobby run off to?" Logan asked Alex. "He was behind us when we left the grave site."

Alex looked off to the small knoll to the left of the driveway. "Here he comes. He's got Murph with him."

Bobby seemed to be giving Father Murphy a hand as they trudged through the ever-deepening snowdrifts. The priest used his cane to pick and plod his way forward, but Bobby held him by one hand and guided him carefully down the slope of the nearby knoll.

When they reached the Pathfinder, Bobby said, "Logan Walker, meet Father Murphy. He said Brian asked him to pick up the manuscript from you."

Murph greeted Logan with a warm smile. "Nebraska weather, huh?" he said, chuckling. "It almost makes this seem like a covert ops mission, right? Brian asked me to retrieve the story from you, including perhaps the flash drive with the original on it?"

"Sure," Logan said, turning toward the Pathfinder. He reached inside and drew out a large manila envelope, which he handed to Father Murphy.

"Thank you, Logan," Murph said. "I will see that Brian and his associates receive this. Brian will contact you when it goes to press. Oh. I almost forgot this…"

He tucked the envelope beneath one arm and removed a small white envelope from the inside pocket of his winter jacket. "This was what Frankie wished to leave you. I hope it is compensation enough for all the time and effort that went into writing this book. I'm looking forward to reading it. Perhaps, if you are available, you could sign it for me?"

Logan took the envelope, tucking it into the inner pocket of his own winter jacket. "Sure, though you might not like what you read."

Murph offered him a curious look. "No, I'm sure I'll enjoy reading it. Frankie and I had some very long talks, and in the end, I would like to say I understood him, his flaws and weaknesses."

A strong gust of wind swirled snow around them. "Whew!" he gasped. "This is a bad one. Sorry, I would like to talk more, but we best get out of this weather. Nice to meet you, Logan."

Bobby took Murph by one arm as he walked him over to a dark blue Buick parked some distance away. Logan and Alex stood there in the blowing snow, watching Bobby help the priest into his car.

"What's his story?" Logan asked.

Alex said, "Tell you later. Bobby gets sensitive if I seem like I am badmouthing Murph."

Alex opened the door for Bobby as he came running back, then climbed into the back seat, shaking the snow out of his hair. As Logan joined them, slipping into the driver's seat, he noticed Alex casually flicking snowflakes out of Bobby's long locks.

That evening Logan sat at his desk, drink in hand with wood crackling in the wood stove behind him. The envelope from Father Murphy lay before him, a few inches from his keyboard.

Logan stared at it.

Took a sip of Crown and Seven.

Stared at the envelope some more.

Took a longer sip of his drink.

Relished the flavor as he swished it around inside his mouth.

Continued to stare at the envelope.

Sat there, anticipating opening the thing, but decided to patiently wait.

Drank three more sips before reaching down to pick it up.

The sudden ring of the phone startled him.

He picked up the phone and answered.

"Hi, Logan," Alex said, trying to sound casual. "You doing okay out there in the wilds along the river? Betcha got your stove stacked full, right? It's a cold one tonight. Bet you wish you had some good company, being all alone out there like you are. If you want, I could drive out there to visit?"

Logan sighed. "Oh, no, Alex, this snow is so deep, you wouldn't even make it out of your driveway, let alone make it out here. I'm fine. Really."

Alex bit back a sob. "Oh, okay, Logan. Sorry, I didn't mean to bother you. Guess I'll let you go now."

"Uh, Alex?" Logan said, thinking it best to soothe him before just cutting him lose. "Just curious. But about this Father Murphy fellow? What's his deal?"

Alex sounded a little more chipper as he said, "Murph? You want to know about Murph? Yeah, I can tell you what I know. But Bobby knows him way better than I do."

Which sent off a warning bell in Logan's head. "Oh, so he's that kind of guy, huh?"

"No, not what you're thinking. Not that kind of guy, really."

"So," Logan said, "he's not like Frankie?"

"According to Bobby, thirty-some years ago there was an investigation because some boy killed himself. Bobby swears Murph was counseling the kid. The kid told Murph he was in love with him and wanted a relationship with him. Bobby swears Murph refused to touch the kid and even suggested he see another priest. The kid wigged out, went home after Murph's rejection, and shot himself.

"The investigators tried to pin the kid's suicide on Murph, but there wasn't any evidence. Father Murphy has been trying to save kids like that kid ever since. He's the only priest I know who travels to the Old Market offering counseling services to us street kids.

"Bobby says he offered himself to Murph, but they ended up sleeping together. Just sleeping. Bobby said the way Murph let him cuddle up next to him, he had never felt so loved in all of his life. I know someone like you might think it sounds weird, but I envied Bobby every time he got to spend the night with Father Murphy."

"A Catholic priest having anything to do with a young man outside of the church is cause for concern," Logan said. "Alex? Do you hear what you're saying? Bobby and Father Murphy slept in the same bed together. All kinds of things can be misconstrued from that. Bobby might have felt loved, but Murph placed himself at risk, whether there was sex involved or not."

Good Lord, thought Logan, *what kind of priest sleeps with a boy to give him comfort?*

"I figured you wouldn't understand," Alex said, a little tensely. "I probably shouldn't have shared this with you."

"Sorry, Alex, after reading those two journals and interviewing you and all those other boys, my mind has gone on overload. I'm just not ready to hear anything more about..."

"The Lost Boys of the Fallen Gay King?" He gave a sad laugh. "Hey, there's a title for a new book, right?"

"Alex," Logan said, pointedly, "thanks for calling to check on me like you did. I appreciate it. But I need to go now. Have yourself a nice night. We'll talk again in the near future. Good night."

Without waiting for a response, Logan hung up the phone.

He picked up the envelope and a letter opener. He sliced open one end of the white envelope and withdrew the check it contained.

Logan sat there staring at it in stunned amazement for a long while.

Frankie Judson had paid him $900,000 for services rendered.

CHAPTER THIRTY-SEVEN

Noah Standing Bear carried a tray with three steaming cups of coffee in the Lodge of Mahoney State Park. He carefully placed the tray down on the table between Logan and Jenna McGuire. The big Lakota sat down beside Jenna, reaching for the sugar shaker. Once he had doctored up his coffee, adding also a splash of cream from a small pitcher, he took a long, slow sip.

"Good Joe," he said, grinning.

Logan picked up his own mug, glancing at his rather large Indian friend. "You going to keep us in suspense, Noah? Or come right out and tell us?"

"I figured," Noah said, taking another long drink of coffee, "the longer I waited, the more curious you would become. But since Jenna is here on a more serious matter, I will cut to the chase."

Noah looked out the large window to the naked trees lining the bluff face beyond the lodge. He watched a hawk spiraling out over the Platte River. Logan followed his gaze, and he too saw the hawk drifting away into the haze of a sunny winter day.

"The first thing ex-detective Mason told me was Mike Carrol and Brad Helman are going away for a long time. Investigators were able to tie them into the conspiracy to hire Ben Donovan to murder Baxster Crown to silence his accusations against Franklin Judson. Evidently, they cleared Peters and the execs of Odin's Ring corporation. None of Frankie's colleagues or associates can be tied to the murder of Todd Guildman. It was a plan orchestrated by Carrol and Helman. It was those two operating on their own when they contracted Ben Donovan to murder Baxster. The plan was after Ben had offed Baxster, he was to meet a similar fate soon after snuffing you out, as well. Now they are going to pay for their crimes."

Logan nodded. "And Ben? Any word on him?"

Noah narrowed his eyes. He drank another sip of coffee. "APBs have been put out on the man, but so far, he is still MIA. They've even searched a fifty-mile swath along both sides of the river, and searched the drink, but so far, it doesn't appear that Ben drowned or froze to death."

Logan drank his own coffee and said nothing.

"Baxster could not be tied to the murder conspiracy since he was the supposed target of the hit." Noah finished with his information. "Mason claimed investigators grilled him pretty hard about the porn film on that DVD. But the kid simply feigned ignorance about who had hired him. He never mentioned Judson, Peters, or Ridge Majors. Mason said they let him go. However, in a strange twist, Senator Guildman offered to pay for therapy for Baxster."

Jenna shook her head. "Guildman? That's a nice gesture. But why? What stake does he have in Baxster?"

Noah shrugged his beefy shoulders. "That is what ex-detective Mason wanted to know, and although investigators checked out all the angles, they hit a dead end. Just a genuine nice gesture."

Logan and Noah exchanged a long, silent look.

"And my son?" Jenna asked.

Logan looked away from Noah. Alex had clamped up tight, refusing to share any information as to how he knew the two men who'd broken into her house that night. Jenna had been beside herself with frustration. She'd agonized for days over the fact that Alex had known the two investigators.

To even think that her own son had been involved in the same sexual activities that Max had been made her sick to her stomach, and she'd badgered Alex about being truthful with her.

Alex had not spoken to her for the past five days.

Jenna needed to know why.

❖

Logan started out telling her how he had been contacted to write the book about Franklin Judson.

He told her about the boys Frankie had been involved with, about the porn films both Brian Peters and Ridge Majors had produced—financed, he was almost certain, by Frankie.

He explained to her that Frankie was worth over $800 million when he died.

Logan informed Jenna that he had met both Frankie and Brian Peters, as well as several of the gay boys involved in the production of the pornography financed with Judson's money. He spoke specifically about Baxster Crown and his blackmail plot.

He finished, took a drink of his coffee, and waited expectantly.

"What about my son?" Jenna asked. "Where does he fit into this whole scandal?"

Logan wanted to pass along Alex's journal to her. He wanted to let her know her son had been selling himself in the Old Market for quite some time now. He wanted to tell her about the porn flicks he had starred in. He wanted to let Jenna know her son was a young, horny gay prostitute, addicted to sex. She was his mother, she deserved to know these things about her troubled son.

But Alex had confided in him. He had trusted him with his dark secrets. He had expected Logan to use his name anonymously in his book, which he had. He never once suspected that the author he'd shared so much of himself with would betray his trust, especially snitching him out to his mother.

Logan hesitantly said, "Let's start out slow and easy, okay?"

Jenna impatiently said, "Fuck slow and easy. Tell me what my son has been doing."

"Slow and easy," Logan said, staying on course. "First off, did you know your son was gay?"

"Oh, hell no!" Jenna snapped, a look of denial and rage in her eyes. "Alex is not gay! Are you saying he is? How would you know that? Are you saying he is gay like…Max?"

Logan looked over at Noah. The Indian shrugged as if saying, "You are on your own here."

"Like Max?" Logan asked. "Jenna, I'm sorry, but if you can't even accept that Alex might be gay, then I have no business going any further with this talk. You and your son will have to sort this out for yourselves, on his time. I am not interfering in this."

"Fine!" She choked back a sob, and with tears in her eyes, she looked at Noah. "Thought you said he was your friend. Some friend. If he knows so much about my son, then why can't he open up and tell me about him?"

Noah exchanged a look with Logan. He then looked directly at Jenna, asking, "Do you love your son, Jenna?"

"Of course," Jenna said, using a napkin to wipe tears from her cheeks.

"Even if he is gay?"

Jenna's bottom lip trembled. She toughened up then and said, "Yes, I would love him if he was gay. Yes, of course."

"That is good," Noah said, solemnly. "Because when my own mother found out I was, she did not speak to me for the next ten years. It took her that long to come around. Love your son no matter what, Jenna. He needs your support right now, and him being gay is just one of his issues that is going to need your attention."

Jenna said, "So, Alex is gay?"

"Yes," Logan said. "And any other activities he's been involved in is between you and Alex. Love him, accept him, make him feel all right with who he is, and leave it to him to tell you the rest."

CHAPTER THIRTY-EIGHT

B obby took Alex by the wrist and led him to the hot tub inside his parents' gazebo. He slowly worked him out of his T-shirt, then his jeans and his underwear. Alex did the same for him, and both boys stepped over their pile of discarded clothes, climbing into the warm waters of the hot tub.

"Max is being released," Bobby said, "at the end of this week."

Alex scooched along the plastic seat, pulling Bobby over to him. "It's past time. He's been locked up out there for, what? The past four months? We'll have two things to celebrate then. Max coming home, and Logan's book release."

"No shit?" Bobby said. "I wonder how well it will sell? He's changed all of our names, right? I mean, anyone reading it will never figure out it was us, right?"

Alex said, "Yeah. Logan was being real discreet when he wrote it. I'm still not sure what he's told my mom about me, but she has been really weird lately. She's accepted the fact that I'm gay, but she keeps asking me about how well I know Max. She's prying, that's for sure, but there is no way in hell I can tell her about Max or you or the things we did for Brian and Ridge. She would disown me for certain."

"I would claim you if that happened," Bobby said, grinning. He reached down beneath the water and grabbed Alex's slowly stiffening rod. "In fact, I'll claim you right now, my Alex boy!"

They grappled for a time, rubbing up against each other and giving each other long, slow hand jobs. When Alex nearly came in the hot tub, Bobby suggested they retreat to his bedroom in the basement.

"Mom and Dad are out of town for the weekend," he said. "We have the house to ourselves."

"Don't want the house," Alex said, flippantly. "Just you in your bed will do."

They gathered up their clothes as they made their way inside the house. Once inside Bobby's bedroom, Alex pulled a footstool out from beneath his desk.

"Shall we use the stool?" he asked, raising his brows seductively. "Wanna milk the cow?"

For an answer, Bobby took the stool and placed it two feet from his bed. "Lie down!" he commanded, assuming his usual role as the dominator.

Alex lay face down, his face and chest on the bed, his legs resting on the stool. His cock and balls hung down in the space between.

"Spread this on your cock!" Bobby squirted hand lotion into Alex's cupped hand as he gave his second command.

"Slow! Gently! Make the sucker shine!" Bobby ordered Alex, watching him closely as he coated his hard cock with the lotion, performing slow milking motions.

"Slower!" Bobby demanded, and Alex ran his slick fingers up and down the length of his cock.

"Stop!" Bobby said, taking hold of Alex's slick, shiny boner. Alex breathed out little gasps with each slide of Bobby's hand as he went wild with his jacking, milking the cow for all it was worth.

Alex moaned, "Yesssss! Ohhhh, yesssss!" He tensed up as Bobby kneeled there beside him, pumping him while running his tongue up and down Alex's ass cheeks. "Whoa!" he cried out. "Stop or I'll cum, Bobby! Stop, now!"

Bobby twisted his cock head with one last wild downward pull.

Alex glanced over his shoulder at Bobby still kneeling there beside him. He gave him a wild look and reached down to latch onto his erection. "Lie down!" he commanded, surprising Bobby with his firm grip and the tone of his voice.

Alex scrambled up, still holding Bobby's cock in a firm grip. "Lie down! Now!" he ordered, swinging Bobby around so that he could take his place on the stool in the same position.

Releasing his hold on his cock, Alex picked up the lotion bottle. "Grab your ass cheeks with both hands!" he said, quite forcefully, now reversing their roles, a thing he had never done before.

Bobby reached back and did as he was told, spreading his cheeks slightly.

"Spread them farther apart!" Alex growled, overcome with the heady feeling of control.

Bobby did so, and Alex squirted lotion all over his butt ring.

"Ass in the air!" Alex instructed him. "Keep those butt cheeks spread!"

Sprawled there with his face and chest resting on the bed, Bobby tried to do the two things at once. He bucked up slightly to offer his ass up to Alex while still gripping both mounds of his firm ass, opening himself for the invasion that would soon follow.

Alex climbed on top of him, and without a word, he shoved his lotion-slick dick directly into Bobby's ass ring.

"Unnnnnhhhh!" exploded from Bobby's lips. "Ooooooomph! Unnnnnnnhhh! Geeeesus, Alex! What in the hell are you—"

"Quiet!" Alex demanded. "Just lie there and take my cock up your ass!"

"But," Bobby protested, "you're being a little rough, Alex. What is up with—uunnnnnnhhhh! Arrrggg! Motherfucking A!"

Alex plowed into him with wild abandon, humping madly.

Bobby gripped the sheets of the bed and bit down hard on the mattress beneath his upper body while his lower body was smashed flat against the stool as Alex fiercely fucked him.

"Take me all the way up inside you!" burst from Alex's lips as he rose and came down, rose and came down, rose and shoved his cock deeper inside Bobby's ass. "Fuck! Fuck! Fuck!"

"Ooooooooh!" leaked out of Bobby's mouth as the pleasure sensations overcame him. "Ooohhhm! Oh, yeah! Fuck me! Fuck me! Fuck me, Alex!"

Bobby relaxed then and Alex penetrated him deeply, both of them freezing in one position for long moments, both of them throbbing and overcome with the hot and sweaty fucking that Alex was delivering with such fervor and passion. "Oh, God!" Alex cried out. "Oh, Jesus!" Bobby panted.

And then Alex went bunny-humping crazy, plowing his cock into Bobby's asshole, driving deep, his cock head repeatedly striking Bobby's prostate gland, firing off sensational feelings that racked Bobby's lean body from head to toe, from ass to groin. "Cum! Cum! Cumming!" he screamed, with a final "Cummmpppff!" muffled by his mouth planted on the bed.

Before he could shoot his load, Alex released him and commanded, "Up on the bed! On your back! Grab your ankles!"

Whap! echoed throughout the bed room as Alex slapped Bobby's bare ass.

"Ouch!" exploded from Bobby's lips.

"Bobby?" Alex persisted with his demand. "Lie down and pull your legs apart! Now!"

Bobby scooted onto the bed on his back and latched onto both ankles, spreading himself wide as Alex climbed over the top of him. "Easy!" he gasped, as Alex literally rammed his cock up inside him. "Easy—unnhhhhh! Ohhhhhhhmmpf!"

The moment he was buried to his balls, Alex began his wild and crazy fucking once again. Bobby grimaced at first, then relaxed and wrapped his arms around Alex's shoulders and upper back, pulling him close and welcoming his spastic thrusts and his deep penetration.

They lasted for another five minutes. At the end of their rather rough session, Alex went full bore, his movements so fast and erratic that Bobby lost his grip on him and flopped around beneath him like a rag doll. "Oh, yeahhh! Oh, yeahhhhh! Oh, fucking yeahhhhh!" Alex shouted, and then he came, bursting inside Bobby, his cock pulsing and shooting white creamy sperm into his ass cavity.

Bobby rose slightly as his orgasm hit him, trying to keep himself impaled on Alex's cock as he, too, groaned, "Yeahhh! Yeahhhh! Fucking yeahhhhh!"

Both of them looked down to Bobby's cock and watched with exhausted looks on their faces as spurt after spurt exploded from his cock head. The first four blasts came from his rigid pole without any manual stimulation, but the last four cum shots were coaxed out of him by Alex reaching down and jacking him in a mad frenzy.

When both were finished, Alex slowly pulled himself out of Bobby, and they collapsed on the bed beside each other.

It took several minutes for them to get their breath. Several more for either of them to speak.

"Alex?" Bobby said, a little weakly. "What got into you?"

Wiping his sperm-coated fingers on the sheet, Alex peered over into Bobby's eyes and said, "I just wanted to dominate for once. My life is so out of control…I just wanted to know what it felt like to be in control for once."

"Did you like it?" Bobby asked.

Alex shrugged. "Yeah, sort of."

❖

Bobby and Alex picked Max up at the end of that week out at the state hospital. Since his dad refused to have anything to do with him after reading his deposition, Max was basically on his own. His mom was too unstable to take him in at her place. She also had a boyfriend who drank and had a blistering hatred for "goddamned faggots!" So Max had been invited to stay temporarily at Bobby's place, with the agreement that he file for emancipation from both parents. Bobby's dad, being a lawyer, strongly advised this course of action so that legally Max could choose where he wanted to stay.

Thanks to Bobby's mom, Max was welcome there until he could get himself stabilized with a good-paying job or possibly apply for funds for college. With the help and support of Bobby's parents, it appeared Max was going to be okay.

However, as they drove him home that day, Max shared with the other two another problem that had cropped up while he was confined to the mental hospital.

"Ridge actually called me in there," Max told Bobby and Alex. "Posing as my dad, he got one of the techs to put me on the phone. He blasted me! He also threatened to kill me when I got released! The fucker is crazy and he wants payback for all the stuff I put him through! The thing is, I think he might seriously carry out his threat."

As Bobby drove, he and Alex silently contemplated Max's dilemma.

But Max bitterly said, "Ridge Majors, that bastard needs to die!"

CHAPTER THIRTY-NINE

Logan's book was released on St. Patrick's Day. It was simply titled *The Gay King*, and while it would never be a smash hit at Barnes & Noble or a bestseller on Amazon, it did cause a small buzz in Omaha's gay and lesbian community. He held a book signing at the Catacombs bookstore, a place selling new, used, rare, and banned books. So he fit right in with the offbeat clientele who frequented the under-the-street bookstore. No reporters did any stories on the book.

He sold barely over fifty copies but remained cordial, speaking to any who were interested in his book. He signed fifty more after the book signing was over.

Not a big hit in the long run, thought Logan. *But I have been paid well for my work.*

The St. Patrick's Day parade clogged up the two main streets of Jackson and Howard there in the Old Market, and Logan decided he would just settle into the Bullfrog Lounge.

He didn't expect to see anyone he knew as he sank into oblivion with his fourth Irish car bomb, a shot of Baileys dropped into half a pint of Guinness. But he heard his name being called, and he looked up, bleary-eyed, at the lean, dark-haired kid banging frantically on the window overlooking the crowded street beyond.

It was Alex.

He peered in at Logan, desperation in his eyes. He banged on the window again and gestured for him to come outside.

Muttering a curse, Logan staggered his way through the crowd packed into the Bullfrog.

"Max!" Alex cried, nearly panicking. "Max has a knife and he's planning on killing Ridge Majors! You got to help me, Logan Walker! You got to help me find him and stop him!"

❖

Alex led Logan directly into the crowd on the sidewalk of the Old Market. Following the kid's lead, Logan bobbed and weaved his way through the bodies blocking the path. Alex was much more agile and managed to put some distance between them in his haste. Both caught glimpses of Max as he moved ahead of them in a bright red windbreaker, a sharp contrast to the greens worn by the majority of the crowd.

Alex glanced back, his blue eyes searching the crowd for Logan. He smiled in relief when their eyes met, and he waited for Logan to catch up. "Do you see him?" he asked. "He's right there, forty feet in front of us, closing in on Ridge! Oh God, I hope he doesn't do something stupid!"

Logan stepped up beside Alex. "I see him. He's kept a ten-foot distance between him and Ridge. Maybe you're wrong."

"I can only hope," Alex said. "But I wouldn't count on it, Logan. He spooked the hell out of me. We need to stop him."

Max closed within five feet of Ridge, who had no idea he was being tailed by a distraught kid armed with a knife. "He's going to do it!" Alex hissed, glancing from Max with knife in hand back to Logan. "What do we do?"

Logan's first thought was to call out to Max, using that ploy to distract him, but he spotted movement off to the right of Ridge. A huge hulk of a man lumbered in between two startled beer drinking jocks, causing both clean-cut fellows to spill beer from their red Solo cups. One of the jocks opened his mouth to protest, but the large, red-haired giant who had rudely passed between them gave him a glare and the jock remained silent.

It was the biker, the Viking-like Dirk who had been with Ridge the first time Logan had encountered them in the hotel parking garage. *Of course,* he thought. *Ridge Majors might be smart enough to have a shadow, at a discreet distance.*

"Oh my God!" Alex whispered. "Dirk's spotted Max!"

Max made his move. He whipped the hunting knife out of the sheath beneath his windbreaker and made a wild, crazy lunge at Ridge's unsuspecting backside.

Dirk intercepted him, sending a meaty fist directly into Max's solar plexus. The large, grungy biker grabbed Max, one hand latching onto his shoulder, the other grasping the wrist of his knife hand. He swung him around, directly toward Ridge, who had turned.

"Take his knife!" Dirk snapped. "Disarm him, Ridge!"

Ridge snatched the hunting knife from Max, nodding toward a nearby alley. "Move him into the alley, Dirk," he said, loud enough for Logan and Alex to hear him.

It had all happened so fast that people in the crowd simply moved out of the way of the brief scuffle. Dirk said, "Kid's had too much to drink. Needs to retch his guts out. Out of the way, unless you want chunks blown all over you!"

No one in the crowd appeared to have even noticed Ridge concealing the knife by placing it beneath his black leather jacket.

"They'll kill him!" Alex gasped, pulling Logan along behind him through the mob of people in front of them. "They get him into that alley, Max will never leave there alive, Logan!"

Logan twisted his arm out of Alex's grasp. He pushed his way through the crowd blocking his path.

He then spotted a better alternative, the black cane in the hand of the dark-haired man off to his left. As he moved to relieve the man of the cane, he imagined he heard Noah say, "When it comes to facing a man armed with a knife, an advantage is needed. Even a rock or a can of peas in hand is better than facing a knife wielder unarmed. Lots of damage can be done with a knife if it is not removed from the fight in the first few seconds."

And that cane, thought Logan as he lunged forward to snag it from the man's grasp, *is a far better weapon than a rock or a can of peas!*

And yet, just as he reached for the black cane, the tall, lean man spun it out of his grasp and placed a restraining hand on Logan's chest. "Sorry, but I'll need this," he said solemnly, "to stop that."

Logan gaped at the black-haired, middle-aged man, and recognition came to him. *Father Murphy?* he thought. *The priest*

who was in the hospital chapel with Frankie when I first met him!
What the hell is he doing here?

"Murph?" Bobby said, appearing there at the priest's side.
"Ridge is gonna kill Max!"

"No, Bobby," Father Murphy said, "he is not."

The priest darted into the alley. The moment they were free
of the milling crowd, Dirk held Max up and Ridge brandished the
knife.

Logan was about to shout at Ridge when the priest swung his
cane like a sword, lashing out and striking Dirk in the back of his head.
The huge biker groaned in pain and reeled away, releasing Max.

Ridge was just turning to plunge the long blade of the hunting
knife into Max's chest when Father Murphy threw himself between
them.

"No!" Bobby cried out. "No, Murph! No!"

But it was already too late. Ridge brutally stabbed him in the
center of his chest. For a moment, Ridge stood there, the bloody
knife in his hand. But when Bobby launched himself at him, Ridge
fell against the large metal Dumpster behind him, the knife slipping
out of his grasp.

Two plainclothes detectives intervened. While one restrained
Bobby, the other detective checked on the wounded priest.

Still in a slight daze, Max clambered to his knees beside the
dying priest, muttering, "What the hell, Murph? What the hell?"

Thinking it wise to distance himself, Logan simply faded away
into crowd.

❖

Noah Standing Bear phoned him later that night.

"According to my sources," he said, "Ridge Majors has been
charged with murder. Dirk Grill was charged for felony assault. Cops
grilled Max and Bobby for several hours, but no one could connect
Max with that knife. Cops just assumed it belonged to Ridge. They
still can't figure out what Father Murphy was doing intervening
between Ridge and Max, but they are claiming he was some sort of
hero. The three boys were pretty shaken up about Murph's death.

Cops let them go without citing them. Investigators just assumed the boys were in the wrong place at the wrong time.

"I guess Alex told investigators that it was some sort of cosmic justice took place in that alley today. Murph died like Jesus died, dying in Max's place. He actually sacrificed himself, throwing himself between Max and that blade. At least that is the legacy he left behind for Max, Bobby, and Alex, who claimed Murph was like some kind of martyr. Which sparked an argument later between the boys. Investigators were amused that the boys started arguing about saints, you know, like patron saints, Jude of Lost Causes, and Saint Christopher, who's supposed to protect travelers."

He paused, then added, "So, Logan, do you think there is a patron saint for boys like them?"

At this, Logan did not know quite what to say.

"Patron saint?" Logan peered out the window to the dark trees along the river. "Patron saint of lost boys? If there ain't, there should be."

Chapter Forty

It was so quiet in the Fair Haven Cemetery that first morning of spring that Logan felt as if he had passed through a secret portal and stepped into the Other World that Noah was always telling him about. The world between worlds, where unseen spirits gathered, either for great purposes or to do great mischief.

As he walked through the freshly cut green grass, his shoes made tiny sluffing sounds beneath him. It was the only sound he heard, and he felt like he was intruding on the privacy or disturbing the peace of all those whose bones were buried there, either in the ground or in the many mausoleums scattered amidst tall pines.

He stopped for a moment, his ears almost aching in the profound silence.

Into this void there came a muffled sob.

Ahead of him.

From somewhere in the distance, a dog barked, more than likely from one of the dairy farms situated in the rolling hills beyond the iron fence of the ancient cemetery. Another dog barked back.

Peering up into the blue skies, Logan's sun-dazzled eyes took a moment to locate two hawks performing slow, lazy circles five hundred feet above him. "Two hawks," he whispered, "is a good sign. Hawks mate for life, so those two are not alone in this life."

He sighed and added, "Not alone, like I have been these past several years."

The sob came again. It was a little softer this time. Still, it was there all the same. Logan topped a small rise and peered down at the stone gazebo surrounded by dozens of gravestones. It was the final resting place of Franklin Judson.

To his surprise, a golden-haired figure sat on the stone bench located just beneath the stone overhang with the word *Judson* etched deeply on its surface.

Baxster Crown looked up, startled for a moment by the presence of a stranger approaching the burial site of his former lover and mentor. Recognition dawned in his red-rimmed eyes.

He's been crying, Logan thought as he slowed his pace. *For quite some time.*

"Hello, Logan," Baxster said, followed by a long sniffle. "Come to pay your respects?"

Logan shook his head. "No, actually I got a phone call from Alex. He asked me to meet him here. Any chance you know what that's about?"

Baxster got a confused look on his face. "No. Not a clue. I just come out here every week to say a few things. Weird, right? But I somehow feel as if Frankie can hear me."

"You still love the man?" Logan asked him. "After all the things he put you through, you still care that deeply about him?"

Baxster rubbed at his eyes. "I do. Frankie never forced me to do anything. Frankie was kind and gentle, and at one time I was the center of his universe. I will always have that. No one can take that away from me."

He reached into his shirt pocket for an electronic cigarette. He took a puff, releasing the vapor into the air between them.

"You see," Baxster said, "there's a difference between men like Frankie and men like Ridge. Frankie was out to find love, where Ridge was an abuser. Frankie was just making himself available to a lonely kid like me. He was a godsend, where Ridge was just a user. There's a big difference, you know. I suppose I could never justify all the things Frankie and I did, but maybe I don't have to. He made my life better. He was a beacon. I will always remember him for that. Never forget him."

Logan glanced back to see Alex, Bobby, and Max walking down the grassy knoll behind the Judson grave site. Alex smiled when he made eye contact with him. Max drifted over to speak quietly with

Baxster while Bobby wandered over to stand beside a Celtic cross serving as headstone for a single grave. Across the face of the cross was engraved the name *Father Francis Murphy.*

"Talk to you alone?" Alex asked Logan, a sad smile on his face.

Logan followed him as he made his way between the many headstones lined up in even rows across the cemetery. He did not stop walking until he had placed a good distance between them and the other three young men inside the Judson gazebo. Only when he was certain they could not hear him did Alex stop walking.

He sat on a stone bench beside a stone angel. Looking up at Logan, he patted the bench and said, "Sit. Please. I have something to say. If you care to listen."

Logan sat, noticing that Alex kept a respectful distance between them.

"I read your book, Logan," he said, quietly. "It really made me think about what I have been doing with my life. Where I've been. Where I go from here."

Alex fidgeted a bit before plunging ahead. "I need help, Logan. Maybe a therapist can fix me. Maybe one who specializes in sex addiction. But I am willing to listen to someone tell me how to stop doing what I've been doing. To get me off the street. I really wish you would love me and take me in, but I understand if you don't. I just need help in a bad way. Would you be willing to help me?"

Logan said, "Alex, nothing has changed about me taking you in. I cannot be what you want me to be. It's just not me. But yes, I will help you. I'll find a specialist, one who's had success with sexual addictions. Therapist? Psychologist? Some professional that will address your issues."

He paused, then said, "Have you been tested lately? Are you certain that all your risky behavior hasn't already burned you?"

Alex said, "Yes, Brian made us take blood tests all during the time we were filming. I'm negative for HIV."

"*Yet,*" Logan said. "That's the key word. So, let's make sure that you *never* get that. And what about your mom? Any chance you'll ever share with her the activities you've been involved in? Does she play into this?"

"No," Alex said, adamantly. "What she doesn't know will never hurt her. Yes, she's still dealing with me being gay, but to let her know of all the things I wrote about in my journal, she never needs to know that stuff. It would kill her. It would kill the relationship we've developed over the past two months. So, no, Logan, please leave my mom out of this. Agreed?"

Logan slowly nodded. "That is on you, Alex. I'll never say anything to your mom that would damage your relationship with her. Will she know about the help you're getting?"

"Sure," Alex said. "But I'll just tell her I'm seeing a shrink or a therapist because I'm dealing with the fact that I am gay. That would be a good cover for the real reason. Agreed?"

Logan sighed. "Look, Alex, whether or not I agree with your decisions on this matter, I am not responsible for you, for the final outcome on these issues. I'm simply willing to finance this venture to get you the help you need. I'll do so covertly, setting up a fund for you. One that will cover all the costs involved. I'll be happy to do that for you."

Alex looked off to the rolling green hills in the distance. "Whoa, that might be costly. How will you pay for that? I mean, I heard your book is selling steadily. At least the reviews on the Internet have been good so far. I also heard they're making a movie out of it."

Logan said, "Yes, some producer has optioned the rights for a potential movie deal, but nothing is set in stone yet on that deal. And as far as sales go, well, Brian Peters is a cutthroat when it comes to royalties. Ten percent does not make me a rich man. No, let's just say I'll dip into another fund that will more than cover the costs of any help we find for you."

"Another fund?" Alex asked, curiously.

"Yes," Logan said. "Let's call it my fund of the Lost Boys of the Fallen Gay King."

A hawk wheeled into view in the blue skies in front of them.

They watched it spiral lazily into the wind currents, rising and falling as it joined a second hawk soaring out above the distant river.

"Lucky ducks," Alex said, squinting his eyes as he watched the two hawks drifting into black specks above the distant bluffs on the far side of the river. "Hawks mate for life. So as I see it, those two will never be alone. Always hunting, feeding, roosting, flying together. I just wish I wasn't so all alone. Wish I was like a hawk."

Logan narrowed his eyes, nearly losing sight of the two raptors winging their way over the bluffs. "Yes, hawks are lucky, for sure."

And Alex softly muttered, "Yes, they are."

About the Author

Simon Hawk was once a consultant for an AIDS Awareness program. Ironically, it is there that he stumbled upon the threads for this particular story. Those threads led to a complicated tapestry involving rich men, young boys, and the international porn industry. Simon makes his home somewhere in the Midwest. This is his first book.

Books Available From Bold Strokes Books

Backstrokes by Dylan Madrid. When pianist Crawford Paul meets lifeguard Armando Leon, he accepts Armando's offer to help him overcome his fear of water by way of private lessons. As friendship turns into a summer affair, their lust for one another turns to love. (978-1-62639-069-0)

The Raptures of Time by David Holly. Mack Frost and his friends journey across an alien realm, through homoerotic adventures, suffering humiliation and rapture, making friends and enemies, always seeking a gateway back home to Oregon. (978-1-62639-068-3)

The Thief Taker by William Holden. Unreliable lovers, twisted family secrets, and too many dead bodies wait for Thomas Newton in London—where he soon enough discovers that all the plotting is aimed directly at him. (978-1-62639-054-6)

Waiting for the Violins by Justine Saracen. After surviving Dunkirk, a scarred and embittered British nurse returns to Nazi-occupied Brussels to join the Resistance, and finds that nothing is fair in love and war. (978-1-62639-046-1)

Turnbull House by Jess Faraday. London 1891: Reformed criminal Ira Adler has a new, respectable life—but will an old flame and the promise of riches tempt him back to London's dark side...and his own? (978-1-60282-987-9)

Stronger Than This by David-Matthew Barnes. A gay man and a lesbian form a beautiful friendship out of grief when their soul mates are tragically killed. (978-1-60282-988-6)

Death Came Calling by Donald Webb. When private investigator Katsuro Tanaka is hired to look into the death of a high profile lawyer, he becomes embroiled in a case of murder and mayhem. (978-1-60282-979-4)

Love in the Shadows by Dylan Madrid. While teaming up to bring a killer to justice, a lustful spark is ignited between an American man living in London and an Italian spy named Luca. (978-1-60282-981-7)

In Between by Jane Hoppen. At the age of fourteen, Sophie Schmidt discovers that she was born an intersexual baby and sets off on a journey to find her place in a world that denies her true existence. (978-1-60282-968-8)

The Odd Fellows by Guillermo Luna. Joaquin Moreno and Mark Crowden open a bed-and-breakfast in Mexico but soon must confront an evil force with only friendship, love, and truth as their weapons. (978-1-60282-969-5)

Cutie Pie Must Die by R.W. Clinger. Sexy detectives, a muscled quarterback, and the queerest murders…when murder is most cute. (978-1-60282-961-9)

Going Down for the Count by Cage Thunder. Desperately needing money, Gary Harper answers an ad that leads him into the underground world of gay professional wrestling—which leads him on a journey of self-discovery and romance. (978-1-60282-962-6)

Light by 'Nathan Burgoine. Openly gay (and secretly psychokinetic) Kieran Quinn is forced into action when self-styled prophet Wyatt Jackson arrives during Pride Week and things take a violent turn. (978-1-60282-953-4)

Baton Rouge Bingo by Greg Herren. The murder of an animal rights activist involves Scotty and the boys in a decades-old mystery revolving around Huey Long's murder and a missing fortune. (978-1-60282-954-1)

Anything for a Dollar, edited by Todd Gregory. Bodies for hire, bodies for sale—enter the steaming hot world of men who make a living from their bodies—whether they star in porn, model, strip, or hustle—or all of the above. (978-1-60282-955-8)

Mind Fields by Dylan Madrid. When college student Adam Parsh accepts a tutoring position, he finds himself the object of the dangerous desires of one of the most powerful men in the world—his married employer. (978-1-60282-945-9)

Greg Honey by Russ Gregory. Detective Greg Honey is steering his way through new love, business failure, and bruises when all his cases indicate trouble brewing for his wealthy family. (978-1-60282-946-6

Lake Thirteen by Greg Herren. A visit to an old cemetery seems like fun to a group of five teenagers, who soon learn that sometimes it's best to leave old ghosts alone. (978-1-60282-894-0)

Deadly Cult by Joel Gomez-Dossi. One nation under MY God, or you die. (978-1-60282-895-7)

The Case of the Rising Star: A Derrick Steele Mystery by Zavo. Derrick Steele's next case involves blackmail, revenge, and a new romance as Derrick races to save a young movie star from a dangerous killer. Meanwhile, will a new threat from within destroy him, along with the entire Steele family? (978-1-60282-888-9)

Big Bad Wolf by Logan Zachary. After a wolf attack, Paavo Wolfe begins to suspect one of the victims is turning into a werewolf. Things become hairy as his ex-partner helps him find the killer. Can Paavo solve the mystery before he runs into the Big Bad Wolf? (978-1-60282-890-2)

The Moon's Deep Circle by David Holly. Tip Trencher wants to find out what happened to his long-lost brothers, but what he finds is a sizzling circle of gay sex and pagan ritual. (978-1-60282-870-4)

The Plain of Bitter Honey by Alan Chin. Trapped within the bleak prospect of a society in chaos, twin brothers Aaron and Hayden Swann discover inner strength in the face of tragedy and search for atonement after betraying the one you most love. (978-1-60282-883-4)

Tricks of the Trade: Magical Gay Erotica, edited by Jerry L. Wheeler. Today's hottest erotica writers take you inside the sultry, seductive world of magicians and their tricks—professional and otherwise. (978-1-60282-781-3)

Straight Boy Roommate by Kevin Troughton. Tom isn't expecting much from his first term at University, but a chance encounter with straight boy Dan catapults him into an extraordinary, wild weekend of sex and self-discovery, which turns his life upside down, and leads him into his first love affair. (978-1-60282-782-0)

In His Secret Life by Mel Bossa. The only man Allan wants is the one he can't have. (978-1-60282-875-9)

Promises in Every Star, edited by Todd Gregory. Acclaimed gay erotica author Todd Gregory's definitive collection of short stories, including both classic and new works. (978-1-60282-787-5)

Raising Hell: Demonic Gay Erotica, edited by Todd Gregory. Hot stories of gay erotica featuring demons. (978-1-60282-768-4)

Pursued by Joel Gomez-Dossi. Openly gay college student Jamie Bradford becomes romantically involved with two men at the same time, and his hell begins when one of his boyfriends becomes intent on killing him. (978-1-60282-769-1)

Timothy by Greg Herren. *Timothy* is a romantic suspense thriller from award-winning mystery writer Greg Herren set in the fabulous Hamptons. (978-1-60282-760-8)